DI022140

INVISIBLE LIFE

INVISIBLE LIFE

The Fifth Anniversary Edition

E. Lynn Harris

DOUBLEDAY

NEW YORK LONDON TORONTO SYDNEY AUCKLAND

PUBLISHED BY DOUBLEDAY
a division of Random House, Inc.
1540 Broadway, New York, New York 10036

DOUBLEDAY and the portrayal of an anchor with a dolphin are trademarks
of Doubleday, a division of Random House, Inc.

Invisible Life was orginally published by Consortium Press in 1991. The Anchor Books
edition was published by arrangement with Consortium Press in 1994.

*This novel is a work of fiction. Names, characters, places, and incidents either are
the product of the author's imagination or are used fictitiously. Any resemblance to
actual persons, living or dead, events, or locales is entirely coincidental.*

Book design by Brian Mulligan

The Library of Congress has cataloged the Anchor Books edition as follows:
Harris, E. Lynn.
Invisible life / E. Lynn Harris. — 1st Anchor Books ed.
p.   cm.
1. Young men—United States—Fiction.   2. Afro-American men—Fiction.
3. Bisexuality—Fiction.   I. Title.
PS3558.A64438I58   1994
813'.54—dc20   93-8731
CIP
ISBN 0-385-49463-7

FOR

Randy L. Johnson and *Richard S. Coleman*

and Five Ladies Who Make a Difference Daily

My mother, *Etta W. Harris*

My grandma, *Bessie Harvey*

My aunt, *Jessie L. Phillips*

My friend, *Lencola Sullivan*

My inspiration, *Dellanor Young*

IN LOVING MEMORY

Dionne Harold

William Rhodes

Larry J. Stewart

Connie Garrett Abbensetts

Calvin A. Brown

Cary Allyne

Rory Gautt

Dwight Hollis

Greg Googer

Walks like a duck,

quacks like a duck,

must be a duck . . .

But then again,

it might not be a duck . . .

—anonymous

THE BEGINNING

or The End

Protected by a crisp, cloudless sky, I sipped iced tea on the dusty wooden deck of my parents' home. There was a trace of heat; no humidity. It was a few days after my twenty-ninth birthday and I was pondering the next step in my complicated life. While deep in thought, but savoring the Southern tranquillity, I heard my father come through the sliding glass doors. He quietly placed a large envelope, addressed to *Raymond Winston Tyler, Jr.,* on the wrought-iron table, gave me a half smile and returned through the doors. I immediately recognized the familiar feminine handwriting and the New York City postmark. I quickly ripped open the envelope, ignored the card and began to read the letter on the soft pink stationery.

Dear Raymond,

I decided it was time I responded to your letter. How could this happen? Never before have I received a letter filled with so much pain, yet so much love.

The last six months have been like a wild roller coaster ride, full of extreme highs and lows. I find myself numb over the recent events. Why did it happen to us? . . . Why can't we live in a perfect world? . . .

Before continuing to the next page, I laid the letter down, noticing that the moisture from my iced tea glass had caused the name on the envelope to blur and dissolve into an ugly black mess, bringing to mind my current life. As I studied the envelope, I asked myself, How did it happen?

ONE

There is something poetic about falling in love. The tingling sensation lingers like the lyrical words of a Langston Hughes poem. There is something romantic about the changing of seasons. A romance reminiscent of an unending summer, or one as fleeting as spring and fall. Whenever I think back on the loves of my life, I am often reminded of the seasons. There are four seasons. I have been in love four times.

It was summer when Sela, my girlfriend, and I drove the five hours back to campus. On this beautiful day, there was no way of knowing that my life, like the season, would soon change. My black Volkswagen was filled to capacity with our clothes, books, albums and items that we couldn't live without during the summer vacation. As we drove down Highway 17, the heavy August sun beat down on us. The Alabama sky was a shimmering summer blue. State troopers were out in numbers trying to catch the fancy cars exceeding the speed limit, giving special attention to cars with THE UNIVERSITY and Greek-letter organization stickers.

Sela and I were both especially excited this year because for me it was my senior year and I would finally be heading to law school, while Sela, now a junior, was moving into her sorority house after a couple of years in the dorm. In the midst of the excitement and happiness, I was feeling a bit melancholy because this was going to be my last year. I was going to miss Sela and my fraternity brothers, who kept my life at this lily white university interesting and fulfilling.

My fraternity, Kappa Alpha Omega (ΚΑΩ), was one of the three black fraternities on campus. While the white fraternities and sororities were going through rush, which we never understood, we were planning a big party to welcome back the black students. We would get a head start on pressing the freshman girls to become our sweethearts and persuading the top black freshman men to pledge ΚΑΩ.

We decided to have the party at the house of one of our advisors, who was also one of the few black faculty members at the university. He owned a huge old rustic house outside of town surrounded by trees so large they cast an indelible shade over the two tennis courts and aqua-colored pool. It was the type of house I dreamed of one day sharing with Sela.

Since I was the social chairman of my fraternity, Sela and I arrived early to make sure that everything was set. We checked the music and food, and made sure the keg of beer was ice-cold. Sela looked beautiful in her white tennis outfit. It was a pleated short skirt with a matching top that looked wonderful against her vanilla wafer brown complexion. Her long black hair was pulled together with a crimson satin ribbon that flowed down her back. Her face, with deep dimples and almond-shaped hazel eyes, was accented by an open smile.

As I watched Sela help our sweethearts prepare for the party, I thought back to the time almost six years ago when I had first laid eyes on her. It was the annual citywide basketball tournament and about five of my football teammates and I went over to North Birmingham to Northeast High for a game.

Northeast High was like most of the high schools in Birmingham, an all-black basketball team and a cheerleader lineup of blue-eyed blondes, with the exception of a pair of identical brunette twins. As my eyes made it to the end of the line, I saw the most beautiful black girl I had ever seen. She had two thick ponytails, one with a gold ribbon and the other with a light blue ribbon, that matched her uniform perfectly.

Whenever there was a time-out, Northeast's pep band started to play and the cheerleaders ran onto the court and started their well-rehearsed pom-pom routines. The black girl on the end was spectacular. She appeared to be using her ponytails and high kicks to conduct the band. As her kicks got higher, her ponytails flew in her face, temporarily blocking her view but never causing her to miss a beat. Her blue, gold and white pleated skirt twirled like a kaleidoscope against her light brown skin.

As the band played the theme from *Shaft*, the cheerleaders and crowd chanted in unison, "Go Chargers . . . Beat those Bears . . . Go Chargers." I became mesmerized by the cheerleader from the opposing school. I became so wrapped up in her that I wanted to cheer for Northeast High instead of my own school. While I watched the cheerleader's every move, someone came up behind me and put his huge arm around my neck in a playful strangle. When I was released, I turned and recognized Bruce Grayson, one of Northeast's star football players.

"Ray Tyler, what are you doing in my neck of the woods?" Bruce asked.

"I'm over here to see my boys kick some Northeast butt," I joked.

Bruce and I had met during the summer when we both were

training at the Presidents Health Spa downtown. After talking for a couple of minutes, I asked Bruce who *this vision of ebony beauty* was. He told me her name was Sela Richards and that she was his play little sister. During halftime Bruce introduced me to Sela. When he left the two of us alone, I became so nervous, not knowing what to do or say, that I put my hands into my orange-and-white leather football jacket, took them out and placed them in my tight-fitting blue jeans and just kept staring at Sela. When I finally found the courage to ask Sela for her phone number, one of the girls on the cheerleading squad came up and grabbed her, telling her it was time for the second half. She smiled at me. "It was nice meeting you," she said, and ran off with the blue-eyed blonde.

During the second half I thought of ways to approach Sela after the game. Before the game ended, Bruce came up to me and gave me a little piece of paper.

"Sela asked me to give this to you," he said, smiling. I looked at the paper and there they were: the seven digits that would lead to my first love.

That night I couldn't sleep for thinking of Sela. I got up at 6:30 A.M. the next morning and called her at 7:15, before I left for school. Our first date was that evening at Baskin-Robbins. Our romance blossomed quickly, even though we lived in different parts of the city and went to different high schools. I attended every Northeast game they had in the city, often borrowing my father's car to take Sela and some of her cheerleader friends to basketball games outside the city. I gave Sela my football jacket and she gave me her tiny gold cheerleader megaphone chain with the Northeast emblem. It was not long before I had fallen in love with the first female in my life other than my mother, grandmother or favorite aunt.

*   *   *

It didn't take long before the party started jumping. A sweet rain had lifted the dizzy August heat. Since ΚΑΩ was the largest black fraternity on campus, we always had the initial party and almost every black student on campus would be there, even those book-worms who probably wouldn't attend another party all year.

It was great seeing everybody, catching up on what had hap-pened during the summer, and seeing the latest dances that people brought back to campus.

As the night wore on, I noticed a tall, muscular guy who seemed to be attracting a lot of attention from all the females. He stood against one of the banisters looking unapproachable, not saying a word. He was dressed in white linen and looked too mature to be a freshman. From his muscular body I could tell he was a jock, but he wasn't with the athletes at the party. Sela and her sorority sisters gathered in a clique, laughing and flirting with the stranger. He danced with a couple of them. I could tell from the way he danced and from his haircut, extra short on the sides, that he was not from the South. No, this guy was East Coast *for real.*

The party lasted until the wee hours of the morning, and after the beer ran out, we switched to ΚΑΩ punch, a combination of fruit juices and pure grain alcohol. The next morning I woke up with one of my worst hangovers ever, but I had to get up to drive to Birming-ham and catch a plane to New Orleans for my cousin's wedding. Why Terrence and Beverly chose August instead of June was a complete mystery to everyone in the wedding party. While on the Delta flight to New Orleans, I had a dream that bothered me. I didn't quite remember all the details, but the stranger from the party the night before was in it. He was visiting the campus to see if he might want to come to school next year. All during my stay in steamy New Orleans I thought about the dream. I was puzzled as to why I was dreaming about a guy I had seen only once and to whom I had never spoken a word. My return flight to school went smoothly and didn't include any illusions about the stranger or Sela, whom I dreamed of often when we were separated.

The football season rolled around, and with it, much cooler weather. Fall was advancing against the backdrop of an immense sky; braids of yellow, red and teal leaves created delicate hues as beautiful as the sweaters worn by my classmates. September flew by, and on the first Friday in October, I was in the locker room at the athletic complex after hitting some tennis balls with one of my frat brothers, Trent Walters. Trent finished his shower and started back to the frat house, where we always gathered before starting the weekend of partying.

This was the weekend of our first home football game, so there would be some serious parties. ΚΛΩ was giving a party too, but this weekend we would be competing with the two other black fraternities for attendees. After I finished dressing, I headed toward the exit of the locker room. I was looking down at my shoes, trying to decide if they needed shining. While trying to adjust my collar from the back, I bumped into a hard body.

"Oh, excuse me," I said. "I wasn't paying attention to where I was going."

"Sure, no problem," the stranger said.

When I looked up at him, my mouth dropped open. It was him! The guy from the party, the guy in my dream.

"Do you have a comb?" he asked.

"Excuse me." I was in a complete state of shock. Was I seeing and hearing him correctly?

"Do you have a comb?" he repeated.

"A comb," I repeated as I tried to regain my composure.

"Yes, a comb."

"I don't think so. Let me look." I suddenly became very nervous.

He was staring at me as I frantically looked in my gym bag for a comb.

"It doesn't look like I have one," I said. "I'm sorry."

"No reason to be," he said. "Thanks anyway."

As the stranger walked away, I stood in the same spot, speechless, not knowing what to do next. Suddenly the stranger stopped and turned around toward me.

"Where is the closest place you can buy liquor around here?" he asked.

"Duncan County, about thirty-five miles away. Do you go to school here?" I asked.

"Yes, unfortunately I do."

"Why say it like that?"

"Well, this place is different."

"Yes, it is. Where are you from?"

"Philadelphia."

"Philadelphia?" I asked, a bit surprised.

"Ever heard of it?"

"Of course! How did you wind up down here?"

"Football scholarship."

"Oh."

"My name is Kelvin Ellis," he said, extending his massive hand toward me.

"Raymond Tyler," I said as we shook the regular way and then went into the black-power handshake.

"Where are you from, Raymond?"

"Alabama."

"The whole state?" he asked with a smile, exposing almost perfectly white teeth.

"No, I'm from Birmingham."

"I've heard of Birmingham." Kelvin and I had now walked out of the locker room toward the enormous football stadium that anchored the athletic complex while talking about school and the game tomorrow.

"What position do you play?" I asked.

"Defensive back."

"Are you playing tomorrow?"

"No. I sprained my ankle this week. That's why I was down in the locker room in the whirlpool, getting treatment."

"Oh."

"Do you have a car?" he asked.

"Yes."

"How much would you charge to run me down to Duncan? I've got to get some brew."

"Nothing. I have to go down anyway to pick up some beer for my fraternity. What dorm are you in?"

"Westview, the athletic dorm."

"Okay, be outside in about thirty minutes. I'll be in a black Volkswagen."

"Great!"

I got into my car. I wanted to see if Sela wanted to ride to Duncan with me and my new friend. While I was driving, I began thinking about the dream I had had about Kelvin. Should I tell him? No, he would think I was weird. I began to hum the theme music from "The Twilight Zone" to myself as I pulled up in front of the Delta Sigma Theta sorority house. I went inside and asked the girl at the desk to page Sela Richards.

"Sela Richards, Sela Richards, you have a guest downstairs," she called over the loudspeaker. Five minutes later there was no sign of Sela. I left and went to my apartment, changed clothes and headed toward Westview Hall. When I came to Westview, I could see Kelvin standing against the bike rack. He had changed clothes too. As I approached the dorm, I blew my horn and rolled down my window.

"Get in," I said.

"You don't have to say it but once." He smiled.

As we drove down the highway toward Duncan, I could feel Kelvin staring at me. When we talked, he looked me straight in the eyes. I wasn't sure why, but this made me feel a bit uneasy. We talked about sports, school and, of course, females. We stopped at the first liquor store in Duncan. Kelvin purchased a case of beer and I bought two cases, plus a six-pack for the ride back to campus. While our initial conversation started out tense, after the first beer we both appeared to loosen up.

"Are you dating anyone?" Kelvin asked.

"Yes, Sela Richards. She's a Delta and my HTH."

"HTH?"

"Yes. Haven't you heard of *hometown honey?*"

"Hell no," Kelvin laughed. "HTH."

The time seemed to go by so fast. I became comfortable talking with Kelvin; he was very bright for a freshman. He had a deep baritone voice and a wonderful East Coast accent. He was very pleasant and seemed to know exactly what he wanted out of life. Yes, I thought to myself, a perfect ΚΑΩ pledge prospect.

"What about you?" I asked. "Do you have a girlfriend?"

"Yes, back in Philly. The babes here are so country."

"I guess."

I was driving pretty fast. With the sunroof open, the cool October wind breezed through the car. We had drunk a couple of cans of beer and I started to get a slight buzz, plus I had to piss. "Mind if I pull over? This beer has me running."

"No problem. I can use the stretch."

I pulled over along the side of the road and we both let out some of the beer we had consumed. The oyster-colored sky appeared solid as the setting sun shivered against it and the light breeze blew its own way. Kelvin and I sat on the front of my car and continued our conversation. He told me about growing up in Philly. I shared with Kelvin some of my childhood memories growing up in the South. I couldn't believe how comfortable I felt talking with him. I gave Kelvin my opinion of different people and places on campus and of the virtues of pledging KAΩ. Kelvin seemed interested in most of my conversation, but sometimes he appeared to be staring off into never-never land.

"Do you consider yourself open-minded?" he asked as we got back into my car.

"Yeah, I do."

"How open?"

"Pretty open." As we got closer to campus, Kelvin's questions became more personal. I wondered what he meant by "open-minded."

"Do you sleep with your girlfriend regularly?" he asked.

"Often enough. It's hard sometimes with her in a sorority house and me in a one-bedroom apartment with a roommate. But my roommate and I have worked out a system."

"A system?"

"Yeah. We have signals. Like this weekend he has to vacate the premises. He will either break the dorm rules and stay with his girlfriend or he'll stay with one of our fraternity brothers."

"Oh, I see."

"Would you like to come by my apartment and help me finish this beer?" I asked.

"Sure, why not. I'm out of football for a few weeks."

"Okay, man, let's do it."

"I'm game."

Once we reached my apartment, I gave Kelvin another beer. I was putting the rest in the refrigerator when he walked into the kitchen.

"Nice apartment. How much is the rent?"

"Two-fifty."

"Two-fifty? You're kidding."

"No, two-fifty."

"A place like this near Penn would cost three times that."

"It would?"

"Yeah, it would. Raymond, can I ask you something?" He was staring at me again with his light brown eyes with their curling black lashes. There was an ardent look about them. No man had ever looked at me this way.

"Sure."

"What did you think I meant when I asked you if you were open-minded?"

"I don't know. I really didn't think about it."

"You didn't?"

"No, I didn't. What did you mean?"

"Well, I'm not sure the good people of Alabama are going to be able to deal with me."

"Why?" I asked.

"Because I'm bisexual," Kelvin said.

"You're what?" I asked, almost spitting out the beer I had just swallowed.

"Bisexual. I make it with guys and girls. Haven't you heard of it?"

"Yeah, sure, we had sissies at my high school."

"Do I look like a sissy to you?"

"No, of course not, but . . ."

"But what?"

By this time I was getting nervous. Kelvin was standing very close to me, literally blocking my path to the living room and front door. Should I run or should I hit him? I just stood there and continued to talk, trying to change the conversation. "You want to go grab a pizza?"

"You're avoiding my question."

"No, I'm not . . . it's just that . . ."

"It's just what?"

"Well, Kelvin, you're a good-looking guy. You could probably get any girl you want."

"And I do."

"Don't you like girls?"

"I love women. Nobody eats trim better than me."

"Trim?"

"Yeah, you know, pussy."

"Oh. Then tell me, Kelvin, why in the fuck would you want to mess around with a man?"

"Variety is the spice of life."

"If you say so."

"So, Ray, tell me. Have you ever made it with a guy?"

"Hell no!" I protested.

"Don't get bent out of shape, Raymond."

The questions and the conversation were making me agitated. I wanted to appear more sophisticated. Maybe this was an East Coast thing. Did Kelvin guess about the one time I had experimented with my cousin Marcus, when we were both around nine years old? We had really only compared the size of our growing peters. How could he possibly know that?

I looked Kelvin straight in the eyes. "I'm not bent out of shape. That shit's not my style."

"Maybe you haven't run across the right man."

Trying to avoid Kelvin's eyes, I looked down at the gold shag carpet. When I decided to look up, I noticed Kelvin's erection bulging through his jeans and became even more nervous. What had I gotten myself into? This guy was bigger than me. There was a brief, uncomfortable pause. The silence was as heavy as one of my grandma's homemade quilts.

"Well, man, we better head back toward campus," I said.

"Sure. Come here for a second—there's something in your hair."

Without thinking, I moved closer to Kelvin. With the palm of his hands, he softly rubbed my entire face. I quickly pulled back.

"What the fuck are you doing?" I shouted.

A slight smile flickered over his face and he said, "Your skin looked so smooth that I had to touch it."

I didn't respond, silenced by his stare. His eyes were deep-set and defiant. Then he touched my nose and moved his fingers down to my lips. I don't know why, but I didn't stop him as he cupped my face and suddenly kissed my lips. I couldn't believe it, but it felt so natural. It was the first time I had ever kissed a man. I had never felt a spasm of sexual attraction toward a man. Honest to God. But his kiss. I had never kissed anyone like this, not even Sela. Before I was conscious of it, I was kissing Kelvin back and putting my arms around his waist. His force left little room for hesitation or resistance. I felt his strong body press toward mine—and an erection in my Jockey underwear, just aching to come out. I finally managed to pull back when I realized my sex was now full and hard, pressing against my navel. Kelvin looked down at me, gave a half-cocked grin and then pulled me toward him once again. This time there was no resistance.

What was happening? This sinful, sexual longing. This was wrong. Everything in my head screamed *no!* Yet my body was saying *yes*. We stood in the kitchen kissing nonstop for almost an hour.

"Where's your roommate?" Kelvin whispered in my ear.

"Don't worry, he'll call first," I said.

All of a sudden I felt Kelvin's hands touch my sex and then, with a single motion, his hands unzipped my jeans, releasing my throbbing penis. We continued to kiss passionately as he led me to the bedroom. Everywhere he touched became sensitive. My nerves became raw, tingling with unknown enjoyment. The movement of his body against mine felt as sensuous as powdered sheets. Moments later we were both butt-naked, lying on the edge of my twin bed. We managed to stop long enough to push the beds together.

On that night, the first Friday in October, I experienced passion and sexual satisfaction that I had never in my twenty-one years dreamed possible. Until that Friday evening in October, sex with females was all that I knew. I never imagined sex with a male. Sure, I had noticed or envied guys with great bodies while playing high school football, but I never thought of it in a sexual context. I had never before given a man's body such lofty regard as I did with Kelvin. How would I have known that rubbing two male sexual organs together would bring such a complete feeling of ecstasy?

I woke up nude and with a slight hangover. *Oh my God*, I thought as I sat straight up and jumped out of the makeshift bed. What had I done? Where was my overnight guest? I slipped my jeans on and ran from the bedroom through the kitchen and into the living room to see if the front door was locked. Thank God it was. What had happened to Kelvin? As I walked back toward my bedroom, I heard a knock at the front door. Could that be Kelvin? I put a sweatshirt on and quickly opened the door.

"Are you ready?" Sela asked as she walked through the door.

"Ready for what?"

"The game, silly. Doesn't my uniform tell you anything?"

Sela was the only black pom-pom girl at the university and she was all decked out in her red-and-blue uniform.

"What time is it?" I asked.

"It's eleven-thirty and I have to be at the stadium by noon."

"Oh shit, I must have overslept."

"What did you get into last night?" she asked.

"What?"

"Are you deaf? They told me you came by the house, but when I called you, I got no answer. I was at a party at your fraternity house last night and nobody had seen hide nor hair of you."

"I was studying."

"On a Friday night?"

"Yes, the LSAT is next Saturday."

"Oh well, should I wait on you or not?"

"Go ahead. I'll meet you at halftime."

"Okay, can I have a kiss?"

"No, not now," I said, pushing Sela away. "I have morning breath and I haven't brushed my teeth."

"Suit yourself. It's not like I haven't tasted your morning breath before," Sela said as she grabbed her purse and left the apartment in a huff.

After Sela left, I began to panic. What if Kelvin had set me up and now everybody on campus knew about last night's escapade. What if he told one of Sela's sorority sisters or, even worse, one of my fraternity brothers. I would have to drop out of school or transfer to A-State or Auburn in my senior year. I thought about the humiliation my parents and fraternity would feel. I would probably be kicked out. Should I go to the game or should I stay here and map out a plan of denial? I suddenly felt sick to my stomach. I quickly rushed to the toilet.

After some thought I decided to go to the game. By the time I reached the stadium, it was almost halftime. The few people I ran into seemed to act normal, nothing out of the ordinary. As I approached the section where my fraternity brothers were sitting, they all stood up and started clapping. What was the deal? There they were all standing up clapping and chanting, "Ray, Ray, Ray."

"What's up?" I asked.

"We're glad you could grace us with your presence," Kenny Adams, the president of the fraternity, said. "Where have you been?"

"What do you mean, where have I been?" I asked defensively.

"I'm just running a little late." I looked at my ticket stub and located my seat.

"Sorry I asked. We just missed you last night," Kenny replied. I gave Kenny a firm look, wondering if he knew Kelvin. Maybe he was gay and this was a part of some plan he had devised. No, Kenny wouldn't do that, I thought. Why was I being so paranoid? Did I have reason to be? Maybe. Maybe not.

During halftime Sela came up to our section, grabbed my hand and said, "Can I have a kiss now, Mr. Tyler?"

"Sure!"

As I kissed Sela in front of my fraternity brothers and the stadium filled with a crowd of over eighty thousand spectators, I thought everything seemed normal. Maybe last night had never happened, it was just a bad dream. Or was it a nightmare just beginning?

After the game Sela and I went to our usual after-game restaurant, Ben's Bar-B-Que, which had the finest food in town. We could only afford it about once a month. The restaurant was filled with the aroma of Ben's famous barbecue and the sounds of french fries and onion rings hitting hot grease. It always had a diverse mix of people. Black students, white students, alumni and the local folks. Ben's served the best onion rings I had ever tasted and the beer was always ice-cold. Being the only black pom-pom girl, Sela was something of a local celebrity. Several alumni always came over to our table to talk and gawk at her. Most of the time they simply ignored me. I didn't mind, especially today. I had my own problems.

I kept thinking about the night before. What had happened? Why had I let it happen? Why had I enjoyed it? After we left Ben's, we headed to my apartment to finally spend some time alone and to get in our weekly lovemaking. This was an event that I usually looked forward to, but on this Saturday I didn't want Sela to touch me. Maybe I didn't feel clean or maybe I now viewed my body differently. Once we got back to the apartment, I grabbed a beer from the previous evening's excursion to Duncan. Sela went into my bedroom and changed from her uniform into tight-fitting jeans and a red cashmere sweater. I didn't bother to change from my starched khaki slacks and stiff white oxford shirt. I sat on the sofa, gazing at the television, not really aware of what was on. Sela came in and sat on my lap in an obviously romantic mood. We started kissing, and just when I started to loosen her bra, there was a knock at the door.

"Are you expecting anyone?" Sela asked.

"Not that I can think of," I answered.

I got up, tucked my shirt back into my pants and opened the door. When I opened the door, there he stood. Kelvin. *No, I guess last night was not a dream.* A wave of shame suddenly came over me.

"Hi. I'm sorry . . ." Before he finished his sentence, Kelvin noticed Sela sitting on the sofa and quickly stopped his words and his approach into my living room.

"Hi. I'm sorry, I must have the wrong apartment. I'm looking for Linton Johnson's apartment," he said.

"Do you know the apartment number?" I asked.

Kelvin had a strange look on his face. It was a mixture of surprise and disappointment.

"Fifteen-J," Kelvin said.

"Oh, you're at the wrong building. J is about two buildings over. Hold on a minute, I'll show you where it is."

"Gee, thanks. I'd appreciate that."

I hurried back to the sofa, where Sela sat looking at me. Kelvin stood in the doorway looking away from the apartment. I slipped on my brown penny loafers and avoided the curious look on Sela's face. As I walked out and closed the door behind me, Kelvin turned to face me.

"Man, I'm really sorry," he said.

"Oh, don't be ridiculous. It's no problem. Let's walk out by my car."

"I didn't mean to leave so early this morning, but you looked like you were sleeping so soundly that I just couldn't wake you up."

"Why did you leave so early?"

"I forgot to tell you that even though I'm not playing with the team, I still had to attend a mandatory team breakfast and I didn't want any questions if someone happened to see me leave here so early in the morning."

"So what time did you leave?"

"Just before sunrise."

"I was beginning to worry. I didn't know what to think. I thought maybe last night was a dream."

"Well, it was a dream for me. A dream come true," Kelvin said.

"Don't say that. We have to talk," I said, looking away from Kelvin.

"When?"

"Well, definitely not now. It will have to be Sunday or Monday."

"How about Sunday at four?" Kelvin suggested.

"I don't know, it's hard to say."

"You do want to see me again, don't you?"

"Yeah, no. I mean, I'm not sure."

"Well, you think about it. I'll be standing in front of the student union at four sharp. I'll wait fifteen minutes, then I'm history."

"That sounds fair," I said.

"Later."

"Okay. Later."

As Kelvin walked away from the apartment parking lot, I wondered why I was being such a jerk. I started to call his name out loud and tell him to come back so that we could talk when I suddenly heard someone call my name.

"Ray!" Sela yelled out.

"Yeah," I said, still watching Kelvin walk up the hill and disappear into the neighborhood, heading toward campus.

"What are you doing?"

"Hold on, I'm getting a book from my car." I walked over to my car and realized that I didn't have my car keys. Even worse, I looked in the window and saw that there were no books anywhere. I turned away from my car and walked back toward my apartment. I noticed that Sela had a puzzled look on her face.

"What was that about?" she asked.

"What?"

"I mean, he looked like he knew you."

"Well, we both have seen him before. Remember the party at the beginning of the year? His name is Kelvin Ellis."

"Oh yeah, my soror Cinda Shepard is crazy about him. They've been out a couple of times."

"Who is Cinda Shepard?"

"You know her."

"Is she that brown-skinned sister with the bad weave and green contacts?"

"Yeah, but she's a sweet girl and really smart."

Sela and I went back into the apartment and picked up where we had left off. Things went normally, or so they seemed. I don't know what I was thinking. Maybe that I wouldn't be able to get it up or that I would think of Friday night with Kelvin. Sela still excited me and I loved waking up with her in the mornings, her head lying against my chest.

Saturday night went by swiftly, and on Sunday morning Sela and I attended church. During the altar call I was tempted to throw myself on the altar to repent for Friday night, but I resisted. After dropping Sela off, I looked at my watch. Four o'clock. I drove my car down Sharp Street toward my apartment and away from the student union and Kelvin. I was at a stoplight that seemed to stay red forever when I suddenly found myself turning right instead of left, in the direction of the student union. As I reached the student union, I saw Kelvin leaning against the front door. I could tell he spotted me immediately. Before I could blow my horn, he was walking toward the driver's side of my car.

"Get in," I said.

"Are you sure?" he asked.

"Come on now, Kelvin. Quit playing."

"Okay, I give up," he said, grinning, as he got in on the passenger side.

"Where to?" I asked.

"You know this place better than I do."

"Let's go back to the scene of the crime."

"Your apartment?"

"No."

"Where?"

"The stadium."

"The stadium?"

"It's usually empty around this time."

"Let's go!"

We drove into the parking lot of the stadium and went around through the fence that students used on game days. It was empty, with the exception of a few football players running around the track. We went high up into the stadium so that we couldn't be recognized and no one could hear our conversation.

The sky above was clear and blue and the wind seemed to blow harder the higher we climbed. We sat opposite each other on the hard aluminum bleachers. It seemed as though we were in a vacuum, sitting alone in the enormous empty stadium.

"So, what's up?" I asked.

"You."

"What did you want to talk about?"

"Friday night."

"What about it?"

"Was that really your first time?"

"What do you think?"

"I think so."

"Why?"

"I can just tell."

"How?" I asked curiously.

"Trust me, I know."

"I bet. I heard you're dating Cinda."

"Cinda who?"

"Cinda Shepard."

"We've been out a couple of times, nothing special. I told you, I have a girlfriend back in Philly. Her name is Paula Wyatt."

"Oh, and do you have a boyfriend too?"

"Don't be silly. I've told you about that sissy shit."

"Well, this is all new to me. What do you mean you could tell?"

"Yeah, I realized that, but you're easy to read."

"What do you mean I'm 'easy to read'?"

"Don't worry about it. That's just an expression. I just had this feeling about you when we met, kind of like a sixth sense." Kelvin paused and then continued, "I don't think anyone else would pick it up unless they were *in* themselves. Raymond, I think you're pretty special and I would like to become your friend even if we don't ever sleep together again. I promise not to interfere with your relationship with your girlfriend, Selee."

"You mean Sela?" I snapped.

"Yes, whatever. But Friday night has to be our secret. You know I plan to be a big football star in this place and something like this could end it all."

"Who am I going to tell?"

"I don't know."

"Well, don't worry. This is a secret I'll carry to my grave!"

"Can I ask you a question?" Kelvin asked seriously.

"Oh boy, here we go again," I said with nervous laughter.

"No, be serious. Was I the first guy to ever approach you?"

"Yeah. Do I look like a sissy?"

"That's not what I mean. It's not about that sissy shit. Look at you. You're an attractive guy. I can't believe that Friday was the first time."

"Well, trust me, it was."

"I believe you, Raymond. It's not the end of the world."

"I don't know if I agree. I mean, nothing like this has ever happened to me," I said.

"Raymond, if it hadn't been me, it would have been someone else."

"You sound so confident. I don't think it will happen again."

"We'll see. Is it okay if I have your phone number?" Kelvin asked.

"I don't know if that would be cool. I have a roommate."

"What do you think I'm going to do? Call him and tell him what went down?"

"No."

"Then stop tripping. I just want to keep in touch. There is nothing wrong with a friend calling a friend. Right?"

"I guess you're right. It's 332-8971. And yours?"

"I don't know," he teased. "I've got a roommate."

"Now who's tripping?" I asked.

"It's 332-9981."

"Thanks, I'll write it down when I get back to my car."

"Raymond, you know one time doesn't make you gay."

"It doesn't?"

"No, Raymond, it doesn't."

"Well, we better get out of here before they think we're trying to burn this baby down."

"Burn it?"

"Yeah, my freshman year the black students demanded that the band stop playing 'Dixie' and the cheerleaders stop carrying Confederate flags. When they refused, there were several flag burnings by the Black Student Union."

"Man, what have I gotten myself into?"

"Are you talking about the flags or me?"

"Both," Kelvin said with a lighthearted smile.

I dropped Kelvin off by Westview and headed for my apartment. As I drove, I became filled with so many tortured feelings about Kelvin and Friday night. When I arrived at the door, I could hear the stereo in my apartment blasting a new song, "You Give Good Love." The first time I had heard it was early Saturday morning as Kelvin and I lay with our backs to each other. I thought to myself that it was such a beautiful song. When I walked into the apartment, my roommate, Stanley, was washing dishes.

"How was your weekend?" he asked.

"Okay," I said. "Who sings this song?"

"It's a new singer. Her name is Whitney Houston. She used to be a model, and Ray, she is so fine. Look at the cover. The album is as good as she looks."

"I love that song. Yeah, she is beautiful." Great, I thought to myself, women still look good to me.

"I've been playing the album constantly. Anything special happen this weekend?" Stanley asked.

"No, not really, just a typical weekend in the country."

TWO

As the fall semester progressed, so did my relationship with Kelvin. I guess you wouldn't really call it a relationship. Sometimes we would meet and study in the library, walk around campus and wind up at the stadium talking about things I couldn't talk about with anyone else, especially Sela. It was easy talking with Kelvin. When we talked, I felt as though we were the only two people on earth.

Sela was still important to me and I was convinced that I still loved her and would eventually marry her. But Kelvin excited me in ways that were hard to explain, let alone understand. At times the guilt was unbearable. This relationship was totally against everything I had been taught. My happiness with Kelvin was sometimes replaced with disgust, depression and disappointment when I wanted to be with him but instead fought those feelings and spent the time with Sela. There were periods of extended remorse on both our parts, days when I avoided Kelvin like I avoided visits to the dentist. I was certain he had days when he felt the same about me. Our relationship was like a fickle faucet that ran both hot and cold. You never knew what to expect.

Kelvin's football career was off to a promising start, as was his reputation as a ladies' man. There were times when we saw each other at campus dances and he was often with attractive girls. I would become jealous, but these were feelings that I had to keep inside.

Once we were together, we would talk about my jealousy. I think he got jealous seeing me with Sela, but he never let on. Kelvin always reassured me, explaining that I knew about the females in his life but they would never know about me. It was our secret.

I often wondered why this had happened to me. Would this relationship and the new revelations I experienced with Kelvin change the carefully laid plans that my parents and Sela had mapped out for my future? How would I make room in my life for this? My schoolwork was not affected by this new relationship. In fact, my grades were perfect. The only difference was that the relationship forced me to reconsider staying in Alabama for law school and giving up my dream of leaving for an Ivy League law school education.

My relationship with Sela remained the same. As far as she knew, Kelvin was no more than a face in the crowd. She was busy with the football season and her sorority. We continued to do things that we always shared. Our lovemaking was frequent and passionate, and when I experienced difficulties getting in the mood, I would conjure up thoughts of my lovemaking sessions with Kelvin. It wasn't hurting anyone and Sela seemed satisfied. I assumed she was satisfied. I sometimes wondered if it wasn't an act. I mean, I had always heard all this stuff about women faking orgasms. At least with Kelvin and me the proof was there. He was a sexual cyclone.

*   *   *

It was the longest we had ever been apart since we met. Ten whole days. It was the first time I could remember that I wanted Christmas and New Year's to come and go. I wasn't even interested in what Sela or my parents had gotten me for Christmas.

Sela's parents surprised her for Christmas with a new Ford Mustang, so she decided to drive to Atlanta to pick up one of her Delta sorors. As luck would have it, a huge snowstorm hit town, and while I made it back in my car, I wondered if Kelvin's flight would get in. The airport was small and I could see him stuck somewhere between Alabama and Philadelphia.

I found myself pacing around the one-bedroom apartment that I still shared with Stanley, who had to be one of the straightest brothers in my fraternity. This was the first time I could ever remember being alone. My roommate or Sela always seemed to be around, but on this day I didn't want to be alone. Where was Kelvin? Suddenly the phone rang and my heart started to race as I let it ring again. I couldn't be too anxious.

After the fourth ring I grabbed the phone and there was a dial tone. Who was it? No one besides my parents knew that I was back in town. I had given them some excuse about my scholarship money being in question and my needing to get back early to get the mess cleared up.

Maybe it was a wrong number or maybe it was Kelvin. Then a terrible thought came across my mind: what if it was Sela? Maybe she had decided to surprise me and show up on campus early. She wouldn't dare.

Now I was a nervous wreck. What if it had been Kelvin? Maybe he thought I couldn't get away from my family, or that I had gotten stuck in the snow, which was now about six inches deep. Almost half an hour later the phone rang again. This time I didn't wait and I picked it up in the middle of the first ring.

"Hello," I said quickly.

"Hello, Ray, is that you?"

"Yeah. Where the hell are you?"

"You'll never guess."

My heart started to beat at a rapid rate. "Where?"

All of a sudden Kelvin started to laugh out loud. "I'm in the dorm, you nut. Hurry up and come get me!"

"Don't play with me like that. I'll be there in ten minutes."

I grabbed the black leather jacket my father had bought me for Christmas, checked for my car keys and headed out the door. When I reached my car, I couldn't believe what had happened. Snow covered every inch of my black Volkswagen. The only way I knew it was my car was because other than it, the lot at my apartment complex was empty. Most of the students who lived there were still away for the holidays. I looked at the streets and saw that there were no cars and the snow was still falling very fast. After removing all the snow from my car, I tried to start it. The car would not turn over. I tried over and over with no luck. It was frozen solid.

Depressed, I went back into my warm apartment and picked up the phone to call Kelvin. Before I even dialed, I heard his voice on the other end.

"Where are you?" he asked.

"Guess what?" I said. "My car won't start. It's frozen stiff."

"What are we going to do?" he demanded.

"I don't know," I replied reluctantly.

"I can't wait to see you! I've missed you something terrible. I even have on my black bikini underwear," he added.

I could just imagine his muscular brown body fitting perfectly into his black bikini underwear and I knew then that nothing was going to keep me away.

"Start walking. I'll meet you halfway," Kelvin said.

"Are you crazy? Do you know how far that is?"

"Don't worry. I'll make it worth your while," he said softly.

"I'm leaving now," I replied hurriedly.

I didn't realize how far I had walked until I noticed the full moon looking over the snow-covered grounds of the beautiful campus. It was like a ghost town: no students moving around, no campus buses or cars, no lights or shadows in the huge dormitory windows.

As I reached the bottom of the hill, I could see Kelvin coming around the bend. Though he was all bundled up, he looked fantastic to me. As he got closer, I could see his sparkling smile beneath the snow-covered purple skullcap that covered his head and most of his face. Before I knew it, I was running and sliding toward him and he was running and sliding toward me too. Within moments we were doing the unthinkable. Embracing in front of the university president's red brick house. All of a sudden we both fell and started rolling around in the snow, still embracing each other. There we were, acting as though we were the only inhabitants in this picturesque college town. Two able-bodied black men, in a town where most of its citizens were as white as the snow that now covered it, kissing like nothing else mattered but that moment. I looked up at the transparent sky and suddenly realized the importance of that moment; my lust for Kelvin had slowly turned to love. Never, in any of my most romantic dreams, had I ever imagined a night as perfect as that cold winter night.

My final spring semester at AU sailed by with the speed of a Carl Lewis one-hundred-yard dash. While I had become comfortable with the sexual relationship with Kelvin, I was not prepared for an emotional relationship. The more I began to care for Kelvin, the more frustrated I became with the demands of my now strained relationship with Sela. Oftentimes I started fights with Sela for no apparent reason, at least in Sela's eyes.

There were times, however, when I needed Sela, not just for public appearances, but because deep in my heart I truly cared for her. Times when I only wanted to be wrapped in her small arms, lying there, looking at her, smelling her. I thought of the countless times I had told Sela I loved her and really meant it, but I couldn't understand why it was impossible to tell Kelvin just once. Was it possible to be in love with two people at the same time? One Friday evening Kelvin did the impossible. We were sitting in my apartment about to start our second six-pack of beer. Kelvin slowly walked from the kitchen to my stereo just as the last notes of Whitney's "You Give Good Love" faded away. Kelvin fumbled through my album collection for a few minutes and then said aloud, "I found it."

"What?" I asked.

"Just listen," Kelvin said as he put his finger to his lips. "Shhh."

Suddenly the room was filled with the sounds of LTD's "Love Ballad." I will never forget how, just as Jeffrey Osborne was about to proclaim the depth of his love, Kelvin gently lifted the needle from the album, gazed at me and proclaimed, "I love you."

The room was bathed in silence as I sat on the sofa, staring at Kelvin. I was dumbfounded; my stomach was quietly turning somersaults. I knew I loved him too, but I couldn't say it; instead, I smiled and murmured, "*I know.*"

Decisions, decisions. It would have been easy had I only been accepted to law school at AU. Instead, I found myself accepted at Howard, Columbia, Harvard and, of course, AU; this made my decision more difficult. Choosing a school to further my education was one thing, but trying to satisfy my educational goals and both relationships made my decision even more complicated.

The only person willing to voice an opinion was my father. He favored Harvard. I wanted Howard and Washington, D.C. Sela had always assumed that I would go East for law school. Kelvin mentioned that he wouldn't mind transferring to Howard. I compromised and chose Columbia. I was on my way to New York City.

THREE

Alabama and the university were miles and years away—
they had become my past. Parallel to the distance and the days, my
relationships with Kelvin and Sela were also things of the past. It
was hard to believe, but I was now entering my sixth year of living
in New York City. Who said I wouldn't last?

After a slow start in law school, I managed to finish in the top
half of my class and secure a job with one of the top New York
firms. I received several offers from all across the country, including
one from my father to join his firm.

I had new friends, a new apartment and a new attitude about
life. My life was totally different from the one I had lived down
South. I no longer considered myself straight . . . but was I completely gay?

If it were not for holidays, birthdays and necessities, like underwear and socks, I would never enter a department store. I would

just simply order all my clothes through mail-order catalogues. At least while living in New York, I was not subjected to mall mentality. All the major stores were located on New York's busy streets. It was Friday evening, and after leaving my office a little early, I stopped by Saks Fifth Avenue to pick up a robe for my best friend, Kyle, before he left for home for the holidays.

Kyle and I planned to meet as usual, around six-thirty, at the Nickel Bar, to start our Friday night ritual of drinking and chasing the boys of New York City. We would always start at the Nickel Bar, grab a bite to eat, go home to change from our business attire to jeans and then reconvene in the Village or up in Harlem at the Cotton Club if it was gay night.

After picking out a silk robe for Kyle's Christmas present, I waited an awfully long time for the salesman to get approval on my credit card. Was I over my limit? I didn't think so, since I had just sent a large payment.

Staring straight ahead waiting for the salesman to return with good news and Kyle's wrapped gift, I suddenly noticed the back of a man's head across the counter, directly in front of me, and I also noticed a light brown birthmark right above his neck. No, it can't be, I thought. As the tall, well-built black man reached for the young lady at his side, he turned around and we were face-to-face.

"Kelvin?"

"Ray?"

"How are you doing?" I stammered, obviously in a state of shock.

"Fine. It's been a long time," he said.

"Yeah, almost six years." For a moment we both just stood there looking at each other. A layer of sweat started forming on my forehead when suddenly I heard another voice.

"Kelvin," the voice said. "Honey, aren't you going to introduce us?"

"Oh," Kelvin stammered, "I'm sorry. Ray, this is Candi,

Candance Wesley, my fiancée. Candance, this is Ray—I mean, Raymond Tyler."

"It's a pleasure to meet you," Candance said as her lips parted in a flash of perfect white teeth. "Where do you two know each other from?" she inquired.

"School," Kelvin said quickly. "Undergraduate school in Alabama."

"Yes," I said. "Many, many years ago."

"I heard you were living in New York," Kelvin said. "What law firm are you with?" he asked.

"Clay, Wilson and White. It's in the 767 building, right around the corner. And where are you these days?"

"Oh, Candance and I live in Washington, D.C. Candi is in her final year of medical school at Howard University and I'm coaching football at one of the high schools down there."

"Oh, a doctor?" I asked as I finally took my eyes off Kelvin and turned my eyes toward Candance.

"Well, I'm not a doctor yet, but hopefully very soon." Candance smiled. As shoppers moved around us, I had to stop myself from looking at Kelvin. He appeared even more handsome than I remembered. His brown, cocoa-colored skin now included a thick black mustache that covered the top of his large, exquisite lips.

All of a sudden so many memories rushed into my mind that I felt more sweat forming, not only on my forehead but now in the palms of my hands. I wanted to loosen my tie to be able to breathe more comfortably. I had so many questions that I wanted to ask, but I just stood there waiting for him to say something.

"We came up to complete our Christmas shopping and wrap up our wedding plans," Candance chirped in. "My family is from Mount Vernon, so you'll definitely have to come to the wedding," she said.

"Oh yes," I replied. "When is the big day?"

"June twentieth," she said.

"June twentieth?" I repeated, almost choking.

"Ray, are you all right?" Kelvin asked, reaching to grasp me, but abruptly stopping his motion.

"Oh yeah, I'm fine," I said. "June twentieth is—"

But before I could finish my sentence, Kelvin jumped in and said, "Isn't that your birthday, Ray?"

"Yes," I said quietly. "And you're December twelfth, right?"

"Yes," he replied bashfully.

"What a coincidence!" Candance laughed and said, "Now we will have two reasons to celebrate."

"Yes, I guess you're right," I said.

Now I was purposely avoiding Kelvin's eyes.

"Well, come, sweetie," Candance said. "We have to meet Daddy at seven o'clock. Ray, it was a pleasure meeting you and I look forward to seeing you again real soon. Maybe you can come to D.C. sometime to visit. It's a shame you guys live this close and don't see more of each other."

"Yes, I'd like that."

I began to study Candance's face and realized what an attractive young lady she was. Candance was delicate, with auburn hair that was pulled back into a shoulder-length ponytail, nice light brown eyes that were almost identical to Kelvin's and striking features that complemented her small face and petite figure. Her skin tone was a yellowish brown-waffle color.

"It's great seeing you, Ray. You look great," Kelvin said.

"Well, I try. It's great seeing you too; here's my card. Give me a call real soon so that we can talk about our days at old AU."

"I will," he said nervously, his eyes again avoiding mine. "Merry Christmas and all that stuff," he stuttered.

"Yeah, Ray, Merry Christmas," Candance added. "Come on, Kelvin, we're running late," she said.

"Merry Christmas to you guys and belated Happy Birthday, K."

Kelvin suddenly looked at me and for a moment a familiar smile crossed his face. "Yeah, thanks, Ray," he said as his light brown eyes looked straight through me.

"K! How cute," Candance giggled. "I'll have to remember that, Kelvin."

As I watched the two of them walk out of Saks hand in hand, I realized that the store was now packed with people doing their last-minute Christmas shopping. I suddenly became aware of the sounds of the holiday season as they filled the large department store.

"Mr. Tyler," the salesman said, "your package is ready."

"Oh, thank you," I said as I headed toward the doors facing Fifth Avenue and my meeting with Kyle.

As I walked out of the store, I instantly realized that I was running late and would have to catch a taxi, which would be almost impossible on this cold Friday evening. It didn't matter that I had on my best blue suit, a silk scarf and my black cashmere overcoat. I was still black and a taxi would be difficult to catch in front of Saks, with all the white ladies waiting on taxis too.

I looked at my watch, and since I still felt a little warm, I decided to walk to the Nickel Bar. As I started uptown, I decided to take the route through Central Park. The lights in the park made it easy to see the heavily clothed joggers, homeless people and matronly society ladies walking their dogs, which wore outfits as fashionable as their owners'.

Walking through the park aroused thoughts that went back to my senior year in undergrad—the many good times I shared with Kelvin, our plotting ways to spend time together. I also remembered the last evening we shared, the night before my parents came up for graduation. I had given Sela some flimsy excuse about spending time drinking with my frat brothers. She was so busy planning dinner for my family after the ceremonies that it didn't seem to matter to her what I did or whom I was doing it with. I was leaving the next day for New York and a summer job Pops had found for me.

My last evening with Kelvin turned out to be quite unpleasant. He told me he was going to start dating women exclusively. Deep down I was angry, but I told Kelvin I was in agreement; he and I both dated women. Damn, Sela and I had dated since my junior year in high school and Kelvin never interfered with our relationship. The first few weeks I was away, Kelvin and I talked every day. There was a letter or card at least twice a week. He talked about coming to New York on his way home and he seemed really worried that I would meet someone else. He wasn't worried about another woman but another man.

When school started, Kelvin stopped writing and returning my phone calls. Sela once casually mentioned that rumor had it that he was dating a blonde Tri Delta, and because Kelvin was so good-looking, all the black girls on campus were furious.

Though she never questioned me in depth, Sela had always wondered why Kelvin and I were no longer friends. I brushed it off, telling her he was just a dumb jock and I had more important things with law school and all.

As I walked up Broadway, I stopped to enjoy the lights and the fountain at Lincoln Center. I stuck my hands deep in the pockets of my cashmere overcoat and pulled out a shiny new penny. I dropped it into the fountain and thought back to my unexpected reunion with Kelvin as the penny found a place at the bottom.

Married, I thought to myself, Kelvin, *married?* I chuckled out loud at the thought and wondered if his future wife knew what I knew. My trip took me past several of my favorite restaurants, and before I realized it, I was on Seventy-second Street. As I turned the corner, I suddenly felt the brisk winter wind. I quickened my pace toward Columbus Avenue, and moments later I was lined up behind several handsome black men going through the thick mahogany door that led to the Nickel Bar. I smiled to myself and thought, Boy, do I need a drink.

When I opened the door to the small, dimly lit bar, I immediately spotted Kyle sitting on his regular stool at the end of the bar close to the door. He had a drink in one hand and a cigarette in the other. He was surrounded by several admirers, who seemed to be hanging on his every word. When Kyle looked up from his drink and saw me coming through the door, he immediately put down his cigarette, motioning me toward him and his audience.

"Bitch, where have you been?" Kyle quizzed me.

"Kyle, don't start with that 'bitch' crap," I ordered.

"Okay. Answer my question."

"You'll never guess."

"You look like you've seen a ghost."

"Well, not quite, more like a vision from the past."

"Who was he?" Kyle asked quickly. "Anybody I know?"

"Give me a minute to check my coat and catch my breath, please. Order me a drink," I demanded.

"Excuse me," Kyle snapped at the bartender, waving his left hand in the air and twirling around with a single motion on the barstool. "A Stoli on the rocks for my friend and make it quick before I have to read this bitch."

"Please, Kyle, not today. I'm in no mood to read you back," I pleaded.

Three drinks later, the Stoli had settled and was taking effect. Kyle and I were both laughing out of control at my previous encounter with Kelvin and Candance.

"Chile, these confused boys give me fever. How long do you

think that marriage is going to last before Mr. Kelvin starts sneaking out on Miss What's Her Name?" he asked.

"Her name is Candance, Kyle. Anyway, Kelvin was pretty much a ladies' man back on campus."

"Yeah, and so was I," he snickered. "Are you still in love with this guy?"

"I don't really know. He was my first, and to be honest, my heart started to beat faster the moment I saw him today. I mean, it was like the first time I saw him years ago."

"Are you going to call him?"

"I don't think so. I'm going to leave well enough alone. That was then; this is now. Come on, let's change the subject. Where are we going tonight?" I asked, purposefully changing the subject.

"We will pick this conversation up later, my dear," Kyle said. "Right now I see a gorgeous guy in the corner with big hands and I'm going to give him a Christmas greeting. Watch my stool."

Kyle moved toward the back of the packed narrow bar; off to meet his next conquest.

While Kyle was on his mission, I moved from the corner barstool and walked around the bar to see if I saw any familiar faces. The Nickel Bar was always crowded, but Fridays found the Nickel jammed packed with good-looking and not so good-looking black men in business suits and jeans, all looking relieved that another workweek had ended. I located a spot against the wall that was strategically situated, where I could keep one eye on Kyle and the other on any interesting faces that might catch my eye.

As I sipped my drink, I eavesdropped on the conversation of two men standing close by. "Miss Thing, I can't believe you didn't work that fine man," the guy standing next to me said to his friend in a high-pitched voice. "He wasn't my type, Miss Honey. Did you see those hands? Trust me, he's not the one," the other giggled. I wondered if these guys talked like that most of the time, and if they did, where did they work?

The Nickel Bar had not changed since the first time I had come in almost three years before. A real fear came over me the first time I entered. I remember feeling as though I were walking through a dark tunnel into a secret world. The music was loud and aggressive. Beating faster than my heart.

One of my law school classmates, Peter Davis, had invited me to the Nickel Bar one evening for a drink after one of our study group sessions. Peter failed to mention that the Nickel was a gay bar, and even though I knew New York had several such places, I had no idea that there were all-black gay bars. I was convinced that this was Peter's way of trying to find out what my deal was without directly asking me. It became obvious, once we arrived, that Peter was a regular at the Nickel. Everyone from the bouncer to the coat-check guy knew him. How Peter could have such an active social life and stay on top of law school was amazing to me. It was on this outing with Peter that I met Kyle. Peter was in the back of the bar talking with a friend when I noticed a very attractive guy. He had nice, short, curly hair. No Jheri curl but naturally curly black hair, called *good hair* down South. He had a sandy-colored complexion that was void of any acne, razor bumps or hair. His teeth were so perfectly straight that you guessed he had spent years wearing braces or had spent a lot of money for caps.

Kyle Benton was an original. He had graduated from Princeton University but hated being called an Ivy Leaguer. The first evening we met, Kyle told me that we would be friends for life. When I asked him how he knew that, he simply replied, "I'm psychic." I laughed so hard that my sides began to hurt. Kyle appeared to be quite comfortable with who he was. A black man and gay. This sometimes made me a little bit uncomfortable. When I asked him how long he had been gay, he laughed, "Chile, I've been a sissy since I was in my mother's womb."

Prior to our meeting, I found myself staring at Kyle for about an hour. I could tell that he saw me staring, so I decided to look down into my drink and glance around at other guys in the bar. I caught him looking over at me and even noticed him smiling in my direction. I lifted my half-empty glass to my lips, and casually looked in the direction where he was standing, when I realized he was no longer there. I started toward the back of the bar to find Peter when I felt someone grab the back of my shoulder.

"So do you have a name?" he asked.

"Excuse me," I said, slightly startled.

"Do you have a name?"

"Yes."

"Well, what is it?"

"Who's asking?"

"The QIB," he said, very seriously.

"The QIB?"

"Yes, the QIB."

"Who's the QIB?"

All of a sudden Kyle couldn't contain his straight face. "The QIB," he laughed. "You haven't heard of the Queen's Information Bureau?"

By now he was holding his stomach from laughing so hard as I stood there with a dumb look on my face.

"I'm sorry," he said, "but you looked so serious. I couldn't resist. I'm Kyle Alexander Benton, or KAB, like in taxi." He reached out his hands to greet mine.

Now I was smiling too. "Hello, I'm Raymond Tyler," I said as I extended my hand toward him.

"Your pleasure, I'm sure. What are you drinking?"

"White wine."

"Oh, how Mary Tyler Moore of you, Mr. Tyler." Kyle smiled as he motioned for the attention of one of the waiters. "Let me buy you a drink," he offered.

"Sure, thank you."

A couple of hours later, I felt as if I had known Kyle for years. He was smart, funny and self-assured. He kept asking me to say certain words because he loved hearing the remains of my deep Southern accent. Suddenly we heard the disc jockey announce last call and realized how fast the time had gone.

"Let's exchange numbers," Kyle said.

"Sure, I'd like that."

"I work on Fifty-second and Avenue of the Americas, so we should get together for lunch soon and decide if we are going to be friends or fuck buddies," Kyle stated very matter-of-factly.

"Excuse me?" I asked, startled.

"I'm just playing with you," he laughed. "Let's just be friends. Lord knows I've had enough one-night stands to last a lifetime."

"I'd like to be your friend," I said as I began to look around the now brightly lit bar for Peter. The bartender was counting money in the cash register and the bouncer was giving us a get-the-fuck-out look. When I found Peter, the three of us headed toward the Seventy-second Street subway stop, laughing like old friends at the night's events. Once we reached the station, Kyle gave me a big hug and went to the side of the tracks going downtown. Peter and I caught the first express train heading uptown. Once on the train, Peter rambled on and on about who he thought was gay in our law school class. I saw his lips moving but didn't hear a word.

"What are you smiling at?" Peter inquired.

"Who me?"

"Yes, you."

"Life." I smiled. "Just life."

*   *   *

Kyle quickly became my first openly gay friend. At times the relationship was trying, while at other times Kyle was like a breath of
fresh air in a smoke-filled room. He became my mentor in terms of
teaching me about the gay world. Sometimes he would look at me
in amazement at my naïveté about the gay life. It was completely
different from the world I was used to. Different in many aspects,
including language. I felt like I was learning a foreign language.

Everything and everyone was referred to as Miss, Miss Thing this
or Miss Thang that. There were often used words like *trade, size
queen, B-boys, butch queen, read* and *clocked.* These words were
often punctuated with a quick finger snap or pop, and almost every
gesture was exaggerated. Kyle was a master at all the wiles and ways
of the black gay community.

Most of the time I felt as though I were in a different country,
not really fitting in. But by now I didn't feel a part of the straight
world either. My transition to the black gay community reminded
me of high school, when I was one of twenty-two blacks in my
freshman class of eight hundred forty-three. All my new white classmates were different from the kids at my all-black junior high on
the east side. I mean, the way they talked, the things that made
them laugh and the things they considered important were totally
opposite of what I was used to. Down South, Kyle would definitely
have been labeled a sissy. I told him on countless occasions that I
would have gone in the opposite direction had I met him in high
school or college. He would simply reply, "And I would have read
you for filth."

"Didn't the boys you grew up with tease you?" I once asked Kyle.

"Not after I had worked them," he replied with confidence.

With Kyle, I no longer had to keep secrets about my feelings. I
could say what was on my mind and not worry about what my

girlfriend, fraternity brothers or my parents thought. I could always count on Kyle to make me laugh whenever I had a bad day at school or (once I had finished law school) at the office. Even though I had felt close to Kelvin, we never talked about gay things. It was always school, sports and girls. At first we were just two guys fucking; later, two men who loved each other and who enjoyed a sexual relationship. We played the same head trips with each other that occurred in male-female relationships and sought the same kind of security. Even though Kelvin and I shared a great many secrets, there was no one I could talk to about him.

My relationship with Kyle wasn't about sex, but friendship. About removing the guards I had learned to put up to avoid letting people in. Although I had had close male friends all my life, Kyle was the first person who I believed loved me no matter what. With Kyle, I became more comfortable with who I was and whom I had become. I faced my insecurities with a newfound knowledge. Life in the black gay community was not for the weak or the weary. It was not for sissies.

"Earth to Raymond," I heard Kyle say.

"What?"

"Where are you, mister?"

"Oh, I was just thinking about something," I said.

"I want you to meet someone. This is Rock."

"Rock?" I asked.

I now noticed that Kyle had returned with the guy he had spotted in the club earlier. He was an oatmeal brown-skinned guy in a black leather bomber jacket and skintight jeans that hung suggestively low in the front. He was decent-looking, well built and tall. Definitely Kyle's type.

"Is that your real name?" I asked Rock.

"No, it's Willis."

"How did you get Rock out of that?"

"It's a long story."

"I'm sure," I responded sarcastically.

Kyle had this stop-being-a-bitch look on his face, so I stopped my questions.

"What time are we supposed to meet JJ?" Kyle asked, rolling his eyes in silent commentary.

"At ten o'clock. I told her we would meet at the Popeyes on Seventy-second and Broadway. Is Rock coming with us?"

"Ask him," Kyle responded smartly. "He can speak."

Before I could get a word out of my mouth, Rock looked strangely at Kyle and then turned to me. "I have to go up to the Bronx and pick up my little girl. It was nice meeting you guys. Kyle, I'll give you a call before you leave."

As Rock walked out the front door, I looked at Kyle and shook my head, trying to register my disapproval.

"Don't you say a word, bitch. And yes, I said 'bitch.' You know, you're such a snob."

"Who me?"

"Yes, you."

"But Kyle, a baby! Did he ask you for Pamper money?"

"You know, bitch, you're not funny. Let's just get the fuck out of here before we're late. Besides, I'm starving and I can taste that greasy chicken right now."

We buttoned up our coats, got our briefcases from the coat check and headed for the streets beyond the door. The wind was blistering now and the temperature seemed like ten below. A light rain had begun to fall and the sky suggested snow. The street was filled with people going in and out of the different shops, restaurants and apartment buildings that lined Seventy-second Street.

Popeyes Famous Fried Chicken was located close to Broadway, right across the street from the subway station. Once we reached Popeyes, we could see JJ already had a spot in the long line.

"What trouble have you two been into?" JJ asked as she gave us both a big hug.

"Just the usual," Kyle said. "Ray's being a bitch."

"No, I'm not," I said in my defense.

JJ, or Janelle, was the female member of our trio. Most people would label her a fag hag; most of her close friends were gay men and she hung out in gay bars. She would correct you in a minute if you implied that she might be gay herself, although she had several lesbian friends.

JJ was attractive in her own way. Her skin was paper-sack brown. She had a narrow face, a small pug nose, thin lips and extremely short well-kept dreads. Janelle wore very little makeup, just a little blush and lip gloss, and dressed with a layered look; probably to hide her child-bearing hips. JJ had dropped out of Sarah Lawrence College during her senior year and was now working as a secretary at the William Morris Agency, so she always had great gossip. I had met JJ shortly after my first term at Columbia. I was at a midtown cabaret, Sweetwaters, enjoying Cissy Houston in concert, realizing where Whitney got her pipes from, when the waitress brought me a drink and said a young lady at the bar had sent it over. After Ms. Houston's set, I asked the waitress to point the young lady out and I went to the round bar to thank her. After polite conversation JJ suggested that I join her for a nightcap. Three drinks later and a ceaseless flow of laughter was the only thing that separated us. With a long Virginia Slims cigarette in one hand and a brandy in the other, JJ said, "Every man I meet these days wants to get in my pants, Raymond, but to be honest with you, I wouldn't mind if you wanted to too."

I took a long gulp of my drink, took a deep breath and replied, "I'm sure that would be nice, but uh . . . uh, Janelle, I'm gay or I guess you could say bisexual."

"I know that, honey, so is it your place or mine?"

"So you want to *get down* with me?" I asked in a deep Southern cadence, obviously sounding very *country*.

"*Get down?*" JJ screamed. "What's that?"

"Oh, you know," I responded, embarrassed but too tipsy to acknowledge it.

"You mean *fuck?*" she questioned.

"Yeah."

I couldn't ever recall having a young lady use the term *fuck* in conversation with me. But then again, JJ was unlike any young lady I had ever met. Although she wasn't my type sexually, I became enchanted with her wit and confident demeanor. We did share that one night of lovemaking and it was quite an experience. JJ wasn't passive like the other ladies I had been with. She took charge in bed, instructing, directing and even placing the condom at the appropriate time. As I separated her thighs and started my approach into her, she stopped my movement and said, "If you can't eat it, you can't fuck it." Like people say, you learn something new every day.

While the evening as a learning experience was quite enjoyable, it never happened again. We never talked about it, nor did we allow it to get in the way of our fast friendship. It was a secret that we kept even from Kyle.

"So what's on the agenda tonight, kids?" JJ asked.

"Let's go to Keller's," Kyle suggested.

"I want to go uptown to the Cotton Club," I said.

"Is it gay night?" JJ quizzed.

"I think so," I said.

"Let's go to Keller's. We haven't been to the Village in a long time," Kyle repeated, making it quite clear that Keller's was where he wanted to go.

"Okay, but let me get some of this barnyard pimp. I'm starving," I said.

The three of us ordered chicken and rice and grabbed a nearby table. We talked about the previous week and the upcoming holidays. Kyle would be going home to nearby New Jersey and JJ was going to the Caribbean islands with some mystery guy, or so she said. I had not yet decided whether I was going to make the trip down South. The holidays just didn't seem to be the same since I finished law school. My mother was begging me to come home, if only for a couple of days. I figured she and Pops would have some new young lady that they wanted me to meet. Or, even worse, they'd drag Sela over, despite the fact that she was practically engaged to a guy she'd met in Mobile.

I thought about telling them that I was busy with work and maybe I would just fly down Christmas morning and come back the next day. Maybe I was trying to avoid the inevitable conversation with my father about what he viewed as a phase I was going through. New York would be lonely during the holidays despite all the millions of people. Kyle's mother, Peaches, who was such a sweet lady, was pleading with me to come to Jersey and a couple of associates from the office had invited me skiing. I just didn't seem to be in the holiday spirit. In spite of having two wonderful friends, I felt lonely.

"Let's get a bottle of champagne and celebrate the holidays before we head downtown," Janelle suggested.

"That sounds great," I said.

"You know, kids, this will be the last time we will be together this year, so let's send it out with a blast," Kyle said.

"What about New Year's Eve?" I asked.

"Oh, Ray, I'm sorry. I forgot to tell you. I've decided to drive

with my mama down to North Carolina to see my grandma. She's
getting old and this may very well be the last holiday season we get
to spend together," he said.

"Oh shit, now what am I going to do?"

"Get out your phone book and call some of that trade you
know," Kyle said.

"Yeah, I'm sure you'll find someone to keep you warm," JJ added.

"I can't believe you two are going to leave me up here alone. A
little ole boy from the South," I said, trying to look as pitiful as
possible.

"Chile, ain't nothing little about you," Kyle laughed.

"I know that's right!" JJ declared.

"Come on, you guys, let's get this champagne and head for the
Village. I'm not even going home to change clothes," I said.

We finished our chicken and went into the first liquor store we
spotted. Nothing seemed to taste as good as Popeyes fried chicken
after a few drinks. We decided to buy a bottle of Korbel. We debated getting something more expensive, but since we were going
to drink it out of the bottle, it didn't make a lot of sense. We kept
the chilled bottle in the brown paper sack and took turns drinking
it as we walked across Broadway to the subway that would take us
directly to Christopher Street a few steps from Keller's. Once we
reached the Village, we were toasted, laughing at almost everything
and everyone, trying to sing a soulful version of Donny Hathaway's
"This Christmas."

Keller's was packed; it was smaller than the Nickel and had a huge
pool table that took up half of the room. There was also a jukebox,
but no DJ. I recognized some of the people I had seen earlier at the
Nickel Bar and a few new faces. Keller's was all black, with the
exception of a frighteningly frail white bartender with a red Santa's

hat. The clientele was a little bit different from that of the Nickel Bar due to the large number of hustlers who frequented the place. It was a cruise bar in the true sense of the word.

"Merry Christmas and what can I get for you?" the bartender asked.

"Two Stoli's on the rocks and a white wine. You don't have champagne, do you?"

"André's."

"Forget it. Let's just stick with the first order."

Kyle and JJ found a spot in the corner near the men's restroom—make that the unisex restroom, since it was the only one in the bar. You could not move without brushing up against someone and you could barely hear the jukebox for all the voices speaking at one time. Kyle was showing JJ his new robe and trying to find out whom she was really going to the islands with. Kyle and I had bought JJ a hot pink swimsuit that she just loved, but she was not giving in on telling us whom she was traveling with. Kyle went up to the bar to order another round of drinks while I looked to see how long the line was for the restroom.

"Don't order anything else for me, Kyle, I'm already too high," I said.

"Oh, come on, just one more."

"Okay, but this is it."

"What about you, JJ?"

"Order me a brandy," she replied.

I pushed my way toward the restroom line, which included about three people. As I was standing there waiting on my turn, I looked up as a very attractive guy was making his way out of the small, one-stall restroom. He was very tall, with smooth charcoal black skin. He didn't have a single hair on his face, with nice full lips that surrounded his white teeth. His ears were a little large, but they looked perfect with his full face, large chocolate eyes, slightly pug nose and closely cropped coarse hair. He smiled at me as I looked at him, up and down from head to toe.

"It's your turn," the guy directly behind me said.

"Oh, I'm sorry, I wasn't paying attention."

"Yes, I see," the small-framed guy said, laughing.

I quickly went into the restroom, relieved myself and rushed out into the bar to try to find the vision I had just seen. He would take my mind off the holidays and seeing Kelvin. Before I had the chance to look for him, I heard Kyle call my name. "Ray, over here. I have your drink."

When I spotted Kyle and JJ, I noticed that they had now been joined by the guy I cruised coming out of the bathroom.

"Thanks, Kyle," I said as I reached for my drink, purposely avoiding the eyes of the group's new member.

"Ray, this is Quinn. Quinn Mathis. We just met," Kyle said.

"Hello," I said, now looking straight into his dark eyes.

"Hello," he said as he extended his well-manicured hand. "Are those your eyes or contacts?"

"They were mine the last time I checked."

"Well, I'm sure you've been told this before, but you have beautiful eyes."

"Thank you," I said with a forced smile.

As I looked away from Quinn and toward the front door, I noticed a familiar face from earlier in the evening. It was Rock, or Willis. He spotted Kyle and the rest of the group and started to push his way toward us.

"Well, we meet again," Rock said.

"Hello, Rock, or is it Willis now?"

"Rock," he said.

"Excuse me," Kyle said. "Ray, come here a second." Kyle pulled me away from the group and whispered in my ear.

"What do you think of Quinn?" he asked.

"He's great-looking."

"Yeah, I know that's right, but I've promised Rock that I would spend some time with him."

"You'd rather spend time with that, rather than Quinn?" I asked, with my eyes moving from Quinn's direction to Rock's.

"Why don't you talk to him?"

"I don't know. Maybe he's another one of those confused boys. Look how he's all up in JJ's face. Probably because she's the only female in the place."

"Push that bitch out of the way. She's already got somebody."

"I don't know."

"Well, while you're thinking, I'm getting ready to leave with Rock. Make sure Janelle gets in a cab. You know she's drunk and no telling what she'll do."

"Okay," I said as I grabbed Kyle and hugged him. "Merry Christmas and I'll see you next year."

"Yeah, thanks for the robe. Now don't act a fool. Get over there and get that man," Kyle said as he hugged me back real tight and motioned to Rock. The two of them headed out the door of Keller's. I returned to Quinn and JJ, who seemed to be involved in deep conversation. Immediately I felt someone grab my hand. I turned around and realized it was Kyle.

"I forgot to give you this," Kyle said as he handed me a small, neatly wrapped box from his briefcase. "Don't forget to give your parents my best and remember that I love you, bitch." Before I could say anything, Kyle disappeared again.

I was standing in the same spot, looking at the door Kyle had just run through, when I noticed the clock above the door had already passed 1:00. I turned and saw JJ and Quinn staring at me. I went back to the corner where they were standing and paid special attention to the nice gray wool suit that Quinn was wearing.

"So, baby boy, I've got to get home. Merry Christmas," JJ said.

"How are you getting home?"

"The subway."

"It's too late for you to be on the subway. Anyhow, you look high."

"I'll be okay."

"I don't care. Take this and take a cab," I insisted.

JJ took the ten-dollar bill from my hand, folded it and quickly put it in her bra. She grabbed my neck and gave me a big sloppy kiss on the lips that reeked of alcohol.

"Merry Christmas, Ray. I think Mr. Macho Man over there likes you. Be safe, use a condom," she whispered.

"Merry Christmas, JJ. I'll see you soon. Be safe."

"I will."

"Do you want me to hail a taxi?"

"No, I'll be fine. If push comes to shove, I'll just pull up my skirt. They'll stop! You get over there and talk to that fine man."

"I love you."

"I know."

I walked out of the bar with JJ and noticed comforting snowflakes dancing hypnotically as they fell to the sidewalk and began to accumulate. The cold wind felt good. JJ blew a kiss as she climbed into a yellow taxi heading uptown. I started back toward the bar, where Quinn was standing in the same spot, guarding my briefcase and coat. I noticed he had a big smile as I walked in his direction.

"That was sweet of you," Quinn said.

"What?"

"I saw what you did, giving Janelle money for a cab. She was pretty lit."

"Well, I have to take care of my friends."

"Would you take care of me?"

"Sure, if you needed help."

"But you don't even know me."

"Yes, you're right, but you seem like a nice guy."

"Most people think I am. Where do you live, Ray?"

"On Ninety-sixth and Broadway," I said. "What about you?"

"Long Island."

"How are you getting home? Don't the trains stop at a certain hour?"

"Yes. I'll probably just get a hotel in midtown."

"You don't have to do that. I have a pullout sofa and you're welcome to it."

"Are you sure?"

"Yeah, you look harmless, and besides, it's Christmas."

"Yes, it is the holidays. Let's celebrate."

Quinn and I grabbed our belongings, buttoned our coats and headed toward Christopher Street to catch a taxi uptown. The snow, mixed with sleet, was falling at a pretty rapid rate—although you couldn't tell by the speeding cars. I looked up at the sky, wishing for the bright full moon and dancing stars that usually overlooked the Village. After about fifteen minutes and walking five long blocks, Quinn and I were able to hail a gypsy cab.

"How much to Ninety-sixth and Broadway?" I asked.

"Ten dollars," the Puerto Rican driver answered.

"That's too much."

"How much do you normally pay?" he asked.

"Seven dollars on the meter."

"Okay, get in."

I let Quinn get in the cab first. I couldn't help but notice how nice he looked as he climbed into the back of the car. While we were riding up the West Side Highway, Quinn talked about how he loved the holidays and shopping for all his family and friends.

"So where are you from, Quinn?"

"Born and raised in Brooklyn, been living on Long Island about five years."

"You like it?"

"I love it! You're from down South, right?"

"How did you know that?"

"I have my ways, Mr. Big Time Attorney. Besides, I went to college down South."

"Oh, I know now, JJ or Kyle. Which one spilled the beans and what college did you attend? Morehouse?"

"Morehouse? I'll never tell about either one."

"So if you won't tell me where you went to school, then what do you do?"

"You mean for a living?" Quinn asked slyly.

"Yes."

"I'm a broker."

"A stockbroker?"

"Yes."

"Who do you work for?"

"Is that important?"

"No, not really." I wondered why he was being so ambiguous. Maybe I was asking too many questions?

"I'll tell you sometime real soon," he said.

As we reached the corner of Ninety-sixth and Broadway, Quinn pulled out his wallet and gave the driver a ten-dollar bill. I noticed gold cuff links on his white French cuffs and what appeared to be a stainless steel Rolex. I wondered if it was real. I'd seen plenty of fake gold Rolexes but never a fake stainless steel. Besides, the way Quinn was dressed and his nice leather Hartmann briefcase led me to believe that it was real.

"Thank you."

"One good turn deserves another. Let's see, I bet that's your building," he said, pointing to the large two-tier building on the corner.

"How did you know that?"

"It just looks like you, sophisticated."

"You're something else," I said, suddenly feeling very warm inside.

We entered the building and I spotted two big boxes on the guard's desk. The holiday-decorated lobby was punctuated by massive marble columns that extended to the top of the thirty-two-story building. Grady, my elderly black doorman, was taking a nap, but woke up quickly as I approached the desk.

"Merry Christmas, Grady," I said.

"Thanks, Mr. Tyler. Merry Christmas to you too. Oh yeah, these two boxes are for you."

"They are! Can you give me a hand with them?"

"Sure, Mr. Tyler. Go on up and I'll bring them up in ten minutes."

"No need," Quinn piped in. "We can take them up."

Grady gave Quinn a severe look and turned toward me. "You sure, Mr. Tyler?"

"Why don't you bring up the larger one, Grady."

"Yes sir, ten minutes."

As Quinn and I got on the elevator, I pushed 23 and started laughing.

"What are you laughing at?" Quinn asked.

"I don't think Grady appreciates you trying to cut down his tip and Christmas bonus."

"Oh, that's what that look was for."

"Yeah, I think so." We reached the twenty-third floor and walked down the carpeted hallway, where almost every door was adorned with wreaths and different colors of wrapping paper. I reached inside my overcoat to get my door keys and unlock the three locks on the huge steel door with TYLER and 23J sprawled across it.

"This must be you."

"How can you tell?"

"Good guess. Besides, I can read."

We walked inside the dark apartment, which faced Broadway. I flipped on the light switch and quickly dropped my briefcase and ran to the bathroom.

"Have a seat!" I yelled as I unzipped my pants. After I finished, I looked into my bathroom mirror to see how I looked. Not bad for a day that started at 5:30 A.M. and for the experiences I'd had on this Friday before Christmas. Maybe a little drop of Visine would clear up the eyes. I returned to the living room of my spacious one-bedroom apartment, noticing that Quinn was still standing there with the box in his hands.

"Didn't you hear me? Have a seat and set the box on the floor."

"Okay, thanks."

As Quinn sat down on my black leather sofa, I observed how tall he was.

"How tall are you?"

"Six feet six and you're six one and about one-eighty, right?"

"Close. Would you like a drink?"

"Sure, what do you have?"

"Well, a little bit of everything. I've been drinking Stoli and champagne, so I think I'll stick with champagne. Did you play any sports at this alleged college down South?"

"Got any Rémy?" Quinn asked, smiling and purposely avoiding my question. There was a glint of seduction in his eyes.

"Yes, just a corner."

"That's all I need."

"I'll get some glasses. Here, let me take your coat."

"Sure, thank you," Quinn said. Before I took his coat, I looked Quinn straight in the eyes and asked, "Is there any particular reason you are so evasive?"

"No, I just like to keep guys like you thinking. You probably like a challenge and mystery. You're used to getting everything you want. Am I right?"

"Maybe."

"What's going on behind those beautiful eyes?"

"I'll never tell."

Quinn poured drinks for the two of us as I went over and slipped in a Regina Belle CD. I loosened my tie and slipped off my damp loafers. As Quinn walked back toward the sofa, I scrutinized him from head to toe again and thought how handsome he was.

"You like what you see?"

"What?"

"You heard me. Do you like what you see?"

"I've seen better," I replied smartly.

"When?"

"Earlier this evening."

"Well, where is he?"

"Who said it was a he?"

"Like I said, where is he?"

"Mount Vernon, I guess."

"Well, he's a fool."

"You think so?"

"Hell yes, to leave a great-looking guy like you. A damn fool."

With that, Quinn put the brandy snifter down on my glass coffee table and kissed me very gently.

"A damn fool," he said again as he started to unbutton my shirt and loosen the bright red tie that he was wearing. I pushed him back, and when I touched his stomach, I could feel how solid his body was. His waist appeared small in comparison to his broad shoulders.

"Let's talk," I said.

"Talk?"

"Yes, talk."

"We'll talk in the morning," Quinn said as he pulled me up from the sofa and led me through the bedroom door, which was only partially open. I could hear Regina Belle singing sweetly in the background as Quinn grabbed my belt buckle and snapped it open. I was following his lead when I suddenly heard my doorbell ringing.

"You don't have a wife or a lover, do you?" Quinn asked quickly.

"No, that must be Grady. Besides, a wife would have her own key."

I looked through the tiny hole in my apartment door and saw that it was Grady standing outside with the box from downstairs. I made sure that my shirt was buttoned, checked my pants and quickly opened the door.

"Thanks, Grady. Come on in."

"Oh, you're welcome, Mr. Tyler. Are you going to be hanging around for the holidays?"

"No, I think I'm leaving tomorrow afternoon. Hold on a second."

I looked around for my suit jacket and realized that it was in my bedroom. When I went in, I saw Quinn standing in front of the large picture window, which overlooked Broadway. He had removed his shirt and tie and I could see his large chest through his white cotton T-shirt. Quinn didn't say anything. He just stood there, gazing out the window as I searched for my checkbook in my suit jacket. Once I found it, I quickly scribbled out a check and went back into the living room, where Grady was still standing in the same spot.

"Merry Christmas, Grady," I said as I handed him the check. "Thanks a million for bringing the box up so late."

"No problem. Have a safe trip and I'll see you when you get back."

As I closed the door behind Grady, I wondered what he must think of me. He never saw me bring any women up to the apartment, with the exception of JJ, and when that happened, Kyle was always with us. Maybe he thought we were having some wild threesome. It wasn't as though I had a lot of male company either. But sometimes, when Kyle and I went out drinking and I got a little full, my judgment would take leave and I would bring home guys that under normal circumstances I wouldn't give a second look. Grady saw all this, but he never treated me any differently or with any less respect than the other tenants in the building. He probably saw more than any of the other doormen, since he had worked the graveyard shift in the building ever since I could remember.

When I walked back into the bedroom, Quinn had removed his T-shirt to fully reveal a broad chest that had small traces of black hair on beautiful black skin. He had also removed his pants and had on red Calvin Klein Jockey-type underwear that appeared to have been painted on him. The white-rimmed red underwear with CALVIN KLEIN printed on them looked beautiful against his well-defined body. It was only when he was down to just his underwear that I realized that he was slightly bowlegged. I sipped the champagne but didn't taste it, just looking at Quinn, quietly observing him.

"I hope you have some protection," Quinn said.

"Protection from what?" I asked, trying to conceal my smile.

"Don't play with me. Come over here," he said playfully.

As I walked toward Quinn, I thought, What am I getting myself into again? I usually avoided sexual contact on the first meeting like the plague. I didn't know anything about this guy. I mean, a nice suit didn't mean that he was safe, but at least he was concerned with protection. It always surprised me how many people still didn't use condoms. They took the attitude that you had to die from something, and if AIDS had a ten-year incubation period, then there was a good chance that every gay person living in New York had come in contact with the virus. I had to remove that thought from my mind. Besides, I was in high school when AIDS began and I had never been with a man when it started. Kelvin was the only man I had practiced unsafe sex with and he looked healthy.

When I reached Quinn, he began to unbutton my shirt with one hand and release my belt with the other. As he released the hook and unzipped my pants, I began to worry about the type of underwear I was wearing and whether I needed a shower. I grabbed Quinn's shoulder. Suddenly I could see our reflections in my dresser mirror. As my pants fell to the blond hardwood floor, landing around my ankles, I could see my black Jockey underwear against my camel-colored skin and felt relieved. Quinn started to kiss my ears, which drove me crazy. He then took his tongue and started to lick and kiss my nose, forehead and even the tops of my eyelids before he kissed my lips. Quinn's first kiss was gentle. As his soft, full lips touched mine, they felt as warm as his body. I responded with an open mouth, allowing his long, hard tongue to touch the roof of my mouth. Quinn's kisses were long, strong and wet. After we had French-kissed for what seemed like an eternity, he started kissing my chin, my neck and then my chest. His tongue and lips were sending me into a sexual frenzy and I wondered what he would do next. We fell on my neatly made bed, where our seminude bodies lay on top of my black-and-green comforter. Quinn's long legs hung off my full-size bed and he positioned himself so that his head lay on my chest. Without warning, Quinn stopped kissing me and just looked directly into my eyes. For a moment I was frightened, but the longer I stared back into his eyes, the more relaxed I became.

"What's the matter?" I asked.

"Nothing. I just want to lie here for a minute."

"You sure everything is all right? Why did you stop?"

"Before I was so anxious to be with you, but now I think you're right—we should talk. I mean, all I know about you is what Janelle told me."

"I know even less about you. Maybe you even have a lover."

"No, I don't have a lover. What about you?"

"No way. I'm too independent and gay relationships just don't last."

"Do you really believe that?"

"Without reservation."

"I tend to agree with you. Let's just lie here and talk. I could just look into those beautiful eyes of yours for the rest of my life. Maybe I'll discover what's going on behind them."

"I don't think that's possible."

"Why?"

"Because I'm about to fall asleep. I have to pack and pick up gifts for my family tomorrow and you have a train to catch."

"Raymond, can I ask you something?" His tone was serious.

"Sure," I said.

"Have you taken the test?"

"The test?"

"Yeah, the AIDS test."

"Yep."

"Would you mind sharing the results?"

"No, I'm glad you asked. I'm negative. And you?"

"Negative also."

"Good. I'm glad we got that out of the way," I said softly.

Minutes later I looked down at Quinn's long black body and realized that he had fallen asleep. I moved his head away from my chest to the pillow, got up to check all my locks and changed the music, popping in a Whitney Houston CD. For some strange reason Whitney always brought Kelvin to mind, but not tonight. I turned out all of the lights in my apartment and went over to the window. I looked down at the streetlights and Christmas decorations that lined Broadway. The snow had turned to a light rain and I could still see a few people walking down the street. I thought how true it was that this city never sleeps and that at this time tomorrow morning I would be back in my parents' home in the room where I had spent most of my life. I walked into my bathroom and put on my robe, which was hanging on the back of the door. I took the cap of the mouthwash bottle off, poured a little into it and swished it around in my mouth before spitting it out in the toilet. I took an Alka-Seltzer to avoid a morning hangover, brushed my hair and reached for the nearest cologne bottle. I dabbed a little behind my ears and on my chest. I took a final look in the mirror and wondered if Kyle had allowed Rock to sleep over and if JJ had made it home safely. After turning out the lights, I went back into my bedroom and saw Quinn stretched out and sleeping as though he didn't have a care in the world.

The digital clock on my nightstand flashed 5:07, and as I lay down on the pillow beside Quinn, the only light in the room came from the clock and the lights outside my bedroom window. As I found my sleeping position, I felt Quinn's huge arms pull me closer to his warm body and he laid his head on the back of my shoulders. Maybe this is the one, I thought to myself. He's tall, black, handsome and smart. Maybe, just maybe, Santa Claus had paid an early visit to my apartment.

The ringing phone awakened me from a delicious sleep. Who could be calling me this early on Saturday morning and why wasn't the answering machine picking up?

"Hello," I said, whispering so that I wouldn't wake Quinn.

"Ray."

"Kyle?"

"Yeah, Ray, I've got a big problem."

"What's up?" I said as I got up and looked around the room for my robe.

"I need to ask you a favor."

"Sure, but aren't you supposed to be on a train heading home?"

"Yeah, that's the problem."

"What's the problem?"

"Well, you remember Rock from last night?" Kyle asked.

"Yeah, what about him?" I asked, changing to a cordless phone and walking into my small kitchen.

"Well," Kyle said hesitantly.

"What about him, Kyle, what about him? Spit it out."

"The motherfucker robbed me, that's what. He even took my Christmas presents for my mother. I don't have enough money to catch a taxi down to Penn Station, let alone replace the gifts," Kyle said disgustedly.

"He did what?"

"You heard me. I woke up about an hour ago and he was gone with my wallet and this huge Macy's bag with all my Christmas gifts."

"Are you all right? Did you call the police?"

"Are you serious? I don't have a leg to stand on. I did invite him here, you know."

"Do you have his number?"

"He said he didn't have a phone."

"Kyle, haven't I warned you to be careful?"

"Don't lecture me, Ray, I don't need that. I need to borrow two hundred dollars until I get back. Will you do that without a lecture?"

"Kyle . . ."

"Come on, Ray, I know you're right, but I'm in no mood for your holier-than-thou attitude. I just want to forget I ever laid eyes on that low life."

"Okay, I'll meet you at the Citibank across the street from my apartment in twenty minutes."

"Do you have company?"

"Yeah."

"Is it that Quinn guy?"

"Yes."

"Oh my. How was he in bed? He looked like he was hung like a mule."

"Kyle, stop dipping and just meet me at the bank."

"Thanks, Ray, you're a lifesaver."

"Problems?" I heard a deep voice say as I laid down the cordless phone on the kitchen counter.

"Quinn! Good morning," I said, slightly startled. "I didn't mean to wake you."

"No problem. I have to get out of here anyway. Who was that?"

"My friend Kyle."

"Is he all right?" Quinn asked with a concerned look.

"Physically yes, mentally I don't know. I have to run across the street. I'll get you a couple of towels and I'll bring coffee and bagels back."

"You don't have to go through the trouble. I'll just wash my face and leave with you."

"Are you sure? Please wait until I come back," I pleaded. Quinn was standing against the sliding door that led to the kitchen, in his underwear and with an erection. He looked even better in the morning.

"Okay, I'll wait. But be quick."

"I will," I said, slipping on some dirty jeans and one of my bulky sweaters. I found some warm socks in my laundry basket and put on my old Bass Weejuns. Before leaving, I gave Quinn a quick brush on the lips as I grabbed my ski bomber and headed out the door to meet Kyle.

I was standing on the opposite corner of Ninety-sixth Street waiting for the light to change when I recognized Kyle standing by the door of the Citibank directly in front of me. The streets were busy with people, hailing taxis everywhere; people shopping and making mad dashes out of Manhattan. I had planned to give Kyle a good lecture, but when I saw him, he looked so pitiful that I just couldn't. We didn't embrace as we usually did, and Kyle forced a smile.

"Thanks for doing this, Ray. I'll pay you back on my first payday next year," Kyle said.

"That's what friends are for. Are you sure two hundred is enough?"

"Yes. I've got to at least replace the gift for my mama. I'll worry about my grandmother later. Did you like your gift?"

"Of course!"

"Are you going to wear it?"

"If I ever put a hole in my ear or nose," I laughed.

Kyle and I went through our good-byes again and I reassured him that I wasn't upset with him.

"Kyle, I hope you remember last night when making your New Year's resolutions," I said.

"Trust me, Ray, I will. Thanks. I love you."

"Yeah, me too."

I went into a nearby deli and ordered two coffees and a couple of bagels with cream cheese. I wondered how Quinn preferred his coffee and if he liked bagels. I thought about my meeting with Kyle and started to worry about him. Despite his good looks, he always went after guys who were not his equal in looks, economic standing or intelligence. He always called it the Madonna-whore complex:

never dating people he considered his equal, no matter who they were. I remember once when a hot-looking Broadway actor, Tony Martin, was in heat for Kyle. He was a really nice guy and Kyle was considering giving the guy a chance. One day Tony mentioned that he had graduated from Yale Drama School. After that revelation the poor guy didn't stand a chance with Kyle. I think Kyle was that way to protect himself from getting hurt. With guys similar to Rock, there was no chance of falling in love. Men like Tony posed a different type of threat. They would steal your heart.

I paid for the coffee and bagels and headed toward my apartment. I had a lot of things to do before my 6:30 flight to Birmingham. The boxes I had received the night before were from my parents and my little brother, Kirby. They sent them thinking that I wasn't going to make it home for the holidays. It was going to be great surprising them. I was even looking forward to visiting with Pops. All of a sudden I was in the holiday spirit. I rushed back into my apartment building and waited for the elevator. It seemed to take forever. If I hadn't lived on the twenty-third floor, I would have taken the stairs. Taking the stairs didn't seem like such a bad idea. Besides, when an elevator did show up, it would fill quickly with tenants carrying either shopping bags or suitcases. Finally, an empty elevator. I still had to pack and do a little shopping before I headed to JFK. I would need to leave a little early to make sure that my luggage arrived in Alabama with me. Once I reached my floor, I hurried to my apartment. As I turned the keys and opened the door, I expected to hear Quinn moving around the apartment, but it was dead silent.

"Quinn," I called out.

No response. Maybe he was in the bathroom. I set the bag with the coffee and bagels on the kitchen counter and looked around the apartment, even opening my closet doors. No sign of Quinn. Where was he? I glanced in my bedroom and realized that his suit coat and overcoat were gone. The bed was made up and I saw a note on my pillow.

Dear Ray,

Sorry, but I couldn't wait. I had to make the next train. The evening was wonderful and I can't wait to do it again. We have some unfinished business. Have a safe trip, Merry Christmas and get back here in one piece. I already miss you!

Take care,
Quinn David Mathis

P.S. I got your number from your phone. I hope it's the right one.

Yes, Quinn, I thought to myself, it's the right one. I looked at the clock and decided to call the airline to get an earlier flight. I was disappointed but excited at the same time. Quinn had left a note. It wouldn't have been uncommon for a guy just to leave and run the risk of running into me at a later time. Yes, Quinn was different. I packed quickly and grabbed my Walkman and some tapes Kyle had mixed for me, stuffing them into my briefcase. Since I wouldn't have time to shop, I would just give checks and write personalized Christmas greetings on my office stationery. I mean, what else would I have to do on the three-hour flight, except think about last evening and Mr. Quinn David Mathis?

FOUR

The taxi turned the corner on Country Club Lane. I could
see my family's house lit with Christmas decorations along the tree-
lined street. The University Court section of Birmingham was one
of the few black middle-class neighborhoods in the city. Most of
the brick homes had been built in the early seventies and it was an
enclave of black doctors, lawyers, teachers and contractors.

Moore Brothers Construction Company had built most of these
homes and the home of one of these brothers, Leroy Moore, anchored Country Club Lane. It was the largest home in the neighborhood and it included not only a pool and tennis courts but also
servants' quarters behind the mansion. My parents' home looked
like a cottage in comparison, but we had always been very proud of
the four-bedroom brick house. It was a long way from the three-
room house on the east side we had lived in when I was a small
child. Mom was the primary breadwinner in the family then, while
Pops was working to get his law practice off the ground.

After paying the taxi driver, I grabbed my garment bag and briefcase and headed up the steps to the front door. Although I still had my key, I decided to ring the bell and not give anyone a heart attack by just walking in unannounced. It looked as though both Mama and Pops were at home because both of their cars were parked in the garage. Pops always left the garage door up despite Mama's pleas for him to do otherwise.

I had pushed the doorbell only once when the door flew open and there stood Mama with open arms. Though she had gained some weight in her later years, she still looked beautiful to me. Her pecan brown skin glowed and her salt-and-pepper hair was up in a stylish French roll.

"My number one son, what are you doing here? We didn't expect you," Mama squealed.

"I wanted to surprise you," I said as I gave her a bear hug.

"Ray, Kirby, come quick, look who's here!" Mama shrieked. By now Mama's eyes were starting to fill with tears and I could hear someone come down the stairs at a very fast pace. While I was still hugging Mama and wiping the tears from her eyes, I saw my father walk into the foyer with a rolled-up newspaper.

"Well, look what the cat done drug in," he said.

"Hi Pops," I said, extending my hands toward him. As I was reaching for Pops's hands, I heard Kirby, my nine-year-old little brother, screaming with delight.

"Ray-Ray's home! Ray-Ray's home!" he shrilled. "Did you get the picture I sent you for Christmas?"

Kirby hugged my thighs, since he couldn't quite reach my waist. My father just shook his head with a slight smile on his face.

"Come on into the den. Marlee, let go of the boy," Pops said.

"I just can't believe my number one son is home," Mama said, now wiping away her own tears. "Why didn't you let us know that you were coming home?" she asked.

"Just so I could get this reaction!" I said. "I know how you love surprises."

"Ray Jr., come on in here and let me look at you," Pops called from the den.

"I'll be there in a second, Pops."

"Ray, come up to my room. I want to show you my football uniform," Kirby said, pulling my arms.

"Wait up, Kirby. I've got to go in and talk with Pops."

As I walked into the den, I realized that not much had changed since the last time I had been home, with the exception of a new large-screen television. The Christmas tree was in its usual place by the sliding glass door that led to an outside deck. The same gold sofa sat against the wall facing the television. Pops's well-used leather recliner was in the same spot, with a table and lamp alongside it. Pops was sitting in his chair, flipping the remote control, as I walked into the den.

"So how is New York treating you?" Pops asked.

"It's great."

"How's your job? Have you tried any big cases yet?"

"Not any big ones, but I am getting into the courtroom more than before."

"That's good," he said, looking at the television instead of me.

"How is it down at your office?" I asked.

"Same old thing, just keeping busy. We're thinking about adding another lawyer," he said, occasionally glancing in my direction.

"That's great, just great," I said.

While Pops seemed immersed in the television, I looked at him and realized that he was aging very gracefully. My father was a strikingly handsome man. He had beautiful eyes, not quite green, not quite brown, filled with hardness and confidence. He appeared to be in great shape, with only a small pouch above his once thin waist, and short graying hair. While I was looking at him, Pops put his glasses back on and started reading the *TV Guide*.

"Been to any high school basketball games lately?" I asked.

"No, haven't had the time, but they are having the citywide basketball tournament over at Northeast. It starts the day after Christmas," he said.

"Maybe we can catch a game before I leave," I said, remembering how much Pops used to enjoy going to the games with me before I left for law school.

"Yeah, that would be fun. How long you here for?"

"Oh, just a couple of days. I wanted to get back and catch up on some work."

"Does your mother know that you're here for only a couple of days?"

"I don't think so."

"Well, don't tell her tonight. You know she wants you to move back home?"

"Yeah, I know. Where is she anyway?" I asked, looking for an excuse to get out of the den.

"Probably in your old room," Pops said, still looking through the *TV Guide*.

"Well, I'm going to go in there and give her a hand. It's great seeing you, Pops," I said.

"Yeah, son, it's great having you home," Pops said, still looking down at the *TV Guide*, not once looking in my direction.

I wanted to go over and hug him, tell him that I loved him and that I was really happy to be home. But Pops was not the affectionate type and he really appeared to be into the television. I stood up and looked at him for a second, then headed down the hallway to my old room. When I reached the first door to the left, I saw Mama coming out of the room with linens and some other items in her hands.

"It's all ready for you, baby. You must be tired and I've got to start my turkey for tomorrow," Mama said.

"Thanks Mama," I said, grabbing her and giving her another hug. "It's really great to be back home."

When I walked into my bedroom, I felt as though I had stepped into a time capsule. On the wall were football letters, blue ribbons from track meets, a *Right On* magazine pullout of Vanity and a perfect attendance certificate from the sixth grade. I looked at the dresser and recognized my old hair brush, a can of Pro-Line hair spray and a picture of Sela and me at her senior prom. Sela, I thought to myself and smiled, I've got to call her.

I went to hang my garment bag in the closet and realized that it was now filled with Mama's old clothes. I sat on the bed and turned on the small black-and-white television that was on the table beside the bed. When I pulled back the bedspread and saw the sheets Mama had put on the bed, I smiled. They were the exact same sheets she had used when I came home for weekends from college. Yes, it was good to be home again.

I got up to brush my teeth before retiring and realized that someone was still roaming around the now quiet house. The sounds were coming from the kitchen, and as I walked in, I saw Mama bent over, basting her turkey in the oven.

"Lady, when are you going to bed?" I asked, startling Mama.

"Don't scare me like that, boy. You know you're not too big for one of my good ole-fashion whippings," she said, smiling.

"What all are you cooking?"

"All your favorites."

"Macaroni and cheese?"

"You know it. Come over here and give me another hug," Mama said. As we hugged, Mama reached up and grabbed the back of my head and just rubbed the back of my hair. As she continued to rub, she whispered, "So how is New York really treating my baby? Are you really all right, Raymond junior?"

"I'm doing good, Ma," I assured her. "What's up with Pops? He was kinda quiet tonight."

"Oh, you know your father, not much for words unless he's in the courtroom or entertaining his card-playing buddies. But I know he's glad you're home. Just a few minutes ago before I came out here to check on this turkey, he looked at me and said, 'The boy looks good, don't he?' "

"Maybe he was talking about Kirby," I joked.

"You're a mess, just like him," Mama said as she took a rolled newspaper and swung it playfully at me. "How are Kyle and JJ?"

"Oh, they are fine. Both send their love. How are your third graders?"

"About the same. Some good, some bad. But I want to talk about you. How's your love life?"

"Mama, are you dipping?" I laughed.

"You know I am. Let's get to the good stuff first."

"Nothing really special. Have you heard from Sela?"

"She called me about two weeks ago. The girl looks good and I think she and that new boyfriend broke up. It's not too late, you know."

"Ma, give me back my business. I'm going to bed before you have me married before the New Year."

"Now, that wouldn't be so bad, would it?" Mama asked playfully.

"Good night, Ma. I love you," I said, hugging her very tightly.

"Good night, baby. Let me be the first to tell you Merry Christmas," Mom said, hugging me back.

My mother, at times, was like my best friend. I could talk to her about anything. Even though we had not talked openly about my lifestyle, she knew. When she and Pops came up to New York for my law school graduation, they met Kyle and JJ at my apartment.

Mama loved them both immediately, but Pops was really stand-offish, almost rude. Mama once asked me what the deal was between Kyle and myself and I acted as though I didn't know what she was talking about. I told her we were just friends and that was it.

I called her once late at night in tears. I was in my second year of law school and I had become involved with my first live-in relationship. The guy's name was Julian, aka *the lover from hell*, and when we broke up, I took it really hard. Kyle never liked him, so he wasn't much in the way of offering sympathy. So I didn't really have anyone else to talk to. I mean, Kyle would listen, but he was more interested in getting me to go to the bars to meet someone else.

I wasn't totally honest with her about the relationship. I had Mom thinking Julian was a girl simply because I changed his name to Julie when referring to the fact that my current love had left me for someone else. I had been drinking the night that I called her and I used *he* instead of *she* a couple of times. Mama, like myself, avoided confrontation, so she didn't say anything. She just listened like she always did with Pops.

She gave me a speech about never doing anything that I was ashamed of, that she and Pops would love me no matter what. That no matter what choices I made in life, I should always stick to them. I didn't have the heart to tell her that there were some things you didn't have a choice about.

No black man in his right mind would choose to be gay. I had always been proud of being black. My parents had instilled a great deal of pride in me regarding my race. When they didn't feel I was learning enough in school, they would give me special assignments. I would have to give them reports on important African Americans at least once a month. I was required to read *Ebony, Essence* and *Black Enterprise* monthly.

The only thing I was told regarding sex was what to do if somebody touched me in my private area. I didn't ever recall hearing the word *gay* or *homosexual* in my home. You heard people call some men sissy or funny, but never gay or homosexual. The first time I made love with Kelvin caused the same kind of wonderment as that which I had experienced when I learned the magic relationship between my hands and my sex. Both experiences caught me by surprise. Maybe my sexual experiences with women were learned behavior.

Christmas Day had always been a big day in our house for as long as I could remember. Even though this was the first time I had been home in years, the day started like so many Christmases of the past. Mama was busy preparing her Christmas dinner and Pops was fixing the gadgets he had bought for Kirby. This year it was video games for Kirby, and Mama bought a new personal computer for Pops. Mama's present from Pops was always a trip to someplace after the holidays. After all these years there still appeared to be fire in their relationship.

There was very little under the tree for me, since they had already sent my gifts to New York. With Quinn being over the night before, I hadn't even opened the boxes.

"Merry Christmas, son. I was beginning to think you were going to sleep all day," Pops said as I walked into the family room wearing only my pajama bottoms.

"Merry Christmas, Pops. What time is it?" I asked.

"Eleven-thirty," he replied.

"Where's Mama and Kirby?"

"Went to the 7-Eleven to get cranberry sauce and some batteries for one of Kirby's games."

"Any coffee?"

"Yeah, I'm on my third cup. You see the computer your mama got me?"

"Where is it?" I asked, still not quite awake.

"Look in the dining room. It's a PS/2," Pops said proudly.

"Let me get my coffee first. We have some of those in my office."

"So do we," Pops boasted.

While I was finishing my first cup of the stale-tasting coffee, I heard the door open and Kirby running through the hallway into the den.

"Ray-Ray," he called out. "Look what Santa brought me."

"What is it?" I asked.

"A Gameboy!" he said, holding it up toward my face.

"You must have been a good boy for Santa to bring you that," I said. "Why didn't you wake me up?"

"Mama said not to."

"That's right. I figured you wanted to catch up on some sleep," Mama said as she walked in holding a brown paper bag.

"Good morning and Merry Christmas, Ma," I said, giving her a kiss on the left side of her face.

"Good morning, or should I say good afternoon to you, Mr. Sleepyhead? How did you sleep?"

"Great. Who's coming to dinner?" I asked.

"Oh, the usual. Uncle James and Aunt Mabel, their crew, Mrs. Vance and her family and Cousin Marcus and his family," Mama said.

"Need any help?"

"No, I have everything under control. You just relax."

"Okay. I'm going to take a shower and go help Pops with his Christmas present."

"I thinks he likes it. I started to give you a call when I was shopping for it, but it's the kind we have at school. I knew that's what he had at his office," she said.

"Yeah, I think you got the right thing. Maybe now you'll have him at home more," I said.

"That's not what I had in mind," Mama said, laughing slyly.

After I finished my shower, I went into Pops's office in the basement, where he had moved his new computer and placed it where he used to keep his electric typewriter. His small, cramped office was filled with his and Mama's degrees from Alabama State and his law degree from Howard University. There were shelves of law books and pictures of Mama, Kirby and me when I was in high school. I looked at the picture of me with my football jacket on and wondered if that was the way Pops chose to remember me.

As I looked at the picture closely and then at the picture of my father with Mama, I realized how much we looked alike. I was always told that my green eyes had come from my great grand-mother on my father's side, and that my features were almost identical to those of my great-great grandfather, whom I had never met. While I was studying the picture, Pops came into the office and rubbed the back of my shoulders.

"Long time ago, right?" he said as he went over to his desk.

"Not that long ago," I said.

I don't know if it was because it was Christmas or what, but Pops appeared more relaxed than he had the previous evening. I looked around his office and admired all the citations and pictures that were on the wall. There were pictures of him when he was elected to the school board and clippings of articles written about him and his involvement in the civil rights movement. I thought back to coming to his office when I was in high school to type school papers or just to read some of the books he had on his shelves. Though he never once pressured me, I knew Pops wanted me to become a lawyer. It had been the same way with football and swimming. In fact, Pops never pressured me about anything. He just had this way about him, one that made me think his silence and the way he would look at you were his way of getting you to do things that he wanted. My pops was a man of great knowledge and patience. Eventually he always got his way.

My relationship with my father had changed drastically since my graduation from law school. I think he was shocked at my friendship with Kyle and JJ and my sudden lack of interest in the opposite sex. Though we had never talked about it, I realized that if Mama knew, Pops knew. When I called home and he answered the phone, I would sometimes hang up. When I would speak to him, it was always short and to the point. Most of the time our conversation centered around legal issues or sports. My mother wanted me to take the first step and make peace. I knew Pops would take my new sexual orientation as a personal slap in the face against him. That it would cause him a great deal of pain and concern. Not to mention his anger.

There was always a great deal of worry when I would mention I was sick, if only with a minor cold. As much as I loved and respected my father, I couldn't allow him to run my life. Nobody, not even Raymond Winston Tyler, Sr., got to vote on my life. I acknowledged to myself that my father was the last of a dying breed. A strong, confident, self-made, proud black man.

After Pops and I had been in his office playing with his new toy for a while, we both appeared to have relaxed. Like the old days, we were father and son sharing something in common. Just when we were loading the software into Pops's computer and testing it, we began to hear the doorbell ringing upstairs repeatedly. Minutes later Kirby burst through the door and I could tell that our time alone was about to end.

"Daddy, Ray-Ray, Mama said to come upstairs, company's here," Kirby said, still holding on to his new Gameboy.

"Tell her we'll be up in a minute," Pops said.

"Okay, but she said now," Kirby demanded.

"Let me see that," I asked Kirby, reaching for the toy he was holding tight.

"Promise not to break it?" he asked seriously.

"I wouldn't do that," I assured him.

As I played a few games with Kirby's new toy, he came over and sat between my legs. A few minutes later he had straddled one of my thighs, rocking as if he were on a toy horse.

"Let's play cowboy, Ray-Ray," he suggested.

"Not now, mister. I promise to give you a pony ride later on."

"All right," he said as he giggled and attempted to give me a high five.

"We better get upstairs before your mother puts out a warrant for us," Pops said.

As the three of us started out the door, I felt an instant closeness with my father and my little brother. At first it was like a chill, followed by a sudden surge of warmth. The feeling was electric. All three of our bodies were touching in some way. I had picked Kirby up in my arms and was carrying him out of the office. Pops's arms were around my shoulders, his huge hands palming Kirby's head, and Kirby was playfully pushing him away. As I enjoyed this moment, I wished that things could always be this way between the three of us. It would have been perfect had there been someone there to take a picture of the three of us at that moment. But since there was no one there, except for us three Tyler men, I'd have to settle for the picture in my mind and keep it in my own special memory bank.

*   *   *

The dining room table was arranged to perfection. Mama had made all my favorites. Besides the traditional turkey and dressing, there were a glazed ham, mashed potatoes, stringbean casserole, candied yams, turnip greens and Mama's famous macaroni and cheese. The table was set with the good dishes and crystal goblets filled with white Zinfandel wine. The smell of homemade rolls and rum pound cake came out of the kitchen each time Mama emerged with another piping-hot dish. My mother could cook! Her best dish, and my favorite, was her fabulous fried chicken.

It was great seeing all my relatives and Mrs. Vance from the old neighborhood, who was just like a member of the family. She had been one of my first babysitters and she still watched Kirby at times, but it was obvious that she was getting up in years. She still kissed me on the cheeks and patted me on the butt, as she had done ever since I could remember. My cousin Marcus sat at the opposite end of the table with his wife and two sons, one of whom was around Kirby's age. Aunt Mabel and Uncle James were sitting down at my end. She was a full-bodied woman with an off-black Dutch boy wig. Uncle James was a small-framed man and looked as though he would jump if you said boo. After Pops gave a moving prayer, mentioning how happy he was to have both of his sons at home, all the dinner conversation seemed directed at me and New York. When was I moving back down South? How much was I paying for rent? Had I met any famous people? Had I ever been robbed? I prayed that they would change the subject and talk about something else.

The more wine Aunt Mabel drank, the more she talked and the more questions she asked. She had slacked up a bit with the questions when out of the blue she looked at me and said, "So, Ray junior, when are you getting married?"

"I don't know, Aunt Mabel. I haven't found the right person yet," I answered back between bites of ham. Mama and Pops exchanged glances that I wasn't supposed to see.

"Who was that girl you dated in high school and at the university?" she asked.

"You mean Sela?"

"Yeah, Sela, pretty girl. I mean beautiful. What is she doing now?" she quizzed.

"She's teaching school," Mama said.

"What happened to you two? Why not marry her?" Aunt Mabel asked.

"Leave the boy alone, Mabel," Uncle James said.

"Shut up fool, before I slap you cockeyed," she retorted.

Uncle James rolled his eyes and everyone at the table tried to keep from laughing.

"Let's go into the den," Pops said, getting up from the table. "I have something I want you to hear, James."

I thanked Pops to myself and stayed in the dining room and helped Mama clear the table. When we finished, I went into the den, where the conversation seemed even livelier and louder. Pops had put on a Joe Sample CD that I had sent him last Christmas and was nursing a glass of Old Grandad. He and Uncle James were engaged in a deep debate about who was going to win the upcoming Super Bowl and Aunt Mabel had passed out on the sofa.

I went into my room, closed the door and turned on the television. I dialed my phone number in New York and punched in my secret code when my answering machine picked up. The little voice on the other end announced that I had four messages. As I waited for the first message to play, I noticed Bo Jackson in second-skin shorts on a television commercial. I listened to my messages and watched the television. I discovered that all four of the messages were from Quinn. As I listened to Quinn's eloquent deep voice and watched Bo Jackson's perfect body, I realized that I had developed a noticeable erection in my pants. Bo Jackson's body, Quinn's voice. I could suddenly imagine Quinn's face in my mind—his nose, his eyes, his lips. I put them all together and pictured Quinn's face. It seemed as though Quinn's last message and Bo's commercial ended at precisely the same time. I reached into my pants and removed my penis, placed it into the palm of my hand and beat myself into a guilty pleasure. Relieved, I looked up at the ceiling of this room where I had spent so many nights doing the exact same thing. Only then the pictures in my mind were of Sela or Janet Jackson. *How times had changed.*

FIVE

I had planned to stay at home only a couple of days, but before I knew it, it was Thursday. Five enjoyable days and my visit home had been quite successful. I had been able to spend an equal amount of time with Mama, Pops and Kirby. No questions about my personal life, just work, the family and the good times.

Mama and I had long talks early in the mornings and late at night, when the house was quiet. I even went to the Outlet Shopper's Mall with her to help load purchases. Pops and I went to a high school basketball game and he took me down to his office to show me their computer setup and introduced me to the other partners. Kirby and I played touch football and went to the movies. On the way home we stopped at McDonald's and Kirby told me that he had two girlfriends in his fourth-grade class.

"Two?" I asked, trying to keep my smile hidden.

"Yeah, Tomekia and Shenikwa," he said proudly. I started laughing so hard that I had to grab my sides. I don't know if I was laughing at my playboy of a little brother or the names my peers were giving their children.

Sela and I agreed to meet on the Thursday before I was to leave. I had decided to travel back to New York on Saturday morning. That way I would get back in time for New Year's Day, even though I didn't have a clue as to what I was going to do. With Kyle and JJ out of town, my choices were limited. There were several more messages from Quinn, but he never left a number where I could reach him. In the back of my mind I was hoping to bring the New Year in with him. But without speaking with him directly, I wouldn't take anything for granted.

Sela and I agreed to meet at Lakewood Mall in the middle of town. It was anchored by J. C. Penney's and the new Winfrey Hotel. I arrived about fifteen minutes early and was standing in front of Wendy's when a very attractive blonde walked up to me.

"Raymond Tyler?" she said with a puzzled look on her face.

"Yes."

"Don't tell me you don't remember me?" she said, putting her hand on her hip in a playful huff.

"Margo," I said, smiling.

I reached for her and gave her a big hug and she hugged me back very tightly. "It's been a long time," I said.

"Yeah, I think the last time I saw you was at Debbie Blass's graduation party," she said.

"What have you been up to?" I asked.

"Well, I pledged Chi Omega at Auburn and married Eddie Sudderth. We own a little card store on the lower level of the mall," Margo said. "What are you doing?"

"I live in New York City," I responded proudly. "I'm home for the holidays."

"New York City. Well, I'm impressed. Are you married?"

There was that question again. "No, not yet. I've been really busy with work and all."

"What do you do?" she asked.

"I'm a lawyer, litigation."

"Gee, that's neat. I never knew you wanted to be a lawyer."

"It pays the bills."

"I guess it must be exciting living in New York. Eddie and I have thought about going up there for a visit."

"Here's my card and I'll put my home number on the back and you guys give me a call if you decide to come up," I said, taking a card from my wallet and a pen from my jacket.

"That would be great. You remember Eddie, don't you?"

"Of course. He was our placekicker. Won the game against Central our senior year. Yeah, I remember ole Eddie. Please tell him hello for me."

"I will," she said, slipping the card into her purse.

"You still look great," I said.

"I think you're even more handsome than you were in high school," she said, now turning a light shade of red.

"Thank you."

Margo Lawson had played an important part in my sexual development. She was the first girl, or the first person for that matter, to give me head. It happened quite innocently the summer before my junior year. One evening when she was coming from summer drill team practice and I from football practice, she drove alongside me in a shiny red Firebird and offered me a ride . . . the long way home. When I thought back on it, I realized that it was another secret I had kept from Sela and my parents too. Although by the time I was in high school, black and white kids were getting along pretty well, dating was still strictly taboo. It wasn't as though Margo and I dated. I don't think anyone at Southeast knew, but it did last about six months. The only interracial mixing that did occur happened at night and it was usually some poor trashy white girl and a black athlete.

Margo was white, but she was anything but trashy. She had long golden blond hair and stirring blue eyes. She wasn't shaped like most white girls I knew, meaning she had a wonderful ass. Most people in our class thought she favored Cybill Shepherd and should pursue modeling, but I guess she never followed up on it. I didn't know what her parents did, but they lived in one of the wealthiest sections of town.

"What ever happened to that girl from Northeast that you used to date?" Margo quizzed.

"Funny you should ask. That's who I'm waiting for."

"Are you two still dating?"

"No, not really, but we're still good friends."

"Well, that's just wonderful," Margo said. "Raymond, it was great seeing you, but I better run. If I stand here any longer, my mind is going to wander into the gutter and old times and we both might be in trouble," she said with a sexy smirk.

"You must be reading my mind," I said, now openly flirting with Margo. "It's good seeing you."

Margo reached up and gave me a big hug and gently bit the end of my ear, which caused a nice tingling sensation. Well, I guess I still have it, I thought to myself.

"Take care, Ray. Happy New Year," she said as she swiftly walked toward the north end of the mall.

"Who was that?" said a familiar voice from behind me.

I quickly turned around to find Sela standing within inches of me.

"Sela!" I shouted as I reached for her, swinging her around in my arms. "It's great seeing you! Stand back, let me look at you."

Sela looked more beautiful than when we had dated. Her hour-glass figure was wrapped tightly in a black leather minidress that left very little to the imagination. The years had been very kind to her.

"Look at you, Mr. Big Time New York Attorney," Sela joked. "Give me another hug."

"Where do you want to go?" I asked.

"Let's go to the Winfrey's lobby piano bar," Sela suggested.

Sela and I walked hand in hand into the Winfrey Hotel lobby, both acting like teenagers on a first date. We located a secluded part of the lobby bar, ordered two white wines and just looked and smiled at each other for minutes without saying a word. The trance was finally broken when the waitress returned with two glasses of white wine and set them on the glass-topped marble table that separated Sela and me.

"So, how's Julie?" Sela asked with a smirk.

"Julie?" I asked.

"Yes, wasn't that the girl you were living with?" she asked.

Oh shit, there goes that lie again.

"Oh, I hardly ever see her," I lied, sipping my wine and looking away.

"So who are you seeing, living with or whatever you guys do in New York City?"

"I'm quite single," I responded. "But I heard you're not. What's this lucky dog's name?"

"Dewayne Kelly. He's the dentist taking over Dr. Wade's practice," Sela said.

"Oh, where is he from?"

"Mobile."

"Are you happy?" I asked.

"Most times," Sela said, looking away.

"When's the big day?"

"Well, it's not final yet, but we're shooting for June twentieth."

"June twentieth," I sputtered, my mouth full of wine.

"Yeah, I know that's your birthday. We're thinking about pushing it back to August or even waiting a year. You know, it's tough starting a practice. What's that look about?"

"What look?"

"Now, don't play that shit with me, Ray. It may have been a long time, but you know I know you."

"Oh, I was just wondering why my birthday is such a popular wedding day."

"Who else is getting married on that day."

"Oh, just a friend," I responded. "So what are you doing besides planning Birmingham's biggest wedding?"

"Oh, didn't your mother tell you? I'm teaching ballet at the Arts Magnet High School."

"She mentioned that she had talked to you and that you looked great. Which she was very right about. After that, I don't remember what else she said."

"Well, it's not like the teaching she does. It's more like play than work. How's your job?"

"Coming along. I passed the New York bar and now I'm getting to handle more clients alone."

"Do you like practicing law?"

"Yeah, most days I do."

"Now, Raymond Winston Tyler, come clean. Who are you sleeping with?"

"Sela, listen at you. All the diseases that are out in New York. I take matters into my own hand, if you know what I mean?"

"All the beautiful women in New York and you're still playing with yourself. All you need is a good ole Southern piece," Sela said very slyly and seductively.

"Well, that's life in the big city."

"That chick Julie must have really screwed you up."

"No, not really," I said quietly.

"Tell me about her," Sela urged.

"Sela, come on now, let's talk about something else. How are your parents?"

"Great. They send their love, and wondered why you didn't come by the house."

"Well, I've been really trying to spend time with my folks and Kirby. I mean, my little brother is quite the little man. You know, it's been almost five years since I've been home."

"Yes, I know. Dewayne thanks you."

"What about you? Are you thanking me too?"

"I refuse to answer that on the grounds that it might incriminate me." We ordered more wine and listened to the piano player. Occasionally we would just look at each other and then break out into nervous smiles. Sela looked more sophisticated. She was no longer the little girl with the two ponytails. Her hair was thicker and longer than I remembered. Her makeup was perfect and she seemed to have a little more up top. Yes, the girl had it going on.

As I stared at Sela, I began to wonder how it would have been had my life not changed so drastically during my senior year. I suspected that we would have long been married and would probably have a couple of kids by now. How would they look?, I thought to myself. Living the Great American Dream. I then wondered what it would be like going to bed with Sela. Had she changed? Could I even get it up? Maybe this new guy had taught her a trick or two. I wondered if I should be open and completely honest with her about my new lifestyle in New York. Would she be supportive, or would she be upset and take it personally? We had never really talked about gay people or things of that nature. I wondered whether she had ever been to bed with another woman, if only in her fantasies.

"Where is your mind?" Sela asked, interrupting my daydreams.

"What?"

"What are you thinking about?"

"You don't want to know," I chuckled.

"Tell me," Sela pleaded. "You used to tell me everything."

"Yeah, you're right, but I don't know about this." *Should I tell Sela what I thought or should I just leave well enough alone, pay the check and head back home?*

"Do you miss living down South?"

"At times."

"What do you miss the most?"

"Honestly?"

"Yes."

"Friday nights. You know, playing high school football. Kicking Central's butt. Saturdays when we were away at school, boning with you know who."

"Boning, what's that?"

"You know, the nasty. Haven't you seen Spike Lee's movies?"

"Niggah, please. We do have movies down here," Sela laughed.

"You want to know what I really miss the most?" I asked.

"You know I do."

"You." I smiled.

"Have you ever thought about what it would have been like, married to me?" Sela asked.

"What? Of course I have. More often than you think."

"And what do you think?"

"Come on now, Sela, don't put me on the spot like this," I answered nervously.

"I want to know," she insisted.

"Do you still trust me?" I asked.

"In regards to what?"

"Just trust me."

"For the most part."

"How much time do you have?"

"As much time as I need. I'm not married yet. Besides, I'm not punching a time clock, you know."

"Great. Wait right here and I'll be back in fifteen minutes."

"What do you have up your sleeve?" Sela grinned.

"Trust me, just trust me and promise me that you will wait," I said gently.

"Okay, I promise."

I don't know what had come over me, but I had to be with Sela. I wanted to hold her in my arms, kiss her all over and have her lie against my chest once again. I walked out of the lobby bar, out of Sela's sight, and went over to the front desk of the hotel.

"Do you have any rooms?" I asked the redheaded desk clerk.

"We sure do. How many nights?" she asked with a deep Southern drawl.

"Just one. What's the rate?"

"Well, we have a special holiday rate of forty-nine dollars," she replied.

"What?" I asked, slightly shocked.

"Is that too much?" the clerk asked.

"Oh no. I'm from New York City and I can't believe that price."

"I can give you a nice junior suite overlooking the ice-skating rink in the mall for ninety-nine dollars," the clerk offered.

"Hey, that sounds great. Let's do it."

"How do you plan to pay for this?"

"American Express," I said as I proudly laid my platinum card down on the black marble counter.

"Great. Please fill out this card and I'll get you a key. How many keys will you need?"

"Just one. Is there a florist around here open?" I asked.

"Right around the corner," she said. "Is there anything else I can do for you?"

"Is there any way you could have a bottle of champagne sent up to the suite immediately?" I asked.

"Sure, no problem. I'll call room service for you."

"Thanks a million," I said, dashing in the direction of the florist.

I located the small shop right around the corner from the hotel entrance. The window was still filled with Christmas arrangements and University of Alabama Sugar Bowl balloons. A short, stocky white guy behind the counter greeted me as I walked in.

"Happy Holidays. Can I help you?" he asked.

"You don't have pink roses, do you?"

"No, not now. All we have is red."

"Give me a dozen and fix them up real pretty," I said.

"No problem. Here are some cards that you can write a note on," he said, pointing to the card holder on the counter.

"Thanks."

"Are you from around here?"

"Long time ago."

"Welcome back."

"Thank you. I'm just here for a couple of days," I said.

As he wrapped the roses in a nice bundle, I picked up one of the cards and scribbled out: *To Sela, Merry Christmas and Happy New Year, from the first man (besides your daddy) who loved you and the man you should be marrying. Love Always, Raymond.*

Yes, I thought to myself, that should do it. I took a twenty-dollar bill and handed it to the clerk and rushed out of the store and back toward the hotel. Twenty dollars, I thought to myself. Things down South certainly were cheap. When I arrived back at the lobby bar, I saw Sela sitting in the same spot looking at her watch.

"You're not going to leave me, are you?" I asked.

Startled, Sela turned around and said, "Where have you been?"

I took the box of roses that I had hidden behind my back and handed them to her. I softly kissed her on the cheek and whispered, "To the first girl I ever loved, Merry Christmas."

"Ray, this is so sweet. What are you up to?"

"Up to?"

"Yes, you didn't have to do this."

"But I wanted to and that's just the beginning of the surprise."

"What? Don't make me cry out here in this hotel lobby," Sela pleaded.

"Then follow me," I instructed.

"Where are we going?"

"I wish I had a blindfold, but just take my hand and come with me," I said reassuringly.

I took Sela's small, delicate hand and led her to the bank of elevators on the other side of the hotel bar. When we got into the elevator, I pushed the button with 19 on it. Sela was looking at me with a puzzled look on her face and I just stared, not saying a word, looking at her beautiful almond-shaped eyes and undressing her with mine. Once we reached the nineteenth floor, I read the signs that led to 1923. I took the magnetic key and opened the door.

"After you, madam," I said to Sela, laying out an imaginary red carpet.

"Ray, what's going on?" Sela asked once again.

"Trust me, just trust me," I said.

After Sela walked into the room, I followed her in and was happy that I had decided on the suite. It was decorated with modern black art deco living room furniture, a full wet bar and a big picture window that overlooked the mall and its skating rink. It was like having your own private view of the world, or at least of the mall. The door in the parlor led to a bedroom that had a huge black lacquer king-size platform bed. There were mirrors against the closet doors that made the room appear larger than it actually was.

"This is beautiful," Sela said gleefully.

"Yes, it is. Come with me," I said, taking Sela's hands and leading her back to the living room. We both sat on the sofa and I opened the chilled bottle of Martini & Rossi Asti Spumante sparkling wine.

After popping the cork, I carefully poured the bubbly into the two chilled stemmed champagne glasses.

"Toast," I said. As Sela held her glass to mine, we both smiled warmly at each other. "To the good times, to the old times, to the new times."

"There were some good times," Sela said.

"I can't tell you what you and that dress are doing to me," I said, looking lustfully at Sela.

"Oh yeah, but don't you forget that I'm spoken for," she said.

"I won't, unless temporary amnesia slips in."

"I don't think so."

"Let me look at your life line," I said, reaching for Sela's hands. "Is this the ring?" I asked, looking at the small diamond ring.

"Yes, and I love it."

As I held her hand in mine, I began to rub it very gently. Sela seemed to be loosening up and she kicked off her pumps and curled her legs up under her. When Sela appeared even more relaxed, I slowly removed the champagne glass from her hand, refilled it and laid it against her knees.

"Let me have your feet," I asked.

Without any hesitation she uncurled her legs and laid them in my lap. As she sipped the Asti, I slowly began to massage her feet, starting with her baby toes and then slowly working my way up. Once I reached her knees, I went back to her toes and softly kissed them through her stockings.

"Come here," I said.

"Come where?"

"Here," I whispered as I motioned with my index finger toward my lips, using my other hand to remove the glass from her hand. As soon as Sela started to move toward me, I reached and touched her face. First I rubbed it with the palm of my hand and then without warning I kissed her fully made-up lips. I planted several short, quick kisses on her lips and then I hungrily moved my tongue down into her mouth. Sela kissed me back vigorously and I took my hands away from her face to her knees and the bottom of the black leather dress.

With one motion I reached under her dress and removed her panty hose with the ease a pickpocket would envy. I then moved my lips from Sela's and went back to her now naked toes and put them in my mouth, sucking them as though they were freshly picked blueberries. Minutes later my tongue started an upward motion toward Sela's knees. I stopped long enough to look at her beautiful face and realized that her eyes were now closed and she was licking her own lips as she wrapped her arms around the top of my head, stroking her fingers through my closely cropped hair. Without any protest from Sela, I unzipped the long, hidden zipper on the side of her leather dress and it fell to the sofa.

For a moment I just sat there and gazed at her exquisite body, which was now covered only by a sheer black bra and matching panties.

"What are you staring at?" Sela asked, blushing.

"The most beautiful woman in the world," I replied.

"You're a piece of work," Sela said as she pulled me closer to her and lifted my red wool Polo sweater from my upper body. As she tackled my cotton T-shirt, I hurriedly unbuckled my belt and removed my wool slacks without even unzipping them. With the two of us down to our underwear, we started kissing again—slow, quick, teasing kisses, then long, deep, hard kisses. Sela tasted like the wine and her lips no longer had lipstick on them. Her body smelled of

Lauren perfume. Her perfectly placed hair now went in its own direction. I removed her sheer black bra and lingered with my tongue long and hard over each nipple of her perfectly formed breasts. Sela's nipples grew firm under my touch.

I took my hands and dipped them into the wine bucket and grabbed some ice, which I placed in my mouth, and then started to suck Sela's throbbing breasts. Sela was licking her lips and quietly moaning. I then took a single piece of ice and placed it between her erect breasts and licked it until it disappeared into her petal-soft skin. I had placed my other hand between her long legs. She freed my sex from my underwear and aggressively massaged it. Starting at the top of her forehead with ice in my mouth, I started to kiss and lick every inch of Sela's body until I reached her midsection. When I arrived at that point, I stopped, took the half-filled glass and poured the bubbling liquid very slowly over Sela's pubic hair. She let out a shivering sigh when I took my entire face and buried it in her now naked lap. I then divided her legs and kissed and licked that portion of her body until it was no longer wet from the sweet-tasting Asti, only damp. After a passionate period, I reached down and grabbed her feet, lifting them into the air and placing her toes into my mouth. Sela's moans and face expressed pure pleasure. I picked up Sela's petite body and carried her into the bedroom. She seemed weightless in my arms. I carefully placed her on the bed, then knelt and started with her toes again. All the years we had dated and all the times we had made love could not measure up with what was occurring in this hotel suite. My sex ached with such power that I could feel it growing harder and longer. I suspended my body in the air over Sela's, swinging my sex like a pendulum over her body, using my arms and toes for support.

"Ray," Sela moaned.

"Yes, baby, yes."

"Do you have protection?" she asked in a soft murmur.

"Don't worry, I'll take it out before I come."

"Ray, no, we can't take that chance."

"Please, baby, don't worry. I'll take care of it."

"No, Ray, I want to, but . . ."

"Please, Sela . . ."

"Here, you lay back and let me do the work," Sela said.

I lay back on the bed, staring at the ceiling as Sela took the position I had been in. Starting with my toes, she used her tiny tongue and licked my entire body, lingering at my sex. I gazed around the room in total shock and complete ecstasy. It felt wonderful. Sela attacked oral sex with great intensity. This was the first time she had ever done anything remotely close to this. Where did she learn this, I wondered in my enjoyment? Is this something Dewayne taught her?

"How am I doing, Ray?" Sela asked between her kisses.

"Wonderful, great . . ." I moaned.

When the pleasure got so that I couldn't stand it, I pushed Sela away and rolled on top of her. As I prepared to find my way into her again, I suddenly thought of past sexual partners. No, I couldn't risk endangering Sela. The thought caused my rock-hard erection to disappear.

"What's the matter?" Sela asked.

"Nothing," I lied. "Come here and just let me hold you."

Sela climbed up and laid her face and hair against my sweaty chest.

"Are you sure you're all right?"

"Yeah, baby, I'm sure. I mean, you're wearing me out. I'm not as young as I used to be," I joked.

"You might be older, but you're certainly better. I should send Miss *Julie* a thank-you note." Sela smiled.

Julie, I thought. Julian was good, but as far as I was concerned, he hadn't taught me shit, except how to endure pain and attend law school at the same time. Had sleeping with men made me a better lover with women?

"Do you have to go home?" I asked Sela.

"I'm not married yet. Do you want me to spend the night?"

"Yeah, if you want to," I replied.

"Let me call my parents and Dewayne and then we've got work to do," Sela said.

"Okay, I need to call home too. You know my mother." Sela took the top sheet and wrapped it around her naked body and went into the parlor to use the phone. I looked around the room and asked myself why this had happened. What was I trying to prove? A couple of nights ago I was in heat over Bo Jackson and Quinn. Tonight I was in bed with an almost married woman. I thought it was time for me to return to New York before I ruined other people's lives as I had ruined my own. I knew that this night would not change me the way the night in my apartment with Kelvin had so many years ago. I tried to determine the difference between making love with a woman and with a man. While I had enjoyed this night of passion with Sela, I wondered if I had been too methodical in my lovemaking or if I had allowed myself to just let go as I had done so many times before with male partners. Was making love to a woman now work instead of enjoyment for me?

The morning light filled the bedroom of the suite, reminding me of so many mornings in the past when I had awakened with Sela's head lying against my chest. I looked down at her and realized that she was still asleep. I took my hands and delicately touched her face, causing her to awaken suddenly.

"What time is it?" she asked, rubbing her eyes.

"Nine-thirty. What time do you need to get home?" I asked.

"I told you, Ray, I'm not married yet. How did you sleep?"

"Very peacefully."

"Me too."

"You want to order from room service?"

"Sure, breakfast in bed would be nice."

I reached for my striped boxer shorts, which were on the floor next to the bed. After slipping them on, I headed to the parlor for the room service menu. "What do you want?" I asked Sela as I reviewed the menu.

"Surprise me," she answered.

I ordered breakfast and climbed back into the bed, lightly kissing Sela's lips. She took both her hands and ran them through her tousled mane and then caressed my face with her long, slender fingers. I kept kissing her and holding her close to my body. We would stop kissing and take our noses and press them together. Just when I felt my sex growing inside my boxer shorts, there was a knock on the door.

"Saved by the knock," I groaned.

We took the hot dishes and placed them in the bed with us. I fed Sela and then she fed me. I sat on the end of the bed, sipping the steaming black coffee, and for an instant the room seemed perfectly still. After a long silence Sela looked up at me and asked, "Are you all right?"

"I'm fine. Why do you ask?"

"No reason. Raymond, can I ask you something?"

"Sure," I answered nervously.

"What happened with us?"

"What do you mean?"

"I mean, when you went to New York, you changed. You know, I always dreamed of marrying you."

"And I dreamed of marrying you. I just think the distance and career pressures got the best of us."

"Is that it?"

"I think so. But I can say one thing."

"What's that?"

"I never stopped loving you. But I want you to be happy and I'm not certain that I can give you what you deserve."

"And what do I deserve, Mr. Tyler?"

"Someone who worships the ground you walk on. Someone who loves you more than you love him. You are an incredible woman, Sela, and Dewayne is one lucky man."

"I think a small part of me will always love you, Raymond. I think once you decide what you want, you'll make some young lady very happy."

"Just a small part." I smiled weakly.

"Hey, we better go. Who's taking you to the airport?"

"My entire family, I think. You don't want to take me, do you?"

"I think we should stop while we're ahead. Give me your address so that I can at least send you a wedding invitation."

"What if I show up?"

"You can, but please don't cause a scene," Sela quipped.

As we walked out the door of the hotel suite, I suddenly took Sela's face between my hands and kissed her very softly. There was a look of doubt in her warm eyes and I knew we had left many questions unanswered. But we both had to go on. The time we had spent together would always be special to me and I would never forget her. I pulled her close to me and kissed her one last time, closing my eyes. As I kissed Sela . . . everything was . . . as it had always been . . . the same, and yet it was so very different.

SIX

It was decided that my father would take me to the airport alone. Mama said he had something he wanted to talk to me about. What did he want to talk about? After packing my bags and taking a last look around my room, I went to the garage, where Mama and Kirby were standing, braving the cool winter air. Mama had tears in her eyes and Kirby was pleading with her to let him ride to the airport with Pops and me.

"Now, you call as soon as you get back safe," Mama pleaded.

"I will. You be a good boy for Mama and Pops," I said to Kirby as I palmed his small close-shaven head.

"When can I come stay with you, Ray-Ray?" Kirby asked.

"Real soon, maybe this summer." Pops came out of the sliding glass door all bundled up in my old high school football jacket and his favorite brown hat.

"You ready to go, chief?" he asked me.

"Ready when you are," I responded. Now the tears were coming fast from Mama's eyes and Kirby was holding on to her legs.

"Come on now, Ma, stop crying. I'll be back sooner than you think," I assured her.

"Go on, get in the car," she said as she wiped her tears into her face.

"I love you, Ma."

"I love you too, baby. Take care and don't forget to pray," she said.

"Hey, buddy, take care of Mama and Pops for me," I said playfully, swinging Kirby up in the air.

"I will," he said. As we started for the airport, Pops wasn't that talkative. He just changed the channels on the car radio. When we were almost halfway to the airport, he turned the radio down very low and looked over at me.

"You know your mother turns fifty in May," he said.

"Yeah, that's right."

"Well, I'm planning a surprise party for her and I want you to come back home. Maybe you can bring a friend with you," he said.

"Oh, that will be great. Sure, I'll come back."

"Well, once my secretary and I get all the plans down, I'll have her give you a call and you can let her know who you're bringing," he said.

"Why don't you call me, Pops?" I asked.

"Well, I guess I can do that," he said reluctantly.

"Does it matter who I bring, Pops?"

"No, not really. Who are you thinking about? Some new lady you met? You know, Sela might not like that," he joked.

"No, Pops, Sela's cool. Actually I was thinking about Kyle and JJ. Neither one of them has been down South. I think they would enjoy it and it would certainly surprise Mama. You remember Kyle and JJ, don't you, Pops?"

My father didn't respond. He turned and looked at me very soberly. Then he reached to turn up the radio and put his foot harder on the gas pedal. I looked out the window at the cars passing us and the skyline of the city. I suddenly longed for the Manhattan skyline.

"Is that all you wanted to talk to me about, Pops?" I asked.

At first my father said nothing. I just looked at him, waiting on a response. When I looked away, I saw that we were approaching the airport terminal.

"What airline?" he asked abruptly.

"American."

Once we reached the American terminal, Pops got out to unlock the trunk of his late-model Mercedes. I reached in and grabbed my luggage and set it on the pavement. I reached for my father's hand and he hesitantly extended his.

"I've had a great time, Pops."

"Yeah, me too."

"Pops, are you sure you don't have something else you wanted to talk to me about?"

As he clasped my hand, my father's eyes looked intense, as though something were aching to get out. His eyes appeared as though they had turned emerald green. They seemed to have tiny drops of moisture surrounding them.

"Raymond junior," my father said very sternly.

"Yes, Pops?"

"Your mother"—he paused and we stared at each other—"your mother and I didn't raise you to be no sissy." I looked straight into my father's eyes and fought back the tears that were beginning to form in mine. I forced myself not to drop my eyes.

"I know that, Pops. I know that." Without even a hug or a good-bye, I gathered my luggage and headed through the automatic doors that led me to the airplane that would take me away from this town and my father. As I walked through the terminal, I became oblivious to all the people rushing around me. I was concentrating on keeping the tears in my eyes in place. I could not let them roll down my face. Inside I felt a great bitterness at my father's statement. If I felt this way, then how did my father feel? Somehow I managed to find my departure gate and get on the plane, still very much unaware of what was going on around me. The next thing I remember, the flight attendant was asking me if I wanted something to drink.

"Yes, a double vodka gimlet," I said, coming out of my self-induced trance.

"Rough day?" the blond flight attendant asked me.

"You don't know the half of it . . . I've had a rough life," I responded soberly.

SEVEN

It was a cold gray day in New York. The weather mirrored the way I felt: half snow, half slush. Only in my case I was sloshed after a three-hour flight of vodka gimlets. I quickly grabbed my luggage and got a taxi to my apartment.

I had never been so happy to be in New York with all its traffic and people. Once I reached my apartment, I quickly ran to my answering machine to check my messages. There were three new messages from Quinn, the last two sounding quite urgent, but still no number where I could reach him. To my surprise, there was also a message from Candance, asking me to call her about an extra ticket she had to a Stephanie Mills concert on New Year's Eve.

Stephanie Mills was one of my favorite singers, but I didn't know if I wanted to spend my New Year's Eve with her and Candance. But maybe Kelvin would be there.

As I was rewinding my answering machine and removing my clothes to take a much-needed shower, I noticed a gold ring on the black-and-red oriental throw rug that lay beside my bed. I picked it up and examined it closely. It wasn't mine; besides, it looked like a man's wedding band. *Where did it come from?* Suddenly I put two and two together: Quinn and all the urgent messages. The ring had to belong to Quinn. Was this a ring from a lover or from a wife? I laid the ring on the nightstand and just looked at it. What else could happen before this year was over?

The shower, along with an Alka-Seltzer, cleared my head. I put on my robe and sat on my bed looking around the room. What was I going to do? What if Quinn was married or had a lover? That made him a liar. Lord knows that I ran across enough liars in gay bars. I always told Kyle that anybody you met in a gay bar usually wasn't worth shit. Was Quinn trying to prove my point? Why didn't he call back now that I was home?

The longer I sat on my bed, the madder I got. First Pops, and now this. I needed another drink. No, that would just make me more emotional. Shit, it was the holidays and I needed it. I went into the living room to see what I had in my bar when the phone rang.

"Hello," I said.

"Happy Holidays," the pleasant female voice said.

"Thank you. Who am I speaking with?"

"Oh, I'm sorry, Ray. This is Candance, Kelvin's fiancée."

"Oh, Candance. I got your message and I was going to call you. I just got back from home a couple of hours ago."

"How was your trip?" she asked.

"Great," I lied.

"Well, Kelvin and I have an extra ticket to the Stephanie Mills concert at the Broadway Theater. Are you available?"

"Oh, Stephanie Mills, she's one of my favorites."

"Yeah, Kelvin mentioned that. I have a good girlfriend who's in *Dreamgirls* and she got us tickets."

"How soon do you need to know?" I asked.

"Well, as soon as you can let me know. The show starts at eight and we are supposed to meet Nicole for drinks at B. Smith's before the concert."

"Nicole?"

"Yes, Nicole Springer, that's my girlfriend. I think you might enjoy meeting her."

"Well, give me an hour and I'll get back to you. Let me make sure I have your number."

"Here, let me give it to you. It's 857-5258."

"857-5258. Got it."

"Okay, we'll wait to hear from you. Good-bye."

"Good-bye. Tell Kelvin hello."

"I sure will."

As I pondered whether or not to go to the concert, my phone rang again.

"Ray."

"Quinn."

"When did you get back?"

"A couple of hours ago."

"How was your trip?" Quinn asked.

"Cut the crap, Quinn. What's with all the fuckin' messages and no number?"

"I lost something and I think it might be in your apartment."

"Is it a gold wedding band?"

"Yes. Did you find it?"

"So it is a wedding band."

"Let me explain, Ray. Can I come by in a couple of hours?"

"I'm sorry, Quinn, but I have a date. Call me tomorrow," I said in an unsympathetic tone.

"But, Ray, we need to talk," Quinn pleaded.

"Yes, we do, but not tonight. Call me tomorrow." Click.

Well, that settled it. I was going to the concert. I called

Candance and agreed to meet them at B. Smith's at seven-thirty. I looked through my closet to find something to wear. I put on a Phyllis Hyman CD, which I usually did when I was depressed, and pressed my black tux pants. All the years I had known Kelvin, this would be the first New Year's Eve we would spend together. But it wouldn't be like old times.

I got the impression that Candance might be trying to play matchmaker with this Nicole lady. That's all I needed to further confuse my life. I wished Kyle had been here. He always knew of some hot gay party and that might be just what the doctor ordered.

B. Smith's was a wonderful bar and restaurant in midtown, near all the theaters. It was a bright, open, spacious place with an elegant bar and magnificent African art on the walls. The décor was suggestive of opulence and sophistication, but not blatantly so. It was a frequent gathering place for New York's buppies, especially on Friday evenings. I had been there a couple of times with the other black lawyer from my office, Brayton Thompson. Sometimes we took clients there for lunch.

As I came through the door, I saw Kelvin and Candance at the bar, holding hands and kissing like newlyweds. Oh, this is going to be fun, I thought to myself. Kelvin spotted me and had a strange look on his face as I walked toward the two of them.

"Well, we meet again," I said, extending my hand toward Kelvin.

"Ray, glad you could make it," Kelvin said.

"Yes, we sure are," Candance said as I kissed her lightly on her cheek.

"What are you drinking, Ray?" Kelvin asked me.

"Club soda with a twist of lime."

"Is that all?"

"Yes."

"So, Ray, how were your holidays?" Candance inquired.

"Great, but I'm glad to be back in New York."

"We leave for Washington tomorrow, but I will be back several times before the wedding," she added.

As the three of us sipped our drinks, we chatted about the upcoming year and the concert. I had never seen Stephanie Mills in concert, so I was beginning to get excited. I occasionally glanced out of the huge window that faced Eighth Avenue and noticed that a light rain had begun to fall. While looking out of the window, I saw an attractive lady in a beautiful mink coat get out of a taxi.

"Oh, here comes Nicole," Candance said.

I watched the lady in the mink coat come into the restaurant and head directly to the corner of the bar where the three of us were standing. She and Candance exchanged big hugs and kisses on the cheeks and she then kissed Kelvin quickly on the lips.

"Nicole, this is a good friend of Kelvin's, Raymond Tyler," Candance said as she introduced the two of us.

"Raymond Tyler," Nicole said as she extended a small hand with brightly polished nails.

"My pleasure," I said as I took her hand in mine.

"Oh, don't be shy. Give me a kiss," Nicole said as she gave me a quick peck on the lips.

As she and Candance talked and giggled, I noticed how beautiful Nicole was. She looked like a porcelain Barbie doll dipped in chocolate, with beautiful black shoulder-length curly hair and a lovely face with sharp facial features that made me wonder if she had been under the knife for plastic surgery. Nicole had high cheekbones and her nose and lips looked perfect. Her tawny brown eyes were very large and expressive. She removed her black mink coat to reveal a short black sequined minidress that highlighted her long legs and ample cleavage. With lithe poise, Nicole crossed her legs as she sat on the barstool next to me and Kelvin ordered a round of drinks for the group.

After a couple of sips, Candance and Nicole excused themselves to go freshen up before we left for the theater. It was the first time Kelvin and I had been one-on-one in almost seven years.

"Nicole is beautiful," I said to Kelvin.

"Yes, she is. She's Candance's best friend."

"Oh well, you look great. I like that jacket," I said, admiring Kelvin's caramel-colored herringbone.

"Thanks. It's a Christmas present from Candance."

As we waited for the ladies to return, Kelvin and I engaged in nervous chitchat and tried to appear at ease.

"How do you like coaching?" I asked.

"It's a lot of fun, but I'm thinking about going back to school when Candance finishes."

"Oh, where?"

"Howard or Georgetown."

"You ever run into anybody from AU?"

"Very rarely. What about you?"

"Hardly ever. I saw Sela while I was at home."

"How was she?"

"Doing great. Matter of fact, she's getting married the same day as you and Candance."

"What a coincidence."

"Yeah, that's what I thought."

The conversation with Kelvin went as though we hardly knew each other, much like our first conversation so many years ago: talking but saying very little, especially what was on our minds. Kelvin was playing with the stirrer from his drink and looking around the huge open-spaced bar and restaurant. He looked as though he was getting ready to say something, when the ladies returned.

"Well, we better head out. We don't want to be late," Candance said.

As Kelvin helped Candance with her coat, I assisted Nicole with her heavy mink.

"Thanks," Nicole said with a soft voice and friendly smile.

As the four of us walked out of the bar and prepared to cross busy Eighth Avenue, I reached for Nicole's hand. She looked up at me and broke out in a huge grin and a mischievous look on her face. I suddenly felt myself blushing painfully.

During the opening act of the Stephanie Mills concert, Nicole and I talked and talked. She was a very interesting lady. She, too, was from the South—Arkansas—and was now appearing in a revival of the musical *Dreamgirls*, which was playing at the Ambassador Theater a few blocks away. She told me that she was only in the chorus and was understudying one of the female leads.

I learned that she and Candance had met at Spelman College in Atlanta, where they were both AKAs and roommates. She was very smart, easygoing, and made me feel very comfortable. We hardly heard the singer Christopher Williams, who, as I looked at him onstage, reminded me of Julian, so I was very easily distracted. Nicole suggested that I come and see her show when she took over the lead role of Dena Jones while the regular actress was on vacation. Although I had seen *Dreamgirls* before, I wanted to see more of Nicole. We then exchanged numbers and I promised her that I would come to see the show again. Every once in a while I noticed Kelvin looking over at me and Nicole with a puzzled look on his face.

During the intermission the four of us went out to the lobby for drinks. We talked about the first act and Candance commented on how well Nicole and I were getting along. I looked around the lobby and saw a lot of familiar faces from the bars. I don't know why I was surprised: Stephanie Mills had had throngs of gay fans since her early days in *The Wiz*. When I spotted people I knew from the bars, I simply nodded acknowledgment but didn't say a word. Again, I caught Kelvin's eyes on me when I gave these nods. One guy whom I had talked with in the bars saw me and started in my direction. A nervous tremor went through my body as he approached us. When he got close, Nicole and Candance left to go to the ladies' room without noticing him. *Saved!*

"Raymond," the familiar face said.

"Yes."

"Don't you remember me, Derrick Jeter? We met at the Nickel."

"Oh yeah. How are you doing? This is a friend of mine, Kelvin Ellis."

A startled Kelvin extended his hand with a forced smile and then walked away. He appeared a bit irritated.

"Are you enjoying the concert?" I asked.

"Yes. Are you going to the party?"

"What party?" I inquired.

"Dr. Larry Washington and his lover. It's a black-tie affair up in Harlem," Derrick said.

"I didn't know about it."

"Honey, it's going to be a grand affair. You can come as my guest." I hated it when men called me terms like honey.

"Thanks. When are you going?"

"Right after the concert. We can take a taxi," he said.

"Why don't you give me the address. I'm with a group of straight folks and I don't know what they have planned," I explained.

"Chile, I can understand that. I'll leave your name at the door. Here's the address," Derrick said as he handed me a torn check with the address on it. I wondered why Derrick couldn't just call me Ray.

"Thanks, Derrick. I'll try and make it."

"Trust me . . . you would want to," he said, laughing.

I went over to where Kelvin was standing. "So is that the type of people you hang out with?" he asked sarcastically.

"Excuse me?"

Before Kelvin could respond, Nicole and Candance walked up.

"You guys ready to go back in?" Nicole asked.

"Sure," I replied, rolling my eyes at Kelvin.

The concert was fantastic. Stephanie Mills had the crowd spellbound. I left her performance a bigger fan than before. Ms. Mills was now a close second in my book to Whitney Houston.

After the concert Nicole suggested that the four of us go to JR, a pub in the theater district, for coffee. Even though I had the party uptown on my mind, I agreed to join them.

JR was a place where a lot of Broadway actors met to unwind after their shows. It was a small bar, deceptive in its simplicity. Once we entered, many of the patrons seemed to recognize Nicole and she stopped to exchange pleasantries with some of them as we walked to our table. It reminded me of Sela working restaurants after football games back at school.

While enjoying coffee laced with a little Grand Marnier, Nicole and Candance were busy catching up on people from school. Kelvin and I sat there listening, occasionally glancing at each other. Talk of the upcoming nuptials became my cue to exit. "Well, ladies and gent, this has been a wonderful way to bring in the New Year, but I'm really beat."

"Oh, Ray, you're leaving?" Nicole asked.

"Yes, but we will talk real soon."

"Well, Ray, I'm glad you could make it. You watch after Nicole," Candance suggested. There she went with her matchmaking.

"I will. Kelvin, great seeing you. Give me a call. Maybe we can get together for some boy talk."

"Yeah, sure, I'll do that," Kelvin said.

I gave both Nicole and Candance quick pecks on the cheeks and gave Kelvin a firm handshake. I darted out of JR toward Eighth Avenue into the chilly wind and hailed a taxi heading uptown.

"One Forty-sixth and St. Nick," I instructed the driver.

While riding up Broadway, I relished the busy New York streets. As we approached Eighty-sixth Street, I realized that I was very tired and decided to go home instead of the party. The evening had been enjoyable and I decided to quit while I was ahead.

The taxi driver let me out on the left side of Ninety-sixth and Broadway and I waited for the light to change. It was the beginning of a New Year and I was spending the night alone. As I walked through the lobby of my building, I pushed the button for the elevator. Just as I was about to step onto the elevator, someone called my name.

I turned around and saw Quinn standing before me. "I guess you came for your ring?"

"Yes and to talk. That is, if you will let me."

"I'm not in the mood. Let me go up and get the ring," I said sullenly.

"Ray, please let me come up and explain," Quinn pleaded.

"I don't know," I said, addressing him with the impersonal hostility of a prosecutor offering a plea bargain to a known child molester.

"Please. Just ten minutes."

"Ten minutes. Come on up."

Once we arrived in my apartment, I removed my tie and jacket and Quinn took a seat on the sofa. I grabbed a beer and sat on the sofa opposite Quinn, purposely not offering him anything to drink or a reason to stay beyond his allotted ten minutes. I turned the television on with the remote control and immediately put the MUTE button on.

"So talk," I demanded.

"Where do you want me to start?"

"Hold on one second."

I went into my bedroom and retrieved Quinn's gold band and brought it back into the living room, dropping it in Quinn's lap. "Why don't you start here," I said, with my eyes on the gold band sparkling against his black wool slacks.

With big, apologetic eyes, Quinn began to talk. He spoke slowly and deliberately. Yes, he was married, but he and his wife were having problems. Major problems. They were even considering divorce. They had two small kids, a boy and a girl. His wife didn't know about this side of his life and he just needed somebody to talk to. He assured me that this was not the cause of their problems. His wife was at her parents' home in Virginia to think things over. He said that no matter what happened between him and his wife, he still wanted to pursue a friendship with me. He rationalized the advantages of being involved with a married man. When I asked him to explain, he said, "With everything going on in New York City, you can count on me being faithful to you." Quinn continued by telling me it was a rare occurrence that he even went to the bars and it was fate that we met. He had wanted to meet someone who didn't appear gay, that he could even invite to his office or home. As he talked, I listened intently and began to soften. We had many of the same views when it came to the life and the longevity of gay relationships.

Quinn said he wasn't calling just about the ring: he had thought of me constantly since our meeting. He also pointed out that he had not lied about having a lover. Nothing about a wife had come up. As he talked, I sat on the sofa in silence, occasionally looking at the television or sipping some of the beer from the now warm can. After Quinn finished talking, he stared at the television. His face revealed a restless loneliness. Then he turned to me, watching me for a long time, saying nothing. Then, "So, Ray, will you forgive me and let's start all over as friends?" he said.

"I don't know, Quinn, this is an awful lot to digest."

"I understand. Could I have a beer or something to drink?"

I relented and said, "Sure."

I went to the kitchen and poured two glasses of wine and put in a Luther Vandross CD. I walked back over to the sofa and just looked at Quinn, at the television and around my apartment. Without warning, Quinn pulled me against him, putting himself in my arms as though he was giving me himself to protect. He looked me directly in the eyes and kissed me with intense passion. I felt powerless! Quinn stood up, pulled me up and started to lead me toward my bedroom. Once there, he started to slowly undress me. When he removed an article of clothing to reveal my skin, he gently kissed that portion of my body, until I stood naked in my bedroom. Quinn quickly undressed and pulled me down with him on the bed. We wrestled playfully for minutes, each of us jockeying for position. We tossed and rolled with each other until our bodies seemed to be intertwined. Quinn and I began to make love, gently attending to each other's needs. The lovemaking lasted for hours. Each climax better than the one before. After making love, Quinn lay in my arms and seemed lost in his thoughts.

"What are you thinking about?" I asked.

"Nothing, just wishing," he said.

"Wishing what?"

"That life could be like this forever."

I smiled and brushed his face. We kissed a long breathless kiss and I lay back and surrendered myself to a deep sleep on the first night of the year.

Quinn and I became prisoners in my apartment. The days rolled into nights and time was not a factor. We watched the college bowl football games, played chess, listened to music, talked and became familiar faces to the Chinese and pizza delivery guys. I turned the ringer on my phone off and the volume of the answering machine so low that neither one of us could hear it. The only way I knew that people were calling was from the red digital numbers that indicated how many calls had come in. We ordered a case of Chardonnay and finished it in our three-day hibernation. In between the talks, television and music, we managed to enjoy lustful lovemaking. We took showers together that lingered until the rush of water became ice-cold. Our clothing consisted of robes and old T-shirts.

I learned a lot about Quinn during this time. He had played basketball at Wake Forest University and received a degree in business. He, too, experienced his first relationship with a man during his senior year. Quinn married his high school sweetheart and she was now a bank loan officer when she wasn't at home raising their two kids, Baldwin and Maya. He said he never worried about being found out, either at home or at work. "I don't fit the mode," he remarked.

His only long-term relationship with a man was with his best friend, who was also married. He said the guy had moved to the West Coast and they were just friends now. When I asked him if he was sure his wife didn't know, he replied, "She wouldn't believe it even if Jesus Christ Himself told her."

We talked about how even the smartest of women couldn't detect undercover gay guys. We also discussed how white businesspeople never picked up on it either. I related to him how one of our senior partners was always talking about faggots this and faggots that in our staff meetings. Quinn said that his wife's brother was gay and that he avoided him like the plague. He said he was always polite to him but avoided prolonged conversations or being alone with him. He laughed to himself when he talked about his wife being a real BAP, black American Princess. I shared my airport scene with my father, and Quinn showed compassion I had not expected.

We finally faced up to the fact that we must return to the real world when the beeper from my office went off. My apartment was beginning to smell pungent, similar to a locker room. Grady also slipped a note under my door stating that Kyle had come by a couple of times and appeared worried.

Quinn gave me his office number but wanted to hold off on the home number until he and his wife decided what they were going to do. We decided to take a break from each other for a couple of days and get together for lunch on Saturday to discuss where this relationship was going. When Quinn left, I felt brand-new. I was able to put my problems in proper perspective. I was ready to take on the world, or at least New York City.

EIGHT

January settled in. It was blistering cold. The gray days
became blue. They lingered like a kiss with someone you no longer
loved. Kyle and JJ were back. They were a ray of sunshine through
January's doom and gloom. The three of us decided to meet for
dinner on Saturday evening at Sylvia's restaurant in Harlem. I
talked to both of them on the phone several times to discuss our
plans before we met on Saturday. When I spoke with Kyle, his voice
brimmed with excitement and mystery. I was as anxious about
seeing the two of them and comparing notes on our holidays as
they were me.

I had talked with Quinn a couple of times, but I had to cancel
our Saturday lunch date because of work. One of the senior partners at the firm, Mr. William Clay, called me into the office before
I was due back from vacation. When I walked into his huge office,
he explained that he had a tremendous opportunity for me. In fact,
he was giving me my first big case: a computer software copyright
infringement suit against Tri Tech Telcom, a large computer soft-

ware company. Our client was a computer programmer who had developed a software program that Tri Tech was selling to their customers at huge profits. We would be filing a $50 million lawsuit against the giant corporation. It was my chance to shine.

My initial reaction was that I had been given the case because all the white boys were away somewhere skiing, but I felt that whatever the reason, I was going to make the most of this opportunity. Prior to this case, I had been given only small cases that required no litigation and was limited to writing briefs and doing research for other big cases in our office. There were times when I felt more like a paralegal than a lawyer. I was spending twelve to thirteen hours a day in the office going through documents and preparing for upcoming depositions. I even missed going to the Nickel Bar Friday evening, so I had to show up at Sylvia's Saturday night.

After the long train ride uptown I ran the last two blocks to the popular Harlem eatery. Sylvia's was more like a large luncheonette than a restaurant, with low ceilings, long counters and an adjacent dining room. Before I could take off my coat, Kyle and JJ left the table they were sitting at to come and give me big bear hugs and kisses. As I hugged them back, I shared in our excitement about seeing each other again.

"I was beginning to think you had disappeared," Kyle said.

"Yeah, I can't believe you've been actually working all this time," JJ added.

"Trust me, I've been swamped."

We ordered drinks and scanned the menu of Southern delicacies, each of us taking turns describing what had happened since we last saw each other. Kyle and JJ wanted to talk about Quinn and how that was going. They squealed with disbelief when I broke the news that he was married. I failed to mention my night with Sela or my scene with Pops. Kyle had met some new man that he was being vague about and JJ was complaining about the lack of *real men*.

Sylvia's was always packed and the waitress seemed to take forever. We had been talking for almost twenty minutes before she came back to take our order. JJ and I ordered Sylvia's famous fried chicken. Kyle still hadn't decided and the plump waitress appeared a bit annoyed.

"You still haven't decided?" she asked with slight condescension in her voice.

"Excuse me?" Kyle demanded.

The waitress didn't respond. She stood there holding her white pad and rolling her eyes at Kyle while JJ and I continued to talk.

"Did you hear me?" Kyle asked, raising his voice.

"What?" the waitress replied.

"Miss Thang, you heard me. Are we paying extra for your shitty attitude?" he asked.

"My name is Tawanda. I ain't your Miss Thang," the waitress replied.

"Tawanda, Lawanda. I don't give a fuck. I want to see the manager," Kyle said in an abusive tone.

JJ and I stopped our conversation and looked at Kyle with puzzled expressions on our faces.

"What are you two looking at?" he asked.

"Don't come for me. You don't want me," JJ said.

"Kyle, come on, give the lady a break," I pleaded.

"Fuck that bitch. I get sick and tired of these ghetto bitches giving me attitude for no apparent reason. They don't give white folks their shitty attitudes."

These were the times I found Kyle trying. While I avoided confrontation, Kyle would sometimes look for it. He wasn't a mean person; it's just that I think at times Kyle tried to intimidate women before they intimidated him. When the manager of the restaurant came to our table, Kyle ranted and raved, using his expressive hand gestures and finger pops to explain what had transpired between him and Tawanda. The manager apologized and offered to buy our drinks. This was fine with JJ and me, but Kyle was still simmering. By now, other people in the restaurant were staring at our table. I was beginning to become embarrassed.

"What the fuck are you looking at?" Kyle shouted at some people who had stopped eating and were looking directly into Kyle's mouth. I began to look around to see if I recognized anyone. Chances were slim that I would see anybody from the office up in Harlem on a Saturday night. Sylvia's was such a tourist spot that several white families were in the dining area where we were sitting. I had been there countless times and never experienced the scene Kyle was creating. I found the staff among the best in New York and that included the midtown restaurants I frequented.

After a few more drinks Kyle calmed down, but he and Tawanda continued to exchange icy glances. Kyle looked pleased with himself. I was relieved that they changed waitresses and that Tawanda didn't call Kyle a sissy . . . at least to his face. It would have caused an unusual occurrence. A *hurricane in Harlem*.

We managed to finish dinner without any further incidents. Kyle and JJ wanted to go dancing at Better Days, a club located in midtown. Kyle also knew about a party in Brooklyn. I was tired and was not in the mood for the bars, so I passed. I probably could have been talked into going to a party because I enjoyed gay parties more than the loud dance bars.

The bars were truly meat markets. People didn't speak to you unless they were interested in going to bed with you, and everybody walked around with a snobbish attitude. *Being grand* was the goal while in the bars. Secretly, we all feared rejection. Parties were different, people were more at ease and didn't appear to be out on the prowl. Seduction was more subtle.

"Let's stop at André's and have a drink," Kyle suggested.

"I'm going home. I have to go to the office tomorrow."

"Party pooper," JJ joked.

"Next weekend," I promised.

Kyle and JJ decided to go to Better Days, so the three of us caught the No. 1 train downtown. While riding the train, Kyle started to talk a little more about the new man in his life.

"He is so fine. Light-skinned with gray eyes. Body by God and the dick of death," Kyle said.

"Where did you meet him?" JJ quizzed.

"It's a long story," Kyle said.

"I hope you didn't meet him at the Nickel," I chirped in.

"Fuck you, mister. Don't you concern yourself with where I met him."

When the train reached the Ninety-sixth Street station, I kissed and hugged JJ and Kyle. While I was hugging Kyle, he slipped two crisp new one-hundred-dollar bills into my hands.

"You sure you don't need this?" I asked.

"Trust me, I'm fine."

Once I reached my apartment, I collapsed. I kicked off my shoes, hit the PLAY button on my answering machine and lay across the bed. Two messages from Quinn, one from my mother and a call from Nicole. She was playing one of the lead roles at Sunday's matinee and would leave two tickets for me at the box office. Whom should I take?

"At this performance of *Dreamgirls*, the role of Dena Jones will be played by Nicole Springer," the voice over the loudspeaker said. A collective moan went up from the audience. I'd heard these moans before at Broadway shows, but this was the first time the sigh was for somebody I knew personally.

Minutes into the show Nicole Springer had won me over. She had a stunning stage presence and a beautiful, melodious voice.

When I had last seen the show, years before, I was blown away by Jennifer Holliday's booming voice and Sheryl Lee Ralph's beauty. This cast didn't include Jennifer or Sheryl, but it was exceptionally talented.

I watched Nicole's every move onstage. When she wasn't onstage, I waited with excitement for her return. I hardly noticed all the good-looking men in the cast. Besides, I had seen many of them in the bars.

I had decided to invite my paralegal, Susan Ward, to attend the show with me. We had been in the office working since 7 A.M. and she had never seen the show. I had originally intended to invite either Kyle or JJ, but both of them had hangovers from the previous night. Susan and I had become friendly working on cases before and she was really supportive of me with my first big case. She was attending NYU and planning to go to law school once she finished undergrad. Susan was tall and strongly built, with strawberry blond hair and pale blue eyes. She was attractive in a wholesome kind of way.

Dreamgirls was a welcome diversion from all the documents we had reviewed Sunday morning. As I watched Nicole perform her part to perfection, I questioned why she had made a point of inviting me and leaving two tickets. By the end of the show Nicole had not only won me over but had also won over the entire audience, which gave her a thunderous ovation when she took her final bow. Susan and I waited outside at the backstage door to thank Nicole for the tickets and congratulate her on her performance. When she emerged from the door, she spotted me immediately. Nicole had a big smile on her face and gave me a warm embrace and a kiss on the cheek. Her expression remained intact as I introduced Susan as one of my coworkers. While the three of us stood there talking, I recognized Kyle's friend Tony Martin, who came from the stage door with one of the male cast members. When he first saw me, he had a quizzical look on his face. When he realized that I was with Nicole, he simply nodded acknowledgment and hurried down the street with his friend. If Nicole did see the glances we exchanged, she didn't mention it. She was busy accepting congratulations from well-wishers and saying good-bye to cast members.

One obviously gay cast member came up, interrupted our conversation and said, "Miss Thing, you peed. You were fierce, girl! Miss Brown won't miss any more performances when she hears about this," as he snapped his fingers in the air, laughing.

Though she still looked like the sharp-faced beauty from the first night we met, Nicole didn't have on any makeup. She had washed off her stage makeup and her face was scrubbed clean. Her thick black hair was wrapped in a stylish ball. The sequined dress and mink coat had been replaced by a tight-fitting red sweater dress and a black leather cast jacket. She invited Susan and me to JR for coffee, but we had to decline. There was still a tremendous amount of work to do at the law firm. We agreed to try to get together for lunch sometime the following week. We again exchanged embraces and a sweet, simple kiss and headed in opposite directions.

"I think Nicole is smitten with you," Susan commented.

"Why do you say that?"

"I'm a woman—we know things like that." Susan smiled.

Smitten, I thought to myself. Now surely a woman like Nicole Springer could tell that I was gay or at least bisexual.

Or could she?

The week flew by. Susan and I were heavily involved in the first round of preparations for our upcoming depositions. I had several meetings with the Tri Tech lawyers and I held my own. I had little time for a social life and it didn't seem to matter. Quinn was calling less frequently and Kyle and JJ both had new men in their lives, so

they didn't seem to miss me. Thursday night I called Nicole and we
agreed to have lunch on Friday.

I suggested Ben Benson's Steak House and Nicole promptly
agreed. It was an upscale restaurant in midtown that the partners at
my firm frequented. Nicole was waiting at the hostess's stand, looking absolutely stunning, when I walked in.

"You weren't getting worried?" I asked as I gave her a gentle
embrace and kisses on her cheeks.

"No, I knew you'd make it." She smiled.

We engaged in cautionary conversation while we sipped hot
spiced tea. Just when the waiter was delivering our salads, Nicole
looked at me with a sarcastic smile and asked, "So, Raymond, how
long have you been dating Susan?"

"Dating Susan? Oh no, you've got me wrong! Susan and I are
just coworkers."

"Oh," she responded coyly.

When our entrées were served, out came another question. "So
who are you dating?" she asked while delicately spreading butter on
the sourdough bread.

"No one special."

I decided I'd better not order dessert or the are-you-gay question
might come up.

I enjoyed talking with Nicole. Not only was she beautiful, she
was extremely smart. I discovered that she had come to New York
after becoming the first black to be a runner-up to Miss America
and the first black Miss Arkansas. I was very impressed. She was
truly a Southern belle, a new type of belle but a belle nonetheless.
She had a certain sex appeal that was hard to ignore, a quiet confidence in the way she carried herself that no man in his right mind
could resist. *Dreamgirls* was her first Broadway show and she was in
the process of preparing her nightclub act. She told me she had
been in love once. He was a doctor, but he didn't want to leave

Arkansas. Nicole talked about how hard it was to pursue her career and have a social life.

"All the men I meet are one of three things: white, married or gay," she said.

"You're kidding," I said with a faint smile. An uneasiness seized me, but I tried to appear calm. My eyes drifted away when I heard her say how lucky Candance was to find someone like Kelvin.

"Maybe I'll catch her wedding bouquet," she whispered as if she were talking to herself.

As Nicole talked, I thought to myself how tough it must be for black women these days. I mean, being black and gay was tough enough, but I had never stopped to think how difficult it must be for sharp black women. Maybe that was why she hadn't asked me the gay question. Did she know and just want a new friend or did she really think that I was straight? Or was she willing to take me in my present condition?

"Ray, I find it best to be forward, living in New York, so I have something I'd like to ask you."

"Yes and what's that?" I now felt beads of sweat forming on the back of my neck.

"Would you go to church with me on Sunday?"

"Church?"

"Yes, church. You have heard of it?"

"Sure," I said, laughing. "Sure, I'll go to church with you."

"Where do you live?"

"Ninety-sixth and Broadway."

"Okay. I live in midtown, so I'll pick you up at ten-thirty. Okay?"

"It's a date."

I looked at my watch and realized that it was almost three o'clock. I helped Nicole hail a taxi and headed back to the office. I still had a few calls to make and it was Friday. Kyle and the Nickel Bar would be waiting.

When I was leaving the office, one of the partners stopped me at the elevator.

"How's the case coming, Raymond?" Mr. White asked.

"It's coming along fine, Mr. White."

"Great! Now, Raymond, I told you . . . call me Dan. We're all equals around here."

"Sure, Dan."

"Tell me who that beautiful young lady was I saw you with at Ben Benson's today?"

"A good friend."

"Well, beautiful young lady. You should bring her to the next office function," he suggested.

"I'll keep that in mind, Dan."

The conversation with Dan made me realize that I was getting to the age where people were starting to ask questions about my marital status. Most of the professional gay men that I knew always managed to have a girlfriend that lived out of town . . . like the West Coast or, if you were lucky, Europe. After age thirty-five, the lie changed to "I'm divorced."

The only other black lawyer in the office, Brayton Thompson, was married and his wife, Tracie, often came to the office. I admitted to myself an undercurrent of jealousy and resentment when it came to Brayton. He was living the life I often dreamed of. Smart, successful and married to a ravishing model, with two beautiful children. Brayton had been with the firm about a year longer than I, but he hadn't been assigned any big cases. I once overheard a couple of the partners talking in the men's room, unaware that I was in the next stall. They were discussing who among the current associates would one day make partner. When Brayton's name came up, one of the partners mentioned that he had finished first in his law school class. The other partner remarked, "Yeah, first at Howard, not Harvard."

I hadn't decided if I was going to hang around long enough to be considered partner material, but I knew if I did well on this case, it might start to come up. The firm had one black partner when I accepted my offer, but he was later appointed to the federal bench. In the past I had always brought JJ to office parties and prayed the whole time that she wouldn't get drunk and read somebody. I was also very careful with whom I talked on the phone at work. Everyone at Kyle's office knew he was gay, but even when he called me, we talked in codes, changing *he's* to *she's*. Kyle said there was no way he would put up with corporate bullshit. Being a fashion illustrator meant he didn't have to. I mean, have you ever heard of a black male in the fashion industry who wasn't gay?

As soon as I walked into the Nickel, I spotted Kyle. He still had his coat on and appeared to be waiting on me.

"Don't take your coat off," Kyle instructed me.

"Why?"

"We aren't staying here."

"Where are we going?"

"Down to my apartment."

"Your apartment. For what?"

"I have somebody I want you to meet."

"Who?"

"This new guy I was telling you about, Steve Douglas."

"Steve?"

"Yes, but I want you to act like you just dropped by. He's really secretive. But I want you to see him in case I ever come up missing," Kyle joked.

"Is he a maniac?" I asked.

"No, Ray, I'm just messing with you."

"So what am I supposed to do?"

"When we get close to my apartment, you wait ten minutes and then ring my buzzer."

Even though it was freezing cold, we decided to walk to Kyle's apartment on Fifty-eighth and Ninth Avenue. It always amazed me that no matter how cold it was, the streets of New York were always crowded with people walking. As we walked down Broadway, Kyle chatted nonstop about Steve this and Steve that. How wonderful he was in bed and how beautiful his body was. When I questioned Kyle on where they had met and what he did, he simply replied that he would tell me later. Between his rave reviews of Steve, he mentioned that JJ was going out with the bus driver from the No. 103 bus that she had been riding for years.

"Is he straight?" I asked.

"JJ says he is, but what does that bitch know. She thought you were straight."

"Screw you."

"You wish," Kyle said as he darted into the closing elevator.

I waited about ten minutes and then rang the buzzer to Kyle's apartment. I quickly grabbed the door as soon as I heard the buzzing sound. Once I reached Kyle's floor, I saw him looking out of his door and motioning for me to hurry. When I came within inches of his door, Kyle said, "Ray, what a surprise. It's been months. Come on in."

I rolled my eyes in slight irritation at Kyle as I walked into his small studio apartment. When I walked in, I noticed the back of a beautiful body in black leather pants.

"Ray, this is Steve."

When the guy turned around to extend his huge hand, my mouth dropped open. I realized that I knew Steve from somewhere. But where?

"Hello, Ray," Steve said as he smiled.

After a moment of shocked silence, I extended my hand and said, "Hello." While Kyle was in the kitchen mixing drinks, I continued to stare at Steve. Kyle was right. This guy was an absolute vision. A tall, rock-hard body, with a chiseled face and honey brown complexion highlighted by an engaging smile. His eyes, a catlike gray color, were mesmerizing, not only because of their color but also because of their intensity, demanding my attention.

Kyle returned with the drinks and positioned himself on one of Steve's huge legs. When he stood up, I noticed that his ass was so perfectly shaped that it looked as though it could stand alone, not needing the rest of his beautiful body for support.

I asked Steve questions like what he did, where he was from and so on. He was evasive with his answers and Kyle started to look a bit annoyed. Steve looked extremely sexy, but very uncomfortable. I downed my drink and made up an excuse about having to go back to my office.

"So what do you do for a living, Ray?"

"I practice law."

"What type?"

"Litigation."

"Do you have a card? You never know when I might need a lawyer," Steve said, openly flirting with me.

"Sure, but I can only handle cases assigned to me by the firm," I said as I handed Steve a business card. "Well, it was nice meeting you, Steve. Kyle, give me a call soon."

When I reached the lobby of Kyle's building, it suddenly hit me. That guy's name wasn't Steve. It was Basil Henderson. He played wide receiver for the New Jersey Warriors professional football team. I had seen him recently on ESPN talking about the upcoming playoffs. But what was with this Steve bullshit? Maybe I was mistaken. No, I thought to myself, I would never mistake a face like that. Should I tell Kyle or were they both trying to pull the wool over my eyes? Kyle knew what a big football fan I was; maybe he really didn't know whom he had in his apartment. I did understand that he didn't know shit about football, or any sports for that matter. Maybe Steve, or Basil, was lying to Kyle, or maybe I was wrong.

NINE

Saturdays were becoming my only days to spend with Quinn. We were both busy with work and I had no idea what was going on with his marriage. He didn't say and I didn't ask. I tried to call Kyle several times one Friday night, but he had his answering machine on, which meant he was probably busy entertaining Steve, or Basil.

My phone and buzzer suddenly rang at the same time. I picked up the phone with one hand and pressed the building intercom with the other.

"Ray?"

"Yeah, Kyle, hold on one second. Yeah!" I yelled into the intercom.

"Mr. Tyler, there's a Mr. Mathis here," the doorman announced.

"Send him up," I said, realizing that I still had Kyle on the phone. "Kyle."

"Yeah, what's up?"

"Just the usual. Quinn is on his way up. I don't know what we're going to do."

"Who are you kidding? Probably fuck all day. What did you think of Steve?"

"Oh, nice-looking brother, but we need to talk."

"Talk about what?"

"About Steve, or whatever his name is."

"What do you mean?"

"We'll talk later, Kyle. Quinn's at the door."

"Okay, I may stop by your place later on. JJ and I are going to Needless Markup in White Plains."

"Okay, but call first."

"Yeah, we will."

I greeted Quinn at the door and was very happy to see him. He had on a Wake Forest sweatshirt under his jacket and torn, tight jeans. His beard looked deliciously sexy.

"What's up, Mr. Tyler?"

"You, Mr. Mathis."

We shared a quick embrace and a light kiss on the lips. Quinn had his briefcase with him and we decided to just stay in and catch up on work and each other. We realized that we really hadn't talked in a while, just quick phone conversations. I wanted to ask Quinn how things were going at home, but I resisted. We both seemed immersed in our work, occasionally glancing up and exchanging mischievous smiles. A few hours later Quinn slammed his briefcase shut and announced that he was hungry.

"I don't think I have anything here."

"Let's go somewhere. It's cold, but the sun is out," Quinn said.

"Okay, but aren't you afraid somebody might see you?" I asked in a playful tone.

"So what. We aren't going to be walking hand in hand, are we?"

"Yeah," I said, laughing.

"You're terrible."

We decided to go to Zabar's and just get something to bring back to my apartment. Saturday afternoon found Broadway filled with people walking and shopping in the many stores that lined the popular Upper West Side thoroughfare. We stopped at a newsstand to pick up a *New York Times* and at a record shop before reaching Zabar's. On the way back Quinn mentioned that I appeared preoccupied with something.

"What do you mean?" I asked.

"I don't know. It just seems like you have something on your mind."

"Yeah, I do."

"Anything I can help you with?" he asked with deep concern in his voice.

"Oh, it's nothing."

"Nothing? The look on your face doesn't say 'nothing.' "

"What would you do if your wife or somebody at work found out about this part of your life?" My voice filled with suspicion.

"What, are you planning to call my wife?"

"No, I couldn't do that. I don't have the number, remember. I'm not even sure your name is Quinn."

"What?" Quinn asked in a shocked tone. "Do you want to see my driver's license?" he asked, reaching in his jeans and pulling out his wallet.

"No, Quinn, I'm sorry. I was just thinking about something that happened yesterday."

"Does it involve me?"

"No, and I'm sorry."

"What was it?"

"Oh, it's Kyle."

"What has he done now?"

"Well, he's seeing this guy that I think is a famous athlete."

"And . . ."

"Well, the guy is using a bogus name and I'm wondering if I should tell Kyle."

"Are you sure it's who you think he is?"

"Yeah, I'm pretty certain."

"How did they meet?"

"I don't know that."

"Well, I think you should let Kyle find out on his own or wait and see where the relationship is going. Maybe this guy will tell him. Who is it anyway?" Quinn inquired.

"I think it's Basil Henderson."

"The Basil Henderson that plays for New Jersey? You're kidding."

"No, I think that's who it is."

"I didn't know he was *in*."

"Neither did I."

"Well, you hear rumors all the time about athletes and famous people, but I usually take them with a grain of salt. You know how the kids are."

"What do you mean?"

"You know how they think everybody who's bright and famous is gay."

"Yeah, I think you're right."

"But how did Kyle meet this guy?"

"Only Kyle can answer that."

"Maybe he knows who he is, but I'm not so certain that it's your job to tell him."

"But he's my best friend."

"And he's an adult."

I loved the fact that Quinn was so smart. He was easy to talk to and he viewed things from a heterosexual perspective most of the time. I respected his views. He was right about the fact that gay people labeled a lot of famous people gay. Sometimes they were right, sometimes they were blatantly wrong.

I knew that I didn't want people at my office aware of my sexual life, so I knew that it must be even tougher for people in the public eye. I don't think I was so surprised that a professional football star was gay or bisexual. I knew a lot of athletes who were gay, but they were always undercover like Kelvin. They didn't go to bars, parties or anything that was remotely related to being gay and they always had females on their arms. I guess the burning question in my mind was how Basil and Kyle had met. I mean, Kyle didn't cut corners with anyone; he glamorized his gayness. You either accepted that or he didn't deal with you.

Saturday breezed by and before long Quinn was headed back to Long Island. The day had been pleasant. No lovemaking, just heavy foreplay and much-needed conversation. He didn't mention his wife and I didn't mention Nicole.

Kyle and JJ showed up later in the evening loaded down with packages from Needless Markup (the gay term for Neiman Marcus) and a bottle of wine. We ordered some Chinese food and half watched "The Golden Girls" and "Amen." JJ talked about her new man, Bernard Maxson. She was certain that he was straight as an arrow. Kyle was reserving comment until he met him. Kyle didn't mention Steve but was talking about a Vietnam vet that he had met. I told them about Nicole and how beautiful and nice she was.

"Have you told her your story?" JJ asked.

"No, it hasn't come up."

"She probably knows. I mean, working in the theater with all those kids," Kyle added.

"I don't think she suspects," I answered defensively.

"When do we get to meet her?" JJ asked.

"When do we get to meet Bernard?" I challenged.

"Tomorrow."

"Well, maybe you'll meet Nicole tomorrow too."

"Well, to be honest, I'm not that excited about meeting a bus driver or a beauty queen," Kyle added.

"Queen, be quiet," JJ said. "Ray, it sounds like you like this chick."

"She's nice and very special. But I'm not about to change my religion."

"You better not fuck her. You promised me the next time you got some pussy it was going to be mine," JJ said, laughing.

"JJ, you're crazy. So, Kyle, how's Steve?" I asked, trying to catch Kyle off guard and avoiding JJ's sinister smile.

"Oh, he's okay. Didn't I tell you he was fine? Did you notice the bulge in his pants?"

"Yeah, but you still haven't told me where you met him."

"Hasn't told me either," JJ chirped in. "Why don't you bring him tomorrow?"

"I don't think so. I'm sure he's busy."

"Where did you meet him, Kyle?" I repeated.

"On 'Love Connection,' bitch," Kyle responded with his usual quick wit.

"Is he married?" JJ quizzed.

"I don't think so," Kyle responded soberly.

"So are we going to meet tomorrow with our new spouses?" JJ asked.

"I'd rather perform brain surgery on my mother," Kyle quipped.

"You are sick," I said. "Really sick."

Kyle had a strange look on his face. It was obvious that he didn't want to discuss Steve, or Basil. He was using his quick wit to avoid something. Kyle left my bedroom, where the three of us had been eating, and went into the living room to put on some music. All of a sudden we could hear Madonna blasting away. JJ and I went into the living room and Kyle was dancing by himself as if he didn't have a care in the world. Just smiling and twirling.

"Let's go to the Garage," Kyle said.

"Not me. I've got to meet my man," JJ said.

"Count me out. I've got work to do and I'm going to church tomorrow," I said.

"Church. Chile, you've got to be kidding. I hope it doesn't crash when you walk in," Kyle said, still dancing alone.

"Come on, Miss Thing. Let's go," JJ said, grabbing her bags. "Cocktail kisses," she said as she playfully blew kisses in my direction. "I'll call you tomorrow. We should meet at the Saloon for brunch."

"Okay, just leave me a message."

I locked my door and turned off the blasting music. The food and wine had made me extremely exhausted. I turned off all the lights in my apartment with the exception of a small candle flickering on my bar. I put in the CD soundtrack of *Dreamgirls*, lay down on my sofa and let the music begin to stimulate my thoughts of Nicole.

The ringing of the phone yanked me from a deep sleep. Sunday's bright sunlight was pouring through the large windows in my living room. Completely disoriented, I reached for the portable phone.

"Ray?"

"Yes."

"Are you ready?"

"Ready? Who is this?"

"Nicole. I'll be up in a taxi in about fifteen minutes. Why don't you stand on the left side of Ninety-sixth and Broadway."

"Oh, Nicole, I'm sorry, I just woke up. Maybe we should make it another Sunday," I said, rubbing the matter from my eyes.

"I won't take no for an answer. You have twenty minutes to get ready." *Click* went the phone line.

I rushed into my bedroom to find Nicole's phone number to call her back. There was no way that I could get ready in that short amount of time. When I found her number and began to dial it, it dawned on me that I really wanted to see her. Maybe I could get ready in time. I grabbed a blue suit out of my closet, a starched white shirt and a red paisley tie. Ten minutes to shit, shower and shave and maybe I could make it. As I was getting ready, I thought about my mom and how I needed to call her. I could hear her saying, "Don't go out in that cold weather right after taking a shower."

I was ready in record time. I grabbed my overcoat, my watch, and headed downstairs. As soon as I reached the corner of Ninety-sixth and Broadway, a taxi pulled alongside me. Nicole rolled down the window and yelled for me to get in.

"I knew you could make it," Nicole said and she extended her cheek to my lips for a kiss.

"I don't know how, but I made it. You look beautiful."

Nicole smiled in acknowledgment and instructed the taxi driver to take the Henry Hudson Parkway. She looked even more beautiful than the first night I saw her. Her hair was up in a stylish French roll, which brought to mind a young Diahann Carroll. Her face was perfectly made up and her scent erased the stale odor of the taxi. She mentioned how happy she was that I was joining her and how she knew I would enjoy her church. A black Bible lay beside her black mink coat and I took note of her name engraved in gold on the leather cover. It occurred to me that this was not your standard date, that church and religion were important to Nicole and that her inviting me was important to her. That thought warmed me inside.

*   *   *

Nicole was right. I did enjoy church. I had been to several churches since moving to New York, but never on a regular basis. I think it's one of the first things people rebel against once they leave their parents' home. Growing up in my parents' home, church was not an option, it was the law.

Nicole attended Canaan Baptist, one of Harlem's most famous churches. Its exterior was unpretentious, like an old storefront. When we went inside, I noticed it was large and modern. The church was already packed when we arrived, so we had to take seats in the balcony. Nicole took my hand, smiled and made her way through the worshippers, many of whom seemed to know her very well.

The huge choir rocked with down-home gospel. The minister preached with an exciting vigor that was theatrical. Several times during the service Nicole appeared to be in another place, often standing spontaneously and waving her hand in the air while shaking uncontrollably. She looked as though she was filled with a nervous energy that kept her in constant motion. Toward the end of the service, visible tears filled her eyes, causing her makeup to stream in little black waterfalls down her cheeks. Was this the Holy Ghost? I had seen old ladies in my church back home *get happy*, but never had I seen someone so young and beautiful become *filled* in a church service. I had assumed that these feelings and emotions were reserved for the overweight and the old.

I reached for Nicole's small hands. They felt warm. "Are you all right?" I asked.

"I'm blessed," she whispered with a reassuring smile.

Blessed, I thought to myself. What a way to describe this beautiful Sunday afternoon.

After the services Nicole and I stopped to talk with several of the members. It was much like the scene at the stage door a week ago. Several old ladies came and gave Nicole big hugs and kisses. They chatted about the services and told Nicole that they had seen her in the show or on some TV commercial recently. Many looked at me and then asked Nicole, "Where did you find this handsome young man?" I would smile and hold Nicole's hand tighter.

We decided to take the train downtown, knowing it would be faster, since taxis were at a premium in Harlem on Sunday afternoon. It slipped my mind to check my machine to see if Kyle and JJ wanted to meet. Nicole had to be at the theater, so she suggested we stop at JR for a quick bite to eat. We finished brunch and Nicole invited me to see the show again, only this time from backstage. Even though I had tons of work to do, I promptly agreed.

This time I saw the show from a different perspective. Nicole was performing in the chorus instead of the lead role, so I was able to exchange several quick glances with her as she and the other members of the cast rushed backstage for costume changes.

Again, I noticed several male cast members whom I had seen at the bars. Even though they only smiled without moving their lips, I was becoming very uncomfortable.

Sunday ended without incident. I walked Nicole to her apartment after the show and stood in the lobby of her building, talking with her for hours. When we both noticed that the dark winter dusk had arrived, I gave Nicole a soft moist kiss on her fully made-up lips and took my leave.

TEN

Wednesday, hump day, and Susan and I were falling behind in our preparations for our upcoming depositions. I was deep into reviewing documents when my secretary, Hillary, located me in the firm library.

"Raymond, there's a Steve Douglas on the line. This is the fourth time he's called today. Do you want to take the call?" she asked.

"*Steve Douglas?*" I questioned. "Did he say what it was in regard to?"

"No, he said it was a personal call."

"Oh, Steve," I said, suddenly recalling Kyle's mystery man.

"Do you want me to transfer it in here?"

"Oh, that's okay. Tell him I'll be with him in a minute. I'll take it in my office."

As I walked back to my office, I wondered why Steve, or *Basil,* was calling me. I wondered how he had gotten my number until it dawned on me that I had given him one of my business cards at Kyle's.

"This is Raymond Tyler, Jr.," I said.

"Junior, I didn't realize you were a junior," the voice on the phone chuckled and said.

"Yes. Raymond Tyler, Jr. What can I do for you, Mr. Douglas?"

"Ray, please call me Steve. I just wanted to tell you what a pleasure it was meeting you on Friday and I wanted to see if we could get together for a drink before I leave town."

"Leave town?"

"Yeah, didn't I tell you I live in Atlanta?"

"Well, I'm really busy. When did you want to do this?"

"This evening hopefully. I'm staying at the Hilton Towers on Fifty-third."

"That's near my office."

"Yes, I realized that when I looked at your card."

"Have you spoken with Kyle about this invitation?"

"No, it's not what you think. I'll explain it to you, say around six-thirty in the lobby piano bar?"

"Let me get back to you. How are you registered?"

Suddenly Steve began to stutter. "Well, uh, I've already checked out. I'll have to call you back."

"No need. I'll meet you there."

"Great. I look forward to seeing you, Raymond."

"Sure. I look forward to seeing you, *Basil*."

"Great," he replied without thinking. A silence occurred on the other end of the phone and I smiled to myself.

"*Basil*. Are you still there?"

"Yes, Mr. Smart Ass. I'm still here. So you know."

"Yeah, some gay people do watch sports for more than admiring bodies," I said.

"Point well taken. If you change your mind, I'm registered under Basil Henderson."

"I'll see you this evening."

When I hung up the phone, I felt really pleased with myself. I knew I was right. How did Kyle fit in this picture? Did he know Steve's real name? I picked up my phone and pushed the speed dial next to Kyle's office number. When I asked to speak with Kyle, the voice on the other end responded, "Mr. Benton no longer works here."

I instantly became worried. What was going on? I had spoken with Kyle about three times that week and he never mentioned quitting his job. I hit another button that had Kyle's home number on the label. The phone rang several times before the answering machine picked up. "Kyle, call me at the office as soon as you get this message. It's important."

The rest of the afternoon I waited on a call from Kyle. I even tried to reach JJ to see if she knew anything. When I did finally reach her, she was as surprised as I was and said she didn't know what was going on. Just when I was about to leave the office and meet Basil, Kyle called.

"What's up?" he asked in a very cavalier fashion.

"What's up with you? I called your job and they said you no longer worked there."

"Oh yeah, I forgot to tell you. I quit that bitch at the first of the year."

"What are you going to do?" I inquired.

"Don't worry, Ray, I've got a plan. I'm going to start my own business. Let's meet at the Nickel in a couple of hours and I'll explain everything."

"What time?"

"Eight."

"Okay. Oh yeah, your friend called and invited me for drinks. Do you have a problem with that?"

"What friend?"

"Steve."

"Oh no, Ray. Go ahead."

"Kyle, where did you meet him? I know his name isn't Steve."

"I'm not surprised. I'll explain this evening. Now, don't do anything I wouldn't do," Kyle laughed.

Kyle's call and attitude made me feel a little bit at ease. This recent chain of events was becoming more engrossing than my upcoming trial.

ELEVEN

Basil's backside captured my attention as I walked through the huge lobby of the Hilton Hotel. He was bending over signing the T-shirt of a little boy who had recognized him. I walked up behind him and stood there as he held a conversation with the fan. When he noticed the little boy looking at me behind him, he turned to face me. We exchanged perfunctory handshakes and gave each other the once over.

"Ray." He smiled. "I'm glad you could make it. This is Joey."

"Hello, Joey. Are you a big football fan?"

"Yes sir, the biggest!" exclaimed the small redhead.

Basil spent a few more minutes talking with Joey and then suggested that we try the Oyster Bar for drinks and a quick bite. We both ordered Coronas with lime and took seats at a small table next to the window that faced the Avenue of the Americas.

"Nice suit, Mr. Tyler. Perry Ellis?"

"Yes, it is."

"You wear it very well. That tie is too sharp, man."

"Thanks a lot. So, Basil, why the alias?" I asked.

"No particular reason. Is Kyle your friend's real name?"

"I think so. I've known him by that name for over six years. How did you two meet?"

"Didn't Kyle tell you?"

"No, he didn't."

"Well, let's just say it was a mutual friend."

"A mutual friend?"

"Yes, but I don't want to talk about Kyle. I want to talk about you."

"Me?"

"Yes, you know I'm surprised that Kyle has friends like you."

"Why do you say that?"

"Well, let's face it, Kyle's a flaming faggot."

"Say, man, you're talking about my best friend. I put the term *faggot* in the same category as *nigger*. Besides, what are you?" I felt my face redden from anger.

"Ray, I'm sorry. I *deal* sometimes, but I consider myself straight."

"Good for you. Then I don't think we have anything else to talk about."

I reached for my coat and briefcase when Basil stood up and said, "Raymond, I'm sorry. Please don't leave right now."

I slowly sat back down but held on to my coat and briefcase. Basil started to talk about how he had been introduced to the life by a rich alumnus while he was playing college football. He said he did it because he needed the money. "He gave me head. My girlfriend wouldn't."

"So the money made your dick hard?" I asked with a smirk.

"Come on, Ray, give me a break. Put yourself in my position."

"I can't do that," I replied coldly.

As he continued to talk, I noticed how really handsome Basil was. His honey-colored skin was clear and smooth and his eyes sparkled like polished silver bullets as he talked. Basil explained how hard it was going both ways and being in the public eye. He had to be careful whom he talked to about certain things, and eventually he would have to get married. He also said that there were several professional players, both football and basketball, who were *in*, but that it was the most secretive of cliques. He added that track-and-field guys were notorious for being *in*.

I pumped him for names I would recognize, but he politely declined to name names. As he talked, I realized that there were several things to like about Basil, but an equal number of reasons to dislike him.

He would use the word *faggot* as effortlessly as one sprinkled salt on hot buttered popcorn. Every time he used the word, I raised my eyebrows and he quickly apologized. I got the impression that it was a part of his everyday vocabulary.

"So do you consider yourself bisexual?" I asked.

"No, not really."

"Gay?"

"Fuck no."

"Then what did you want to talk with me about?"

"Well, I like the way you look. I mean, you don't look gay." Basil paused and then said, "I was wondering if we could hook up the next time I'm in the city?"

"What does gay look like, Basil?"

"You know." He shrugged. "What about my question?"

"To talk about sports and stuff? Sure, I'm as big a football fan as your friend Joey."

"Is that all we could do?" he asked in an amorous tone.

"I think so. I'm seeing someone."

"Who is he?"

"Who said it was a he?"

I finished my beer and Basil gave me his phone numbers at three different places, including his mom's and his girlfriend's house. When he stood up, I couldn't believe that I was turning Basil down as a potential suitor.

His body was a sculptor's vision. I smiled to myself at how easily 'I'm seeing someone' fell from my lips. Whom was I talking about, Quinn or Nicole?

"So you're still not going to tell me how you met Kyle?"

"No, I better not. If you and Kyle are as close as you say, then I'm surprised you don't know." We again traded handshakes and I wished him good luck on the upcoming football season and his desire for a complete heterosexual adjustment. He let out a hearty laugh and told me he would give me a call and invite me to a game next season. He walked with me out to the street so I could catch a taxi uptown.

"I'm going to meet Kyle. Should I tell him you said hello?"

"Sure, why not. Kyle's cool," Basil said.

"I'll tell him you said that."

As I rode uptown, I wondered what the big secret was about where Kyle and Basil had met. Kyle had a gift for meeting men anywhere he went and I knew most of his other friends. I knew men like Basil didn't frequent bars, but they cruised the subways and other public places. New York City was famous for its *tea rooms*, a term used for the restrooms in the subways. Kyle told me about all the married men he met there. He said that traffic had decreased since AIDS hit the city. Somehow I managed not to become involved in this seedy side of the life, which also included gay bathhouses. I tried hard not to pass judgment on Kyle and others who chose that route. I learned not to be surprised at the number of professional black men who led secret lives. Had I stayed in Alabama, my life would have become similar. There was no way I would involve my family in my gay lifestyle. Besides, I came to realize that it was a lifestyle and not my life.

In Alabama I would also have had to be concerned with fraternity brothers who lived in the city. Maybe this was one of the reasons I loved living in New York City. When you left your place of employment, your life became your own.

For a Wednesday, the Nickel was packed. Kyle was on his regular stool at the end of the bar next to the door. When I went up to him, I could tell from his eyes and his breath that he was highly intoxicated.

"Ray, baby, what's happening?" he asked, his speech slurred. "How did your meeting with Mr. Asshole go?"

"You mean Basil? It was okay. Where did you meet him, Kyle?"

"Didn't he tell you?"

"He said you were introduced by a mutual friend."

"Yeah, right. What do you want to drink?"

"Nothing. What's going on with you and work and who is the mutual friend?"

"I told you. I quit the motherfucker. You don't know all my friends."

"What are you going to do for money, Kyle?"

"Don't worry, I'll be fine."

Kyle called for the bartender and ordered another drink. A couple of guys came over to the corner where we were sitting and Kyle gave them both hugs and kisses.

"Miss Thing, where have you been, girl?" Kyle asked one of the guys.

"I've been around, staying out of trouble," the small, frail guy said.

Kyle talked with the two guys while I looked around the bar. Suddenly I wanted to run out of there. I became fearful that some of Nicole's castmates might come in. It was Wednesday, which was matinee day, and the kids in the different shows often came to the Nickel between shows. When the two guys left, Kyle leaned over and whispered in my ear, "I think he's sick." I just looked at Kyle and shook my head in dismay.

"Kyle, you're getting too full. Let me put you in a taxi."

"I'm fine, Miss Thing, just leave me alone. I'm fine."

"Kyle, I've told you about that 'Miss Thing' shit. We have a deal. Don't ever call me that again, Kyle. I just don't play that shit," I snapped.

"I'm sorry. Cool your heels."

"Are you sure you're going to be all right?" I asked.

"I'm fine. Do you still love me?"

"You know I do, but I'm beginning to worry about you."

"Don't, Ray, I'm okay. I forgot to tell you I met JJ's new man."

"Is he straight?"

"I don't know, but I think she may have lucked up and found one."

"Well, I've got to go. I've got a ton of work to do. We'll talk tomorrow and I'll tell you about your friend."

"Okay, baby, be safe."

"No, you be safe," I said as I gave Kyle a firm hug and kissed the back of his neck.

As I left the bar, I decided to walk and clear my head from the eventful day. I was really worried about Kyle. We had all gotten drunk at some point, but Kyle was beginning to do it regularly. Maybe something was going on that he didn't want to talk about. I thought about the frail guy who Kyle said was sick and felt a sudden anguish for all the people I had met over the years at the Nickel and Keller's with Kyle who had died of AIDS.

I reflected on how most black gay men thought that AIDS was a white boy's disease when it was first brought to the attention of the gay community. Most of us thought when black guys started to die from it, it was because they were *snow queens*.

AIDS was hitting the black gay community with devastating force, and with all the closet black men out there like Basil, it would soon hit the heterosexual community with equal force—not all black men were IV drug users, as the media would have had us believe. I thought about *trade*, men who had sex with other men for money or other motivations. The majority of these men were lower middle class and either married or living with black women of the same class. They usually chose feminine guys as targets and didn't consider themselves gay or bisexual. The women they lived with usually had no idea of their secret lives because of their great sexual prowess. These women thought there was no way these men would mess around with a sissy or a punk. Difficult economic times had caused a lot of these black men to, in fact, mess around with sissies and punks. But as Kyle always said, "A dollar bill doesn't make a dick hard." A sweat broke out on my forehead as I recalled the time I went for an AIDS test. Waiting for the results alone almost killed me. I didn't take the test by choice. My insurance company had insisted upon it when I applied for life insurance. I started to take them to task, but decided I wanted to know. I celebrated for days when I got my results.

When I reached the lobby of my building, I saw Grady sitting behind the desk with roses and a potted plant blocking his view.

"Hi, Grady."

"Hi, Mr. Tyler. These are for you."

"What?"

"Both of these," he said, pushing both the roses and potted plant in my direction.

"Both of them?"

"Yes sir, you're a popular young man." He smiled.

"I guess so."

When I got to my apartment, I anxiously opened the card on the roses.

Ray,

   Now you can't say that a man has never sent you Roses!

Always.
Q

I must have had a smile a mile long on my face as I tore open the card from the beautiful potted plant.

Raymond Winston Tyler,

   Thank you for making my Sunday more of a blessing than it usually is. You're some kinda special. God is so good!

Love,
Nicole Springer

   P.S. Please call

My mood abruptly switched from a depressed state to one of complete euphoria. It couldn't get much better than this.

TWELVE

A cold New Year's Eve dalliance had turned into a warm spring romance. My relationship with Nicole was flourishing faster than the spring flowers. We spent every free moment we had together. The run of *Dreamgirls* was winding down and Nicole had started preparations for her nightclub act. We had not yet consummated our relationship, but we had come pretty close. The first time I kissed her in a romantic way, I felt as though I was tasting heat. Her body was so warm that it oozed a sexual mist. When our foreplay reached the danger zone, Nicole pulled back and explained that she wasn't a virgin, but that the next time she went all the way, it would be for love. I, of course, was very understanding, and in many ways it relieved a lot of pressure that was building within me. Quinn was still very much in the picture and he more than adequately took care of my sexual needs; in fact, he met both my physical and emotional needs without complications. I got the impression that things were going better at home with his wife, but we never talked about it. I had only casually mentioned Nicole, so he assumed he was the only reason I appeared to be floating among the stars. Men didn't appear threatened by women in gay relationships. The truth of the matter was that the combination of the two had sent me into orbit.

My case at the office was still taking up a great deal of my time. We were just weeks away from going to trial. Susan and I were preparing for a trip to Washington, D.C., to do some additional research and conduct depositions with some of our witnesses. Susan and Nicole had become quite friendly. She called Susan when she couldn't reach me and always brought enough food for Susan when she brought dinner to the office. Susan helped me pick out some diamond stud earrings for Nicole's Valentine's present. Kyle helped pick out sexy underwear for Quinn. They both loved their gifts. One of the things I enjoyed about dating Nicole was that she allowed me to spoil her with flowers, surprise dinners and gifts, and I loved seeing the look on her face when I did. She cried when I gave her a tape of love songs that I had picked out and recorded from my CD collection. When Sela and I were dating, I wasn't in the financial position to do some of the things I was now able to do for Nicole. And men didn't seem to appreciate gifts the way women did; the majority of them acted as though you owed them something after sleeping with them. But Quinn's enthusiastic reaction to my gift led me to believe that with him this could be different.

My life was changing and I couldn't ever remember being this happy as an adult. The only disappointment was that I still was not talking with my pops. I wanted to share with him the big case I was working on and to have him share legal strategies with me. I talked to my mom several times and she assured me that he knew that his son was going up against Tri Tech. She didn't say if he was proud or not. She seemed pleased when I told her about Nicole and suggested that I bring her home soon, or if I went to Arkansas with Nicole, that maybe she could talk Pops into driving to Little Rock to meet us. I told her I would get back to her on that. Before hanging up, Mom told me she loved me and that she was pleased I was happy.

Nicole had me in church every Sunday that I wasn't working. I even attended a Bible study class with her on Wednesdays between shows. The group was made up mostly of actors and crew members of Broadway shows and they usually held it in one of the theaters. At one of the Bible study classes I became reacquainted with a dancer named Curtis Bell, whom I had met in the bars years ago. I overheard Nicole tell a friend that since Curtis had become saved, he had given up the homosexual lifestyle. For the first time since my conversion, I wondered if I could change my sexual orientation or at least redirect it. Could you give up the lifestyle and the life? With Nicole, I began to dream old dreams.

Kyle and JJ appeared to be happy with their lives. We got together on Saturday nights and cooked dinner together. JJ seemed to be really smitten with Bernard. He was roughly handsome, with cinnamon brown skin and a well-proportioned physique. He was a very likable, hard-working Southern man who had been driving a bus in New York for almost ten years. He didn't appear uncomfortable around Kyle and me. Bernard was very comfortable with his own sexuality, so gay guys didn't faze him in any way. To add to all these outstanding qualities, he idolized JJ and she seemed like a changed woman. She still drank, but not to excess. Kyle wasn't dating anyone special, but he always seemed to be busy. He didn't seem to mind when I stopped going to the Nickel and other gay bars. He just remarked, "Chile, if you want to live a confused life, then more power to you."

On this night while we were talking about Nicole, I asked Kyle if he had ever been with a female. To my surprise he said, "Yes."

"What happened?" I asked.

"She didn't have a dick and mine wouldn't work," he laughed.

I still found myself worrying about him, but he always reassured me that everything was fine.

Nicole, JJ and Kyle had finally met, although it was quite by accident. One Saturday night after her show, Nicole dropped by unannounced. The three of us were just kicking around drinking wine, listening to music and catching up on each other's love lives when I heard my buzzer. When Grady announced that Nicole was on her way up, panic struck. I didn't know why I was worried, but fear hit me in a way I hadn't felt since I was a little boy sleeping without a night-light. The sense of impending disaster became overwhelming. I begged JJ and Kyle to be on their best behavior, which I knew was going to be a difficult task, since we had been drinking all evening long. Much to my surprise, things went pretty smoothly. When Kyle saw Nicole, he ranted and raved about how beautiful she was.

"I remember you," he said with an excited tone. "I saw you in the Miss America pageant. Girl, you should have won. You were better than all those white girls. Do you know Vanessa Williams?"

Nicole politely thanked him and told him that she did know Vanessa and that she was really a sweet lady. The two of them started to talk about Kyle designing some dresses for Nicole's night-club show.

I could sense that Kyle was starting to feel comfortable with Nicole and this reduced some of my anxiety. JJ was pleasant but cool. After a couple of hours Nicole left, but not before inviting Kyle and JJ to church and the closing-night party of *Dreamgirls*. They quickly accepted the invitation to the party and promised to get back to her on the church thing. I was certain that after Nicole had met Kyle, the gay question would come up, but it didn't. She appeared to really like Kyle and used her beauty pageant charm with JJ. It became quite comical watching Kyle trying to appear straight. Every time he did something that appeared gay, like snapping his fingers or calling Nicole "Miss Thing," he would put his fingers to his lip and look at me and say, "Oh, I'm sorry." I could only smile.

While I had stopped going to gay bars, the opportunity to meet men had not ceased. Having Nicole on my arm was beginning to attract a different kind of man—a kind I would never have met in gay bars. One Friday evening at B. Smith's we met with some of her old classmates who were visiting New York. All evening long a good-looking brother with a clean, boyish face who was with an equally attractive young lady stared at me, causing me to feel uneasy. He occasionally smiled in my direction but appeared awestruck with his date. The moment he saw Nicole and her friends leave for the ladies' room, he came over to where I was standing. We exchanged polite conversation about the weather and all the attractive ladies at the bar. After a few minutes he pulled out a card and suggested that I give him a call and we get together to play tennis or something. He also stated that he felt that we had something in common. When I asked him what that might be, he said with a certain cockiness, "Let's just call it charisma for now."

"I've heard it called a lot of things but never charisma," I replied. He gave me a knowing smile and returned to his companion. I crumpled up the card and laid it in a nearby ashtray. I had gotten to a point where incidents like that no longer surprised or fazed me.

One glorious Saturday afternoon when Quinn and I were spending our time together in my bedroom, I received a call from Nicole. I don't know why, but I picked up the phone on the first ring. Usually I would let the machine pick up when Quinn was there. She said that she had something very important to discuss with me and asked if she could come up after the matinee. I got her to agree to meet me at JR instead at about six. Quinn decided he wanted to meet "this Nicole chick" and invited himself along. I reluctantly agreed and made him promise that he would stay for only one drink and then promptly excuse himself.

We reached JR and Quinn stared silently at Nicole for minutes while she and I exchanged small talk. He quickly finished his drink and said he had to run because his wife was expecting him for dinner. We exchanged warm handshakes and he asked, "Are we on for tennis next week?" Without missing a beat I replied, "Of course we are." He gave me a suggestive wink and left.

I don't know why I was concerned about Quinn and Nicole meeting. I mean, Quinn certainly didn't look gay and I always thought that if they ever got to know each other, they would really like each other. It made me realize that in situations like this, men always had the upper hand. They knew about the women in their mates' lives, but the women didn't know about the men in their mates' lives, at least not everything. I knew more about Quinn than his wife did.

Nicole told me that the closing notice had gone up for *Dreamgirls*, but the show was going on tour for about three months. She went on to explain that she had the opportunity to take one of the lead roles but was concerned with the effect her traveling would have on our relationship. She looked me directly in the eyes and asked, "Where is this relationship going?"

"Going?"

"Yes, Raymond, what are your intentions?"

"Intentions?"

"Yes, how do you feel about us?"

"Well, Nicole, you know I care for you, but . . ."

"But what?"

"I hadn't really thought that far ahead. You know I've been so busy with my case, and uh, well . . . it's something I guess I need to think about," I said, fumbling for words.

"Well, I'm not trying to force you into anything, but I wish you would think about it. My career is important to me, but you've become important to me too."

Nicole sipped her cappuccino with her beautifully shaped, sensuous mouth. I saw consternation in her face as she lowered her eyes toward the coffee cup. My own ambivalence was starting to bother me. Minutes passed with both of us mute. I was wiping the cold droplets from my wineglass when Nicole said, "I've rented a Spike Lee movie, *Mo' Better Blues*. You want to watch it tonight after the show?"

"Sure."

"Okay, well, I've got half an hour, so I'll see you later."

Nicole grabbed her huge black leather bag, came over to my seat and planted a long, deep, sensuous kiss on my lips. As she kissed me, I felt as though she was blowing heat into my cold body; my sleeping sex began to awaken. I caressed her small hands and slowly ran my other hand up and down the small of her back through her black silk blouse and gently kissed her forehead. "Have a good show and I'll see you later."

Nicole didn't say anything as she stood looking at me with her doelike eyes and sweet smile. Her face looked drained of its beautiful coffee color as she walked out the door. I sat at the table for minutes debating what to do next.

Later that night when she showed up at my apartment, we both acted as though the afternoon's conversation had never happened. We popped corn, drank white wine and watched the movie. It played like a movie of my present life, with the lead character trying to make a choice. My situation was a little different, since Denzel was choosing between two women and I was going to have to make the choice between a man and a woman. For the first time I realized I wanted them both.

THIRTEEN

The sun had barely risen above the Upper West Side's tall apartment buildings as I packed for my upcoming trip to Washington, D.C. Susan and I were going to take the Amtrak to Washington so that we could work before we reached the hotel where the depositions were going to be held. I didn't know what to pack or how much I should take. I pulled out my best blue and gray Polo suits and three starched white shirts as I glanced at Bryant Gumbel on the "Today" show.

We could be there for a day or a week. Quinn called late the night before and said he was trying to arrange a business trip to Washington and wanted to know what hotel I was going to be staying at. I could hear hurt in his voice when I told him I was going to be too busy to spend time with him. Nicole called to wake me up, wish me good luck and sing me a soulful version of "Good Morning" from *Singin' in the Rain*. She gave me Candance's number and told me to at least call and say hello. Right before we hung up, there was a brief hush on Nicole's end of the line.

"Nicole, are you still there?" I asked.

"Yes, I'm still here. Have a safe trip . . . Raymond. I love you," Nicole said with her satin-soft voice.

"Me too," I said as I felt my heart begin to smile. I felt good inside, but the words "Me too" evoked memories of my pops. Why was it so hard to say "I love you"?

The train ride to Washington started off very pleasantly. Susan and I went over a list of things we wanted to accomplish on the trip and sat back to enjoy the train ride. I recalled my phone call with Nicole as I glimpsed the houses that stood near the railroad tracks. The houses we passed reminded me of my old neighborhood down South. I began to think about what it would be like to have a home and children with Nicole. We shared the same ideals about the number of children we wanted and the fact that we both wanted to raise our children down South. I pressed my face against the window of the train and smiled at the thought of a little girl that looked like Nicole and a little boy that favored me and my pops.

"What are you thinking about?" Susan asked.

"Maybe you should ask who."

"I don't have to do that. Could it be Nicole?"

"You're on the mark."

"How is that working out?"

"Wonderful . . . marvelous. Does that give you an idea?"

"Yes sir, it does." Susan smiled.

Susan put down the newspaper she was reading and the two of us started to talk about relationships and the office. Susan was living with a guy she had been dating for about three years and she desperately wanted to get married. "I think I might have to ask him," she sighed.

While we were talking, I noticed an attractive black lady sitting in the seat directly across from us. She was reading something from a huge black notebook and periodically she pulled off her glasses and rubbed her eyes. It was clear that she was some type of businesswoman. The conversation with Susan was interesting and lively. We laughed out loud when we disagreed on male-female issues. Over the past months I had become very fond of Susan and found it very easy to talk to her about Nicole.

During a break in our conversation, I caught the young lady looking at me with a very sour look. I smiled and said, "Hello," and she quickly turned her head toward the window of the train. What was that look about, I thought to myself. Did she think Susan and I were a couple? Could she tell that I was gay? Her look was one of complete disgust. At times when I got looks like the one she was giving, I had a hard time figuring out where they were coming from. There had been situations when I was with Kyle and some of his friends, and black women looked at us with pure disdain.

I had gotten similar stares while I was in high school and college. My high school was predominantly white and so were most of my friends. I went to school with whites, played sports and worked with whites. The only things I didn't do with them were go to church and go to bed, with the exception of Margo. My family and I had always attended church in our old neighborhood. I wondered if those looks had played a role in the fact that after law school I had very few white friends. The fact was that high school offered me very few choices for black friends.

In trying to understand the young lady's look of disapproval, I thought of how Susan and I must have looked enjoying each other's company. Maybe she thought I was another black man who had gone to the other side. But what side would she disapprove of the most? Would her reaction have been the same if I were enjoying the same conversation with Quinn? Would she have preferred me to be dating a white woman or dating a black man? Her look disappointed me and I pulled out some briefs and studied them for the rest of the train ride. Susan took the hint and returned to her newspaper.

After three grueling days Susan and I had wrapped up our work. We felt positive that we had enough to win the case and possibly get Tri Tech to settle before going to trial. Since we were both exhausted, we decided to catch a train back to New York the following morning. When I got back to my hotel room, I was getting ready to order from room service when Kelvin and Candance crossed my mind. I looked in my wallet for the number that Nicole had given me before I left New York. I dialed the number and Candance cheerfully answered the phone. We had been conversing for a few minutes when she suggested that we meet for dinner. She informed me that Kelvin was not home from work, but she was certain he didn't have plans and he had something important to talk with me about. She gave me the address of a restaurant in Georgetown and suggested we meet at eight o'clock. "I'm really looking forward to seeing you, Raymond. We have a lot to talk about."

"Great. I'll see you at eight."

I took a quick shower and dashed downstairs to the lobby of the hotel to catch a taxi to Georgetown. We met at a restaurant called Houston's.

It was a dark, noisy restaurant and bar located in the heart of Georgetown. When I arrived, Kelvin and Candance were waiting at the bar engaged in mutual admiration. Candance greeted me with a kiss and seemed really excited to see me, while Kelvin gave me a weak handshake and a patronizing smile. Houston's was packed and the wait was about thirty minutes. I ordered a double vodka gimlet and the three of us stood around the mahogany bar and talked about how our workdays had gone. I told them about the big case I was working on. Candance appeared really interested and asked a lot of questions. She asked me if I ever thought about moving back South and I responded with a definite no. For a brief moment I forgot about life with Nicole. Candance was busy studying for her medical boards and Kelvin talked about spring football practice. Neither one mentioned the upcoming nuptials. By the time we were finally seated, I was beginning to feel a slight buzz.

Candance told me how excited she was about my relationship with Nicole. I smiled and noticed that Kelvin's eyes were drifting around the restaurant, purposely avoiding my eyes. As she talked, I realized how much Candance and Nicole were alike: aggressive yet feminine, the complete embodiment of the perfect woman. They both were sophisticated but possessed unpretentious qualities that I had always admired in my mother. They would both make their man feel as though he were the only man in the world. I could understand why Kelvin had fallen in love with her. Candance's warmth and kindness were totally genuine. Like Nicole, she was as smart as she was beautiful. What was it about women like Nicole and Candance and bisexual men? Was it because many of us were very bright and good-looking? Were we more sensitive than hetero-sexual men? What was it about these women that caused gay and bisexual men to forget their secret sexual desires? I asked myself the questions, but I didn't have the answers. After finishing prime rib as thick as the tax code, the three of us ordered coffee and cognac. While I was pouring the golden-colored liquid into the piping-hot coffee, Candance started to whisper and playfully dig at Kelvin's side, causing him to giggle out loud. I had forgotten that he was very ticklish.

"Go ahead, ask him," Candance chided.

"Ask me what?" I inquired.

"Well, Ray . . . Candance and I were wondering . . ." Kelvin paused. The restaurant was so dimly lit that I could not see Kelvin's eyes. His face appeared flushed and for a second he appeared at a loss for words. "We were thinking," he continued, "that maybe . . . well, would you be a groomsman in our wedding?"

"A *groomsman?*" I asked. My stomach began to turn as Candance looked at me with a wide smile.

"Yes, I know this is short notice, but we figured you would be down here with Nicole, and well . . . it would mean a lot to us," Kelvin said in a sullen tone.

"Well, Ray? Please say yes," Candance pleaded. "Nicole is going to be a bridesmaid and of course we will pair the two of you up."

"Well . . . I'm flattered . . . but I may be at another wedding. Can I let you know in a couple of days?" I asked evenly.

"Sure, no problem, Ray," Kelvin said with a relieved look on his face.

I didn't know if I should in fact be flattered or mad at Kelvin for allowing me to be caught off guard like this. A part of me felt flabbergasted. All of a sudden I began to feel very uncomfortable. I picked up the check and gave my credit card to the waiter as Candance started to talk about how excited she was at the prospect of having me in her wedding. The three of us walked out of the restaurant. Night covered the busy streets of Georgetown and the weather hinted that spring was close by. I was saying my good-byes and looking for a taxi when Candance suggested that Kelvin give me a ride back to the hotel.

"What hotel are you at, Ray?" Kelvin asked.

"The Hyatt on Capitol Hill."

"Honey, I've got some studying to do. Why don't you drop me off first and then give Ray a ride back to the hotel," Candance suggested.

"That's not necessary," I said.

"Oh no, Ray, it won't be a problem. Will it, honey?"

"No, it won't," Kelvin said with a blank look on his face.

Kelvin and Candance shared an apartment near Georgetown. We dropped Candance off and I hugged and kissed her. When I squeezed her, I realized that Candance felt thinner than she had in January. I surmised that she was getting ready for her wedding day.

At long last a moment alone with Kelvin. Now that it was finally happening, I began to feel nervous. What did I want from him? Did he want anything from me? As we drove off, the car was filled with silence. Kelvin's eyes stared straight ahead as we drove down Pennsylvania Avenue. He put in a tape and turned to me. "So what do you think?"

"Think about what?"

"About what Candance asked you."

"You mean the wedding?"

"Yeah."

"Kelvin, I don't know what planet you're on, but you could have called me and warned me about this."

"Warned you?"

"You're damn right," I said, raising my voice in an angry tone. I was beginning to get so mad that I knew my face was becoming flushed. I couldn't remember ever being this angry with anyone. Kelvin looked at me helplessly, driving through several yellow caution lights.

"Raymond, I'm sorry. You don't understand."

"Understand what, Kelvin? I don't understand how come you've been acting like a raging asshole ever since I ran into you in Saks. I don't understand why you've treated me like someone you'd like to forget. No, you're right, I don't understand. Why don't you explain it to me?" I asked sharply.

"It's hard. The wedding idea was Candance's. She's really fond of you and you know that Nicole's her best friend."

"Does she know about us?"

"Are you crazy?"

"Answer my question," I demanded.

"Of course she doesn't. Have you told Nicole?"

"I'm not marrying Nicole."

"Why won't you be in the wedding?"

"I haven't said I wouldn't be in it. I just don't appreciate the way you've handled this. Would it have killed you to call?"

"No, but I got the impression you didn't want to be bothered."

"Where did you get that idea? You're the one who dropped off the face of the earth without telling me to kiss your ass or good-bye. I thought our relationship meant something to you."

I noticed that we were approaching the hotel. Kelvin pulled his car alongside the hotel and turned off the motor. He turned off the tape player, released his seat belt and turned toward me. His brown face glowed in the shadowy light from the placid street and his eyes appeared subdued and sorrowful.

"Ray, there's no excuse for how I acted. You know I loved you. There are times when I think I still do . . . but . . ." Kelvin paused, looking out the window on his side of the car. His hands appeared to be trembling; his voice sounded remorseful.

"But, what, Kelvin?" I asked, trying to sound understanding.

"It would never work. It's hard enough being a black man. Why add the burden of being gay?"

"You think we have a choice, Kelvin? Have you given the life completely up? Don't forget you started this shit for me! Do you know how much that night changed my life?"

Kelvin just gazed at me, his handsome face looking painfully serious. Part of me wanted to haul off and smack him cold and yet part of me yearned to comfort him. I realized how badly he wanted to be completely heterosexual.

"I know it hasn't been all bad, Ray. We can choose not to act on our desires. I love Candance and I think I can make her happy.

Maybe you should consider marrying Nicole and then we could be together forever."

"What are you talking about?" I was becoming angry again.

"Just forget what I said, Raymond."

"No, I'm not going to let you off that easy. What do you mean?"

"Well, I know quite a few guys who are married and still deal with males, but it's usually someone their wife is close to also."

I sat motionless and looked at Kelvin. He was serious!

"What kind of life would that be, Kelvin? Is that fair to Candance and Nicole?"

"It's not hurting anyone, especially if they're happy. Besides, we love each other."

"Yeah, once."

"You don't love me, Ray? You told me you'd always love me."

"And I do. I just don't think I'm in love with you. I haven't made the choices about my life that you have. I don't know if I'm going to end up with a man or a woman. To be totally honest with you, I'm appalled at your suggestions. I think you should take a closer look at the choices you're making."

Kelvin reached over and grabbed my hand. His touch was familiar and warm, yet it felt cold. I took my hand and gently rubbed the top of his hand. Kelvin started to edge closer to me. His touch never failed to arouse me. I could feel my sex throbbing against the silk boxers that Quinn had given me.

Slowly and wondrously Kelvin's face appeared to change. I looked into his eyes and it seemed as though the Kelvin I had fallen in love with had returned. The temptation to grab his face and kiss his lips became overwhelming.

"So are you going to invite me up to your room?" Kelvin asked in a provocative manner. He was stroking my hand softly.

I reached up and touched his face. He smiled gently as beads of perspiration started forming on his forehead.

"If only I didn't like Candance so much," I mused. "If only things were different."

I slowly pulled back my hands, removed my seat belt and got out of the car. I leaned on the door of his car and smiled at Kelvin. "Thanks for the trip down memory lane. I'll call you about June twentieth . . . drive safely."

Kelvin looked at me, grimacing as he turned over the ignition. "I do love you, Ray. It ain't over till it's over."

Kelvin drove away from the hotel. I stood in the parking lot for a moment, looking up at the stars gliding across the sky and admiring the March moonlight. As I walked into the hotel, I felt proud of all that I had accomplished on this trip. I would leave with the information needed to proceed with my trial, the assurance that the first Friday in October when Kelvin and I met so many years ago, had not been for naught and the realization that I did have a choice in what happened in my love life. I had fantasized so many nights about being with Kelvin again, and yet when the opportunity presented itself, I found the willpower to resist. First Basil and now Kelvin.

FOURTEEN

"Great job, Ray," read the sign in the lobby of my office. We had won. Tri Tech decided to settle out of court for twenty million dollars. I was the hero of the hour in my office. There were congratulations and looks of awe from my coworkers as I walked into my office. My secretary, Hillary, started clapping when I approached her desk. I liked this feeling. Bill and Dan took me to lunch at the '21' Club to talk about my promising future with the firm. I hadn't felt this wanted since the time they recruited me from law school.

In many ways I was relieved that we had settled out of court. I experienced nightmares about having someone from the bars sitting on my jury. I worried how my *body envelope* would come across to the judge and jury. Would they detect my gayness?

After lunch Dan suggested that I take the afternoon and the following day off, to compensate for all the long hours I had been working. I thanked him and asked that the same offer be made to Susan. Dan happily agreed. I called Kyle to see what he was up to and he suggested that I stop by. He and JJ were taking me to dinner that evening and he suggested we get a head start with the cocktails.

When I arrived at Kyle's, he was still in his robe watching "The Oprah Winfrey Show."

"Is this what you do all day?" I asked.

"Yes, chile. I start with Regis and Kathie Lee, Sally and Joan midmorning, and end my day with my girl Miss Oprah."

"What are you doing about your career and how are you paying your bills?"

"I have my ways."

"Kyle, get serious! What are you going to do? You have bills to pay."

"Take a chill pill, Raymond! Stop being a lawyer."

"Okay, I'm just trying to help. What's Oprah talking about today?" I asked, sitting in a chair covered with dirty clothes.

"Oh, you should enjoy this. It's gay men who sleep with married men."

"Get the fuck out," I said in disbelief.

"Yes, chile, look at these queens."

I started to look at the panel Oprah had assembled and couldn't believe my eyes. There were four guys, obviously gay, talking about how they seduce married men. There was only one black guy and he had not yet mastered the English language. He fit every stereotype of finger-popping, quick-witted sissies I had ever known. I looked at the television and then at Kyle and shook my head.

"What are you shaking your head for? Oprah should have someone like you on her show. This black queen from hell ain't the kind that married men go after. If they wanted a woman, they would stay at home. They're looking for confused men like you, mister," Kyle laughed, and snapped his fingers in my face.

"I know that's right," I retorted. "But I would never go on Oprah's show. Where are we going for dinner?"

"Lola's."

"Lola's? Are you sure you can afford that?"

"Don't worry, JJ is helping. I'm getting ready to shower. Maybe we can stop at the Nickel before we meet JJ."

"No, Kyle, I told you I was through with that meat market."

"Whatever," Kyle replied as he headed to the bathroom.

While Kyle was in the shower, I flipped the channels on the TV. When the phone rang, I called out to Kyle to see if he wanted me to answer it, but before he responded, the answering machine picked up. After the beep went off, the voice of a white man could be heard. "Kyle, this is Dave. I have a client that wants to see you this evening. An executive visiting in town. He's staying at the Marriott Marquis, room 2609. He's top, says he has nine inches thick uncut . . . he would like you to wear a G-string. I told him your fee was two-fifty. Call me ASAP so I can confirm."

I couldn't believe what I had just heard. There must be some mistake, I thought. I was staring at the answering machine as though it were going to say, "Sorry, wrong number," when Kyle walked in with a red towel around his waist and a black one around his head. "Did I hear you call me?"

"Yeah, it was your phone," I said coldly.

"What's the matter with you?"

"Kyle, what are you up to?"

"What are you talking about?"

"Listen to your message."

"Why?"

"Just listen."

Kyle hit the PLAY button on his machine, and when he heard the voice, he immediately hit the STOP button. A look of panic swept his face.

"Go ahead, Kyle, play the message. I think it's important."

"Mind your own fuckin' business, Raymond."

"This is my business, Kyle. What the fuck is wrong with you? Don't tell me this is how you met Basil."

"Like I said, mind your own fuckin' business, Ray. Don't judge my life when you're fuckin' with two people's lives."

"Kyle!" I screamed. "You can't compare the two. You're selling yourself."

"Let's just say I'm getting paid for the pleasure of my company. This is not up for discussion. This is my fucking life, Ray . . . so just drop it and act like you never heard that message."

"But Kyle . . ."

"But shit . . . drop it now, Raymond!" Kyle yelled.

Kyle went over to his stereo, put on Chaka Khan's "Through the Fire" and started to get dressed. He didn't say a word and walked around his studio apartment as though I weren't there. I didn't know what to say. I felt anger and sympathy for Kyle. What would cause him to do this? Wasn't he aware of the danger he was putting himself in? Not only sexual danger but physical danger. I wanted to grab him and shake some sense into him, but I knew there was no reckoning with him when he got into these *don't-fuck-with-me* moods. When he finished getting dressed, he finally looked at me. "Are you ready to go?"

We caught a taxi uptown and sat in the backseat as though we didn't know each other. I was beginning to wonder if I really knew Kyle. What would make him do this? Just when I was going to bring up the call again, the taxi pulled up in front of Lola's. I decided to wait until after dinner.

Walking into Lola's, I thought I had stepped into a dream. There was the sign from my office. I looked around and started to recognize Susan, Brayton, Hillary and, to my surprise, Nicole and Candance.

"Surprise!" they all yelled in unison.

I was dumbfounded as I turned to Kyle and he smiled and said, "Got ya."

Everybody started coming toward me, giving me hugs and saying things like "Great job" and "Way to go." JJ gave me a hug and kiss and Bernard gave me a handshake and manlike hug. Finally Nicole came up and whispered, "I'm so proud of you," then planted a deep wet kiss on my lips. Everybody clapped. This was the first surprise party I had ever had and it made me forget about the afternoon at Kyle's. I was excited and surprised to see Candance. She was back in New York with wedding plans. When she congratulated me, she whispered that Kelvin sent his best. She didn't ask if I had made up my mind about the wedding, which I had not.

"I'm so excited about you and Nicole," Candance said.

"Thanks. I'm pretty excited about it too."

"You should be. I hope you'll be as happy as Kelvin and I."

"Me too. Candance, I never asked where you and Kelvin met."

"Oh, we met in D.C. At Union Station in a bar called Fat Tuesdays. I was there with another guy I was dating at the time."

As Candance continued, her face lit up, her eyes glowing, teeth flashing, beautiful facial features made up. "The first time I saw Kelvin, I knew he was the man I was going to marry."

"So it was love at first sight."

"Absolutely."

Candance and I conversed for a few more minutes before Nicole pulled her away to meet Kyle. Toward the end of the party, Brayton pulled me to the side and told me how proud he was of me and that he was leaving the firm. When I asked him why, he replied, "You're their golden boy now and there's not room for two." I begged him to reconsider and to at least go to lunch with me to talk it over. He said he had already accepted an offer with one of the largest black firms in New York but he wouldn't turn down a free lunch.

The thought of Brayton leaving made me very despondent. In recent months we had become very close. When I first joined the firm, I had shied away from Brayton's offer of friendship because he was *hopelessly heterosexual*. I didn't want any straight friends to keep secrets from and I didn't think he would understand my sexual preference. He had invited me to his home several times and wanted me to join One Hundred Black Men and Big Brothers. I declined all three offers. When I started to date Nicole, I began reconsidering my decision. I had always been active in high school and college, but for some stupid reason I didn't feel worthy enough to be a part of these organizations once I started to live a gay lifestyle. I had not even bothered to affiliate with the graduate chapter of my fraternity because of my gayness. Now I was starting to feel a responsibility to be a part of the black community. My gayness was no longer a deterrent . . . or at least I thought and hoped it wouldn't be.

The night ended with everybody in a pretty good mood after all the celebrating and toasts. I learned that my office was picking up the tab for the party but that only two of the white lawyers had joined in.

Nicole was spending the night with Candance in Mount Vernon and I convinced Kyle that he was too drunk to go home alone and should spend the night at my place. It was my way of reaching out and trying to protect Kyle from Kyle. When I arrived at my apartment, there was a balloon bunch from Quinn; a note saying that even if he wasn't with me tonight in body, his spirit was there; and a reminder that Saturday was coming up.

Kyle and I made coffee and sat in my living room. No music, no TV, just the faint sounds from the streets. I got up to close the blinds. As I returned to the sofa, I noticed that Kyle's eyes were red and filled with tears. I had never seen Kyle cry about anything. I wanted to ask him if he felt like talking, but instead I grabbed him and held him tight as his copious tears dropped onto my starched white shirt. After a few minutes the crying stopped. My best friend was in a great deal of pain. As we held each other, something serene and frightening passed between us.

Quinn looked good and each successive Saturday brought some new realization of that fact. Spring had arrived and Quinn showed up at his appointed time in tennis whites. He broke into a big grin when I opened the door. The sight of him made my knees lock. He looked like a black Adonis, with his muscular body bulging out of the spotless white tennis outfit.

"What's with the outfit?"

"We're supposed to play tennis, remember?"

"You're wild. Come on in here."

We shared a long and tender kiss and Quinn announced that he had reserved a tennis court for us and I had ten minutes to get ready. After a brief protest I located my tennis shorts and matching T-shirt and followed Quinn to the front of my apartment building. He had rented a blue convertible Miata and we took the Henry Hudson Parkway heading toward Harlem. I reclined back in the seat and noticed that the bright yellow sun, ivory clouds and incandescent blue sky looked like a fried egg on an ocean-blue plate. As we drove, the brisk spring wind caused chill bumps on my uncovered arms, but with Quinn so close I still felt warm. Once we reached the park, Quinn looked as excited as a kid with an all-day amusement park pass. We hit a few balls and then started our game. I had forgotten that Quinn was an athlete and I was becoming a bit frustrated when he swept the first two games with relative ease. During the third game I dug in and made a more competitive showing, but Quinn still won. I told him I let him win to make him feel better.

"That's not possible," Quinn said.

"What's not possible?"

"My feeling any better. I'm with you."

There were times when Quinn said things that caused me to blush involuntarily. I had never been with a man who was so kind and romantic. My only regret was that it was usually only one day a week.

We started back downtown and I assumed we were going back to my apartment until we passed Ninety-sixth Street. When I asked Quinn where we were going, he told me to be calm, that he was tired of us hiding in my apartment each weekend and he was in control. I sat back and enjoyed the spring weather as we sped down Fifth Avenue to the Village.

We found a small restaurant with an outdoor patio and ordered a bottle of champagne and hot chicken wings. While we were waiting, I studied Quinn's face and how supremely happy it looked. I had started taking for granted how handsome he was. In many ways, I thought, it was like taking the sun's warmth for granted. I speculated if I was the reason that Quinn was in such a good mood and I began to realize how much I depended on him. When I was with him, problems were suddenly solvable. I talked to him about Kyle without really telling him what was going on. He told me that all I could do was be there if Kyle needed me. He talked about his son taking swimming lessons and his wife going back to school. It was one of the few times he had mentioned his family. It was not as though I thought that they had disappeared, but it made me realize what a small part I played in Quinn's life. While he talked about his family, I gulped down the champagne and suddenly felt a wave of intoxication. Quinn observed this and suggested we go home.

By the time we arrived at my apartment, a sadness settled in and

I knew that Quinn would have to leave soon. Quinn walked over to the wall unit and bent over to put in my Anita Baker CD. As I eyed his every move, the outline of his jockstrap through his white tennis shorts caused an insatiable desire within me. Before he could sit down, I went to him and began kissing him as I had never kissed him before. He responded by swaying seductively against me and within minutes his tennis whites and jockstrap lay on the blond hardwood floor. After hours of vigorous lovemaking, Quinn prepared to leave. I pleaded with him to stay the night, telling him that I needed him and I wanted to wake up with him at my side. He gazed at me with unbelieving eyes and said, "I'm sorry, Ray, you know the deal."

FIFTEEN

Reality paid a visit to my apartment. Kyle and I had
finally talked about what was going on with him. To my astonish-
ment and shock, Kyle was hooked on crack and alcohol. He had
been fired from his job and out of necessity had decided to work for
the escort service full-time. I wondered how I hadn't seen it. I knew
Kyle drank too much, but I had never seen him take any kind of
drug. It made me take a hard look at how much I drank. Kyle
wanted help and I agreed to help foot the bill at a drug rehabilita-
tion center in upstate New York. It was a ninety-day program and
Kyle promised me that he really wanted to clean his life up. As
much as I was going to miss him, I knew this was the best decision.
He was talking about going back to school or moving to Paris after
his treatment.

As shocked as I was about Kyle's secret life, my curiosity was
running rampant over his escapades as a call boy. He had met Basil
through the service. I found that ironic since Basil had said that he
got started in the life when someone paid him for sex. Now he was

paying someone just to keep his identity a secret. Kyle confided in me about a lot of his clients, saying many were famous people in entertainment, sports or politics. Kyle bragged about some of the people he had met through the service. He mentioned that Sundays were busiest, with many of the wives away at church. I admitted I was surprised at how rampant this could be in the age of AIDS. Kyle commented, "Ray, you can be so enchantingly naïve! It's a good thing you've got your JD."

Kyle wanted to go out in style by getting really fucked up one last time and then catching a train out of Dodge to the rehab center. I strongly advised against it, but finally gave in. Just as long as we didn't go to any gay bars. JJ joined us and the three of us started drinking champagne at Sardi's, where JJ announced that she was moving in with Bernard. After Sardi's we went to JR for vodka gimlets and B. Smith's for brandy. Toward the night's end, Kyle and JJ said to fuck with me and headed to the Nickel. I was tempted to join them, but I had made a promise to myself. I gave Kyle a hug and a kiss on the lips and promised to visit the first time he could have visitors. I told him how proud I was that he had the courage to take back his life. His eyes started to tear, but the water stayed in place. He looked at me kindly and said, "Thanks, Ray, for being the best friend a faggot could have . . . pray for me."

"I will, Kyle, each and every day," I said, fighting back my own tears.

The week was turning out to be one of endings and beginnings. Brayton had indeed decided to leave the firm. We met for lunch and he seemed excited about his new opportunity. We spent about three hours talking about the difficulties of being a black professional in today's corporate world. As we talked, I realized how brilliant Brayton was. The firm really hadn't given him a chance. I

shared with him what I had overheard in the men's room and he
didn't seem surprised.

"They just don't have a clue. Howard has produced as many
great lawyers as fuckin' Harvard," he said.

"I know, my pops graduated from Howard and I know he's a
better lawyer than most of the guys in the firm," I added.

My recent triumph was a thing of the past. The firm worked
from the what-have-you-done-for-me-lately principle. While Brayton and I were talking, I wondered if his skin color had played a role
in his treatment at the firm. Brayton was extremely handsome, but
his features and skin color were very ethnic. He reminded me of a
regal African prince and he carried himself in that manner. I was
not so dumb that I didn't realize that white folks were more comfortable with blacks who were closer to them in looks. I had seen
this work all my life. I knew that I benefited from my light skin
color. My mother was dark-skinned and nobody ever thought she
was my mom. She told me how upset my father's parents were
when he decided to marry her. They were worried about what color
the kids would be. Didn't they know that we would be black, no
matter what shade we were?

The same kinds of standards existed in the black gay community. Light-skinned guys were usually attracted to dark-skinned guys
and vice versa. Guys who were obviously gay had a tougher time
because most men were looking for men. There had been a time
when the top student at Columbia's Law School was an unques-
tionably black gay guy. I heard he went on several interviews, but
didn't get offers from the top firms. The day he visited our firm for
an interview, I made sure I was nowhere to be found. Later I felt
badly about not being there for support. I didn't know him, but I
couldn't risk the chance of being found out by being supportive. I
was often critical of blacks who didn't come to the aid of other
blacks and here I was doing the exact same thing on two levels. I

heard from a friend of Kyle's that he was working for legal aid. At least people who needed him were getting the benefit of his brilliance.

In the black gay life, success was based on youth and how you looked. My greatest fear was being old, fat and alone. Once when I shared my concern with Kyle, he replied, "You still have those eyes." It didn't really make a lot of difference what you did outside of the clubs. Money didn't hurt, but being well endowed was a more treasured commodity. I didn't know if penis size was as important to women as it was to men. Now, this didn't mean that being successful was not important to black gay men; it was quite the contrary. They usually just weren't that interested in dating each other. It was like in the straight world, being successful and a decent person did not always guarantee success with one's love life. Being successful and congenial was not an aphrodisiac.

This was not the last time I was going to see Brayton. I was definitely going to work with Big Brothers and accept an invitation to One Hundred Black Men. Nicole was having a lot to do with my change in attitude about myself. I didn't realize the low self-esteem I had developed since coming out. I was still the same person who had always taken great pride in his achievements. Being gay was such a small part of who I was. Maybe keeping my gayness a secret was creating the low self-esteem. But was I gay or bisexual and what was the difference? Many gay men viewed bisexuality with misgivings. The feeling was that bisexuality was a cop-out. That you were one or the other, no in-between. Did I hang on to my bisexuality because it was more acceptable? The bottom line was how I felt about the people I was involved with. I wouldn't allow society's labels to run my life.

*   *   *

I began spending more time with Nicole and less with Quinn. His comment the last time we were together felt as if someone had driven a stake through my heart. *Dreamgirls* closed and Nicole was busy working on her nightclub act, auditioning for commercials and participating in Broadway workshops. Nicole made the decision to pass up the *Dreamgirls* tour. She explained to me that it was time to move on with her career and not become comfortable with one show. Privately I was happy with her decision.

Although she didn't let it bother her, I knew she ran into the *color-struck* issue in her business. She once commented on the number of light-skinned sisters who were getting all the work and recording contracts. In my eyes Nicole not only was more beautiful than those light-skinned sisters but could definitely sing better than the ones you saw on the videos. I guess she didn't really dwell on it, with Candance being her best friend.

We started to spend more nights together—no sex, just heavy petting and cuddling. I think my holding Nicole all night meant more to her than me trying to hump her all night. It was a wonderful feeling waking up with her next to me. I had to make only a few minor changes with Nicole practically living with me. I hid my condoms and magazines. There was one close call when Nicole ran across K-Y jelly in my nightstand. She just looked at it and closed the drawer without comment. I realized that a decision on which direction to go was close at hand. I began to suffer unwelcome agony over the choices I had to make.

The night I fell in love was a balmy spring evening. Nicole was performing at a club called Don't Tell Mama in the theater district. She was on a bill with several other performers. I arrived late and had to stand in the back of the small, cramped club. As I found a spot, I saw Nicole step to the microphone. She looked stunning in a white sequined evening gown that Kyle had designed for her. Her full curly black hair cascaded down her back and she wore the diamond pendant I had given her. It sparkled against her skin and brought attention to her leaping bust line. She looked as though she had been poured into Kyle's masterpiece gown. Chills took over my body as Nicole sang "Poppa, Can You Hear Me?" from *Yentl*, bathed in the shimmering hues of the stage lights. Although she could sing the pop stuff, Nicole adored show tunes and old standards. The lushly arranged ballads she sang unfolded like scenes from a romantic movie. I became spellbound as I looked at and listened to her. I noticed a twinkle in her eyes when she saw me standing in the back. It was as though she were singing only to me. I felt like the most special man in New York. I was in love with Nicole. But did I love her enough to give up my secret life?

After the show Nicole and I went to eat sushi in SoHo. I was not a big fan of sushi, but Nicole loved it. She looked even more sensual when eating it. As I watched Nicole's face, she looked as though she didn't have a care in the world. I had a sudden urge to put her on the table and attack her with the same sensuality with which she ate the raw delicacies. She sometimes stopped eating and looked at me dreamily with a smile that would melt your heart.

"What are you thinking about?" Nicole asked.

"You."

"Is it good?"

"Yes, it is."

"Please tell me."

"Nicole . . ."

"Yes, Mr. Tyler."

"I've been in love before and I know it's a lot more than holding hands."

"I know, Raymond."

"Are you ready to love me and do more than hold my hands?"

"What are you asking me, Raymond?"

"Are you ready to put your trust in me completely?"

"I've already done that, Raymond. I've already done that."

"Nicole . . . I love you . . . I said it and I mean it . . . I love you."

"And I love you, Raymond Tyler."

"You do?" I smiled. The sound of her words caused a tingling sensation within me as her eyes flickered with great warmth.

"You know I do."

"Is that why you're so happy?"

"Yes. Besides, it's so much easier to be happy."

"Are you ever sad?" I asked.

"Rarely."

"When was the last time you were sad?"

Nicole looked around the restaurant as though the answer were at one of the tables that surrounded us. "The Miss America pageant."

"The pageant? Everything I've ever heard you say about your pageant experiences has been great."

"For the most part they were. But it was in Atlantic City that I realized the world wasn't perfect."

"You thought the world was perfect?" I laughed, trying to bring Nicole out of her remorseful mood.

"Yes, my daddy always told me it could be. He did his best to try and protect me from life's harsh realities. But when I was named a runner-up instead of a winner for something I worked so hard for, I felt I let Daddy down."

"I'm sure he didn't feel that way."

Nicole went on, quietly reminiscing, "Oh, he was so proud of me. But later that night I found out that my State director had polled the judges."

"Polled the judges? Sounds like lawyer stuff."

"Sort of. What hurt me about that night was the fact that the two black judges on the panel scored me the lowest. It probably cost me the title. I don't think it would have hurt as much if the white judges did it."

"But look how you bounced back. Look at you, starring on Broadway. I bet you don't even remember who won the title."

"You know, Raymond, I don't," Nicole laughed.

"Nicole, your daddy was right."

"Right about what?"

"Your world can be perfect. I'm going to do everything in my power to make it perfect. I promise."

"Raymond, you've already done that," Nicole said as she took her small hands away from the wineglass and placed them on top of mine. "Nothing could be more perfect than this."

At times I was baffled at the trust women put in men. Although it went against her strong Christian principles, Nicole was prepared to go all the way with me. The night that I confessed my love we went further than we ever had without actual penetration. I had become pretty good at pleasing women with oral sex, thanks in part to JJ's instruction. Nicole's own expertise was a revelation. I found it interesting that oral sex was no longer taboo in the black community, as it once had been. I wondered if the taboo against homosexuals would eventually die. There was a time when black men never admitted to oral sex, but now they bragged about it. It was thought that only weak men or sissies would participate in such an act. Women, on the other hand, didn't seem to frown at performing oral sex. Kyle was of the opinion that women would do anything to hold on to their men. He said that about seventy percent of the black men he knew had done it at least once with another guy. "Little boys would . . . when little girls wouldn't" was his motto.

Before I could expect Nicole to go all the way, I had some issues of my own to solve. Namely, what to do with Quinn. I didn't know if it was possible to be in love with two people at the same time. I didn't know whether, if I continued to see Quinn, I would fall in love with him too. Maybe I was already in love with him. I had come to the conclusion that I was passionately attracted to women and sexually attracted to men. I had to face the fact that no matter how I felt about Quinn, my future was with Nicole.

My silence in the days that followed puzzled Nicole. I was thinking about the decision I was in the process of making. I had to be sure that I was making the right choice. I was both excited and nervous about seeing Quinn. Nicole was spending a great deal of time at my apartment and I wondered how I was going to get rid of her on Saturday now that she no longer had a show to do. Fortunately, Candance was in town and they had planned to spend the day together shopping and going over wedding plans. She casually mentioned the three of us getting together for dinner, but I was very noncommittal. I knew my moods were bothering Nicole, but I was living in a perpetual state of anxiety. The thought of not having Quinn in my life was extremely painful.

SIXTEEN

It's interesting what roses do to women. I sent Nicole one hundred red roses the following day with a card saying a rose for each day she had made me smile inside. My being a jerk for the last couple of days was quickly forgiven. I debated all morning on what to say to Quinn about us cooling our relationship. As I came closer to making a decision about giving up the life for good, I wondered if it was at all possible. Maybe being gay was like being an alcoholic. That with willpower and a little counseling you could just stop, that you would still be gay but just choose not to practice. Nicole and her strong religious beliefs came to mind. Did prayer change things? Whenever I was worried about something, she would simply say, "Let go, let God."

I sometimes prayed for a pill I could take to destroy my homosexual feelings. I would have taken it in a heartbeat. When I went to church with Nicole, I listened intently for answers to my questions. I wondered what you had to feel in order to be saved. Were you saved from everything?

I joined church and was baptized when I was twelve years old. It was not because I felt anything different, but because it was time. Like going to junior high when you finished the sixth grade. I accepted Christ during Vacation Bible School, partly because all my friends did. I remembered how proud my mom and pops had been the day I was baptized. I wondered why Christians just couldn't understand that Christ sent about ten percent of us down the chute just to confuse things. Maybe He had a plan yet to be revealed. That maybe we were the chosen ones. With Nicole I learned how to let go with my faith, no longer being intellectual about religion. I believed that Christ loved me no matter what. That there were no degrees of sin and I would be judged according to my heart.

The things that I would miss about the gay lifestyle were few. If I were going to give it up, the thing that I treasured the most about being gay was still intact, my friendship with Kyle. My sensibilities as a man who respected women and my ability to feel and be sensitive were characteristics I attributed to my gayness. I wouldn't miss the bars or the viciousness of the kids.

I understood that being vicious was just another defense. It was no accident that the most obviously gay men were the ones most vicious and with the quickest wit. Many times I felt sorry for those who couldn't *pass*. The majority didn't seem to mind a bit. Many lived with the additional stigma the bulk of their life. They would read you before you got a chance to comment on their appearance. It didn't matter if you were gay or straight. Nothing and no one were spared their tart tongues.

Grady buzzed to tell me that Quinn and two little ones were waiting for me in the lobby. *Little ones*, I thought, what can Grady be talking about? When I arrived in the lobby, there stood Quinn with his two children, Baldwin and Maya. Quinn was holding Maya in his arms and Baldwin was standing and holding Quinn's legs. This was the first time that I had come in contact with any other part of Quinn's life.

"I'm sorry. I have to drop them off at my sister-in-law's up in Harlem," Quinn explained.

"No problem. This must be Baldwin," I said, reaching for Quinn's son. "And Maya. What a beautiful little lady."

They were both beautiful. It looked as though Quinn had spit them out. There was no denying that these were his children.

"Say hello to Uncle Ray," Quinn chided the two little ones.

As the two gave me shy greetings, I looked at Quinn with a double look . . . *Uncle Ray.* What was that about? As we rode uptown, I felt like an interloper in Quinn's world. He was quite the doting father, talking with Maya and Baldwin as though I weren't there. A part of me respected that and another side of me begrudged him. After dropping Baldwin and Maya off, we drove to the Tower Video store, where we picked up a couple of videos, and stopped to grab a bite to eat at the Saloon. When we had finished eating, I stood at the cashier's stand while Quinn paid the check. On the way out I heard someone call out my name. When I turned, I saw it was Basil. He was on his way into the restaurant with an attractive blue-eyed blonde who looked like a *Playboy* centerfold. We exchanged hellos and I introduced the two of them to Quinn. Quinn was polite but reserved. After a few minutes of nervous conversation, I told Basil it was good seeing him and nice meeting his lady friend, Elesa. As we were leaving, Basil said, "I'm still waiting on that call, Mr. Tyler."

"Yeah, real soon, Basil," I replied.

As we walked toward the car, Quinn asked in an annoyed tone, "What was that about?"

"What are you talking about?"

"Come on, Ray. I didn't know you knew Basil Henderson."

"Well, I really don't. I told you he was Kyle's friend."

"Well, he seemed to know you pretty well."

"We did have drinks once."

"Is that all . . . and why didn't you mention it to me?"

"Quinn, come on now. It was just drinks. Besides, I do have a life the rest of the week."

"Point well taken, Mr. Tyler," Quinn said in a huff.

Quinn didn't utter a word as we drove up Columbus Avenue and back to my apartment. I had never seen him behave like this. Was he jealous? The thought made me smile. When we reached my apartment, Quinn went directly into my bedroom. I grabbed a couple of beers and walked into the bedroom, where Quinn undressed in silence.

"Quinn, we need to talk," I said.

"About what?"

"About this relationship," I responded.

"What, Raymond, are you seeing someone?" Quinn asked.

"You know I've been going out with Nicole. It's getting serious."

"And?"

"Well, I'm thinking about telling her the truth. I'm trying to go back to the other side exclusively."

"Are you crazy?"

"What do you mean by that?"

"Why bring that grief on yourself? Are you trying to give me an ultimatum?"

"An ultimatum?"

"Well, I know you haven't been happy with our situation lately. But you know how I feel about you, Ray."

"No, I don't know, Quinn. Just look at you. We don't talk at all and you come in here and undress. It's like saying, 'Okay, let's fuck, so I can get home to my wife and kids.' How do you think that makes me feel?"

"Raymond, it's not like that. It's just that I thought this was what you wanted."

"No, Quinn. I want somebody in my life twenty-four seven."

Quinn rubbed his face and looked out the window. The silence of the next few minutes seemed like days. Had we finally come to the end of the road? He sat motionless on the bed in yellow silk briefs, pressing his knee into his chest. His eyes appeared bottomless. I walked over to the bed and sat next to Quinn. He took my hand and pulled it to his chest. "What are you saying, Raymond? What do you want me to say? That I love you? Well, I do."

"That's not it, Quinn. I think I'm in love with Nicole and I want to be fair to the both of you."

"And how long do you think that's going to last?"

"At least as long as your marriage," I snapped defensively.

"Oh, fuck this shit," Quinn said as he raised his voice in anger and leaped from the bed.

"Is that how you want to handle this, Quinn? Just fuck it?"

Quinn turned toward me with a look of rage in his eyes. I had not seen this side of him. His body appeared to be trembling and tears were welling up in his eyes.

"Why do we have to stop seeing each other? Do you want me to leave my wife and kids? Do you want me to move here and be with you twenty-four hours a day? I don't think this is about Nicole. I think this is about Basil or some other nigger!" Quinn shouted.

"Quinn, if I keep making room for you in my life, then I'm bound to fall in love with you. I can't do that to myself. I can't do it to those two beautiful kids."

Quinn broke into a nervous laughter. "So you're doing this for my kids. What about me and what we mean to each other? There are times when I want you, Raymond, as badly as I want my next breath."

There was a certain power in Quinn's voice and in his face. As Quinn suddenly started to get dressed, with his jeans halfway up, he sat back on the bed and began to sob softly. I stopped my search for my T-shirt and pulled him against my chest and massaged the nape of his neck as his tears fell onto my naked shoulders. I had a sudden impulse to retract my previous words and tell him that everything was going to be all right, but in my heart I knew better.

"Quinn, let's just take some time and rethink this situation. I don't want to hurt you, but I can't risk getting hurt myself," I pleaded. "This is wrong for the both of us."

"What? Being gay?"

"Not that. Quinn, you're married. Maybe it could be different if the facts were different."

Quinn looked straight ahead in silence. His body felt rigid and hard. He gently removed himself from my embrace and finished dressing and walked into the living room. My body became sick with fear that I had made the biggest mistake of my life. I joined Quinn in the living room, where he was standing, just looking around the room in a daze. He walked toward me with a blank look on his face. He gently touched my face and kissed my lips with such power that the force staggered me. His eyes were now dry but slightly pink.

Quinn looked me straight in the eyes and said, "You want the facts. The facts are that you may be throwing away the best thing that ever happened to you. Your desire for me and other men isn't going away because you think you're in love with some woman. I know because I live that lie every day. With the exception of the

Saturdays I'm with you. What we have is the closest thing to real love that either one of us can ever dream of. I won't let you throw it away, Raymond," Quinn said in hurried sentences.

Quinn gave me a last kiss and embrace and headed out my door without another word or allowing me to say more. I walked to the doorway and Quinn stared at me, then turned away and headed down the long hallway, home. I felt the tears falling from my eyes when I let myself acknowledge my real feelings for Quinn. Perhaps I was going to lose his love because I had not, in the end, believed in it enough. But what kind of life would a weekends-only relationship offer me? Why double the sin? I must admit that Quinn's and my tidal wave of emotions surprised me. I guess I knew that he did in fact love me, but was that love enough?

Maybe I *was* giving him an ultimatum. What if Quinn hadn't been married with two children? What if we were just two single gay men? Would our relationship have stood a better chance of surviving? I knew one thing: with Quinn I felt safe. I could talk about work, sports and things that even Kyle didn't understand. It was a friendship similar to those with my fraternity brothers, but with sex. Torrid sex. Plus an undying devotion to each other and the ability to share a tenderness rare in both men and women. I was pushing Quinn away because I was afraid to love another man that deeply. I think when two men like Quinn and myself meet, there is a fear of losing one's self. Although we didn't play roles, it was apparent that we both were used to being in charge. In previous relationships with men, I had always held back, never giving myself totally. AIDS had a lot to do with that, but in many ways it became a *man thing* with me. I used to listen to Kyle talk about the total rapture he felt when he gave himself to another man. He would describe it like a woman talking about multiple orgasms. It sounded like a dangerous addiction that I could live without. I remember meeting a super-macho guy who supposedly had been turned out in prison. The next time Kyle and I saw him, Kyle remarked that he looked like "a queen without a country."

Maybe Quinn touched buttons within me that I didn't want to acknowledge or believe existed. I had to get out now!

SEVENTEEN

Dreaming old dreams. When I was a senior in high school, I was elected president of the student body. Now, in Alabama this was no small feat, especially since I walloped the most popular white boy in the school eight-six percent to fourteen percent. I was the first black to win such an office at a predominantly white high school. I then dreamed of being the first black congressman from the state of Alabama. It was a dream I actively pursued until that Friday in October some years later. When I gave in to my sexuality, I gave up on my political career. I didn't resent it until I saw openly gay white congressmen being reelected by overwhelming majorities after coming out.

Leaders in the black community would have had you believe that you couldn't be a service to the community and gay too. They viewed black homosexuals as freaks of nature and felt their career options should be limited to hairdressers and interior decorators. I wondered how many leaders the black community had lost because certain men felt that their sexuality made them incapable of leading. It was ridiculous—maybe we shouldn't elect black men who beat their women. Or even black men who indulge in oral sex. Maybe we should just have stayed out of bedrooms we weren't invited into.

I was now thinking that if I married Nicole we could move back to Birmingham and I could pursue that dream. But what would happen if one of my one-night stands resurfaced? What about Kelvin, Julian or Quinn? Maybe I would open my press conference by announcing my former lifestyle and by explaining how the love of a beautiful black woman and former runner-up to Miss America had changed my life. The press would love it . . . but would the black community? Maybe they wouldn't care if I didn't beat them over the head with it. You heard rumors all the time about prominent politicians who were gay but kept it hush-hush. In most cases they were usually married with families. Sooner or later you heard some drunk queen in a bar talking about having been with someone before that person became well known. Maybe I should just concern myself with making the big bucks and forget about helping my people.

Janelle, as she now preferred to be called, and I met for brunch on Sunday. I wanted to find out what was happening with her and to update her on Kyle. We decided to meet at Tuesday's West on Columbus Avenue. It was a favorite of the gang because of the unlimited champagne brunch and super omelettes. JJ looked as though she had lost some weight and she was wearing more makeup than usual. We both passed on the champagne and ordered coffee with our western omelettes instead. We talked about how proud we were of Kyle and how much we missed him. I told her how happy she looked and she broke out into a boisterous laugh, saying, "That's what a stiff dick with a good man on the opposite end can do."

I told her about my last meeting with Quinn and my decision to come clean with Nicole.

"Are you sure that's what you want to do, Ray? I mean, it's admirable, but Nicole strikes me as a true BAP. She might not be able to handle it. Trust me, you'll live to regret it," JJ lamented.

"Nicole's not a BAP. How could she be? She's from a small town in Arkansas," I defended.

"Well all those divas she works with have been rubbing off. And I still don't understand why you have to tell her everything now."

"How would you feel if Bernard wasn't completely honest with you?"

"You know what, I don't expect him to be. I know how men are."

"I just want to start out right. I mean, I could marry this girl."

"But why, Ray? Are you being true to yourself? I know you don't like to admit it, but Quinn makes you happy."

"So does Nicole."

"But you haven't even had sex with her."

"How do you know that?"

"Trust me, you would have said something."

"But I am sexually attracted to her."

"That's because she's an unattainable beauty queen. The movie star type. How are you going to feel when she grows old or when you see another fine man like Quinn or that Steve-Basil guy?"

"You don't understand, JJ—I mean Janelle. Nicole does things for me that no person has ever done. She makes me feel like I could run the world if I wanted to. I'm tired of worrying if somebody is really faithful. I want somebody who may love me more than I love them."

"But is that fair to Nicole or are you being selfish?"

"JJ, with Nicole I think I could give up the life. I like her as a person. I want to take care of her. I want to grow old with her."

"Are you sure you're not doing this for your parents?"

"No," I said sternly.

"So you're not gay anymore?"

"You know that I'm not totally gay. Don't tell me you've forgotten about when we met?"

"No, I haven't. But that's not what I'm asking."

"JJ, I'll always have desires for men. But I'll just suppress them."

"For how long?"

"As long as I'm in love with Nicole."

"Well, baby, you know I wish you well. What I think you should have done is made Quinn yours completely. I'm not certain I believe totally in this bisexual thing."

"What do you mean?"

"Don't play dumb with me. What you two had was special. I think you're afraid to really be happy. I think that if you didn't worry so much about what people thought, you might never go to bed with another woman. That part of your life would no longer be invisible. But what do I know, I'm a fag hag," she laughed.

"Invisible?"

"Yeah, invisible. Think about it. Your life with Quinn was basically invisible to everyone but the two of you. A part of Quinn's life is invisible to his family, especially his wife. You know Kyle may be a bit deranged, but it's all out there for the world to see."

"Invisible," I said out loud.

My conversation and brunch with JJ gave me a lot to think about. I treasured her comments, but only I knew how I felt inside. Nicole made me feel like I had butterflies in my stomach. When I was with her, I didn't think about men. I was not going to give up on the dream of being totally happy with just one person, one woman, no matter what JJ thought. Another man would never be able to give me that. That part of my life would just have to remain invisible.

Nicole and I had plans for the Dance Theater of Harlem and dinner at the Water Club. I had decided to wait with my announcement and give our relationship more time. I just made a promise with myself to devote my affections to Nicole completely. There was a message on my machine from Nicole saying she was running late, but at seven forty-five she still hadn't arrived at my apartment. I called her apartment and her service without results. I debated about going ahead to Lincoln Center and just meeting her there. I was all decked out in my tux and was really looking forward to an enjoyable evening. Just when I was getting ready to leave Nicole a message to meet me, the phone rang.

"Ray." Nicole's voice sounded peculiar.

"Yes, baby. Where are you?"

"The hospital."

"The hospital?" I asked with alarm.

"Don't worry. I'm here with Candance. She fainted at her bridal shower."

"Is she all right?"

"I don't know. I think she might be pregnant. I need to stay here with her."

"Where is Kelvin?"

"Oh, he's in D.C."

"Do you want me to come there?"

"No, thanks, everything will be fine. You go ahead to the ballet."

"No, not without you," I protested. "I'll wait on you. We can go somewhere for dessert."

"It might be too late for me to get back in the city. I may just spend the night in Mount Vernon."

"I'll send a car for you."

"No, I should stay here. I'll see you tomorrow. You go on and have fun. Why don't you take Kyle?"

"Oh, Kyle's out of pocket." I forgot I hadn't told Nicole about Kyle's problem.

"Well, don't waste the tickets. What about your tennis partner?"

"Don't worry, I'll be fine all by myself."

"Okay, I'll call you later. I love you."

"Yeah, me too."

"Say it, Raymond."

"Say what?"

"Raymond Tyler?"

"I love you, Nicole . . ."

"Now, was that so hard?"

"No, it wasn't. I love you, Nicole."

"Good night."

I decided against going to the ballet. As much as I was looking forward to it, I didn't want to go alone. In the past, going to a DTH performance was always an excellent place to meet men. Kyle always knew someone in the troupe and we always got backstage passes. In fact, I had dated a couple of dancers; not for long, though. Although they had wonderful bodies, I found them to be quite fickle. A couple of years back I met a really gorgeous dancer named Trey. He was a Morehouse College grad, very intelligent and easy to talk with, but to my surprise he was straight. It was one of the few times when my *sissy sense* was wrong. Trey fit every stereotype of a gay guy, all of which went to prove how meaningless stereotypes can be.

I picked up my briefcase and decided to get a head start on the

week. I had just been assigned a new case and I had a lot of reading
to do. When I looked at my appointment book, I realized my
mom's birthday was only weeks away. I had not heard from my pops
or his secretary. Was he still planning to give her a surprise party
and was I going?

EIGHTEEN

My sleep was interrupted with a dream of Quinn and Nicole. In the dream they were each pulling me in a different direction. I awoke before I found out in which direction I ended up going. I longed for a dreamless sleep. Besides, dreams never provided answers, just presented opposing views, so reminiscent of courtroom dramas.

It began as a typical Monday at the office; slow as a turtle race. I was having slight difficulties getting into the new case I had been assigned. It was another computer case, but this time there was only a contract dispute. I tried several times during the day to reach Nicole. I figured she was sleeping late in Mount Vernon. JJ called me and said that a friend of Kyle's had phoned her. Rumors were circulating that Kyle was sick. I told her not to worry. AIDS rumors were standard fare these days in the gay community. Anytime anyone disappeared from the bar scene or lost a little weight, rumors started. Kyle was such a permanent fixture in the clubs that his absence was bound to start tongues wagging.

I finally saw Nicole late Monday evening. She came by my apartment in a very tense mood. When I asked her how Candance was, she said that the doctors were running some additional tests. We chuckled at the thought of Candance being pregnant. Nicole's laughter seemed nervous.

I baked some chicken and made a tossed salad for Nicole. While she was eating, I stood behind her and started to massage her shoulders. Her upper body felt very stiff. She explained that she hadn't slept well the night before. I started to share my dream with her but decided against it. Instead, we talked about the perfect world we would create together, just the two of us.

"Why don't you let me give you the Raymond Tyler, Jr., special?" I suggested.

"The what?"

"Don't ask any questions. Go into my bedroom. Take your clothes off and put on my robe. Meet me in the bathroom."

"What?"

"Come on now. No questions. Just do as I say."

While Nicole was in my bedroom, I made a steaming-hot bath and added bath salts and oils. I turned off the lights and lit candles around the edge of the tub. I pulled one of the speakers into the bathroom and put on my CD of Luther Vandross's greatest hits. Nicole came in, gave me a smile and a gentle kiss as she removed the robe and stepped into the hot bath. Her body looked flawless. The tension seemed to leave her face as she settled into the tub.

While on my knees, I started to gently massage her soft shoulders and silky neck. She closed her eyes and lay back, allowing the suds to cover her breasts. My fingers moved from her slender shoulders to her forehead. I gently massaged her face in a circular motion. Her body appeared limp. After a few minutes of massaging, I left briefly and returned wearing only my baby blue silk boxers and carrying a bowl of butter pecan ice cream with strawberries on top.

Nicole giggled with delight as I fed her the ice cream and strawberries. Halfway through the bowl she took the spoon from my hand and started feeding me the now soupy substance. She would teasingly put the spoon to my mouth and then suddenly pull it back. The third time she did it, the spoon slipped from her hand into the water. I started to retrieve it and found my hand between Nicole's soft thighs. She reached down and squeezed my hand and moved it toward her erected breasts. They looked like miracles. I leaned my head over and kissed each one separately. I took my fingers and touched the dark circle of each nipple and then I sucked the nipple hard. When I touched them and sucked them, they seemed as delectable as the ice cream and strawberries earlier. I expected them to dissolve in my mouth. Nicole let out a soft cry. With a smooth motion I stood up and picked her up out of the water. I carried her, wet and soapy, into the bedroom and placed her on my bed. As she lay there nude, I ran my hard tongue up and down her moist skin. Nicole shuddered in ecstasy as her body tightened. I removed my boxers with one hand and lay beside her damp body.

"Are you ready for this?" I asked as I gazed down toward my erect sex.

"Yes," she sighed.

A smile broke out over my face and I leaped from the bed to my nightstand. I looked through the drawer in search of my condoms. Minutes later, no condoms. Everything but condoms. Had Quinn and I used them all?

"What's the matter?" Nicole asked.

"It looks like I've been caught unprepared."

"Don't worry. I've taken precautions."

"You have?" I asked in a surprised voice.

"Yes, silly. I'm on birth control."

Birth control, I thought. What about the other stuff. I didn't have sex with anyone without a raincoat. How could I explain this to Nicole without offending her. I could only surmise that women still worried just about getting pregnant. Weren't they concerned with diseases? What about AIDS? Didn't they know women could get AIDS also? But I knew I was negative, so why was I having all these weird thoughts?

Without further deliberation I began gently to make love to her. Nicole shrieked in ecstasy as I entered and exploded inside her. A sweat broke out over my body as my sex melted like the ice cream we had shared earlier. As I rolled alongside Nicole, I hugged her close, enfolding her. She took her slender fingers and gently rubbed my wet chest.

"Are you okay?" she asked.

"I'm fine." I smiled.

"Perfect!" Nicole said.

I wanted to ask Nicole if she was all right, but I didn't. Everything had happened so fast. A phobia that maybe I hadn't satisfied her kept my sex limp, even though Nicole's legs lay against it. Nicole was too ladylike to complain. While she lay in my arms, I realized that there was a big difference between male and female lovers. There were times after reaching orgasm with a man that I didn't want to be touched anywhere. With a woman it was nice to caress and hold each other. I remembered the first time I made love with Kelvin and how we lay back-to-back, both afraid to turn and face each other. But the feeling of reaching simultaneous orgasm with a man and seeing it . . . was magic. While I was sure that this could happen with a woman, I personally had not experienced it. I pulled Nicole even closer to me and caressed her until she was sound asleep. But my feeling a bit guilty and inadequate caused a restless sleep.

＊　　＊　　＊

As the days passed, I saw very little of Nicole. I became worried that maybe my performance in bed was causing her to examine her love for me. We talked on the phone several times, but she seemed preoccupied with something. She always ended our conversations by telling me that she loved me, and that would ease some of my doubt. I figured that if Nicole felt she was going to have a problem with our lovemaking, we would talk about it.

In my experience, men didn't do this. They really didn't talk about sex with each other; the sex would become silent. The quickest way to end a budding romance with a man was for the sex not to be right. When I was in college, we used to joke at the frat house about how quickly your reputation could be destroyed if a woman said that you couldn't screw. It brought the same stigma as saying a woman was easy.

Men would simply suggest, *Maybe we should just be friends.* I was careful not to suggest this to Quinn. I mean, we were friends and the sex left nothing to be desired. Quinn's physical attributes equaled his intellect.

It started as a typical spring Saturday without Quinn. I was awakened by a soft morning light breaking through the mini-blinds in my bedroom. I had seen Nicole the previous evening, but only for a few moments. She explained that something major was going on that she couldn't discuss but assured me it had nothing to do with us. I decided to rent a car and go upstate to visit Kyle. We had talked and he sounded rested. I missed seeing Quinn but felt that I had made the right decision. When he called, I asked him to give me some time before we tried to resume the friendship portion of our relationship.

There were times when I desperately wanted to talk to him

about work, Kyle and Nicole, but I felt that it wouldn't be fair to him. Deep down I hoped that we really could remain friends and that if I ever married Nicole, maybe he and his wife would be included in our circle of friends. I decided to just send my mom flowers for her birthday, since my father still hadn't called. I figured he didn't want me to come home. We were having a Tyler standoff.

While I was shaving, I thought how nice it would be to have Nicole ride with me. Whenever she was around me, I knew that our relationship would work and that my desires for men could remain in check. As I prepared to leave, the phone rang and it was Quinn. He said that he missed me and suggested that we ride upstate together. He said he already had a rental car and that he could be in the city within the hour. He assured me no pressure, no sex. It sounded innocent and it would be nice to see him. When I said yes, his voice rang with excitement. Since I had some extra time, I decided to make breakfast. The phone rang again; I assumed it was Quinn. It was Nicole. In a hysterical voice she asked me to come to New York University Medical Center and meet her in the cafeteria on the fifth floor.

"What's the matter?" I asked.

"Raymond, please hurry, I need you," she pleaded.

"I'll be right there."

I grabbed my windbreaker and headed out the door and down to the lobby. When the elevator reached the lobby, I saw Quinn coming through the double doors.

"You're not leaving without me?" he quizzed.

"No, there's some emergency with Nicole. I have to get to NYU hospital," I said.

"Come on, I'll take you."

As we drove through the busy Manhattan streets, I was intensely concerned over what could have happened to Nicole. When I remembered that she said to meet her in the cafeteria, I realized that it wasn't she who was in the hospital. An early afternoon spring rain made the city streets look clean and new. Quinn didn't talk much as he sped through the city with the expertise of a New York cabby. I guessed he could see the fear and concern on my face. When we pulled up in front of the massive hospital, Quinn touched my hand and asked if I wanted him to wait.

"No, I'm fine. Please call me later," I asked.

"Raymond, don't worry. Nicole will be fine," Quinn assured me.

"Thanks."

Nicole raced to my arms when she saw me get off the fifth-floor elevator.

"Raymond!" she cried, embracing me tightly.

"What's the matter, baby? Stop crying," I said as I wiped the tears from her face. "Come on, sit down. Tell me what's the matter. Who's in the hospital?"

"Candance," she said, sobbing uncontrollably.

"Candance? What's wrong? Is it the baby?"

"No, Raymond, Candance has pneumonia, a rare pneumonia. The doctors say it's serious."

My heart sank as I listened to Nicole explain how they had transferred Candance to NYU because of the seriousness of her illness. She told me how she had been with Candance and her family all night and all day. I felt my legs become numb as the torrent of words rushed from Nicole's lips.

"Come on, baby, let's go get some coffee," I suggested, wiping more tears from Nicole's face.

"Let me go tell Candi's mom that I will be back."

As Nicole walked away, I called out to her, "Nicole, where's Kelvin?"

"No one knows," she answered in disgust.

When she returned, I ordered coffee. As we drank it, I reassured her that Candance would be fine. I told her that she was at one of the best hospitals in the country. I reminded her of her faith and told her that God wouldn't take Candance away so early in life. Nicole then started to chronicle Candance's illness. It turned out that this was not the first bout that she had had. While Nicole was talking, a terrible thought crossed my mind. AIDS!

The symptoms that Nicole described sounded a lot like what I had heard about AIDS. I wondered whether I should ask if Candance had been tested for AIDS?

"So where did you say Kelvin was?" I asked.

"I don't know what's going on. I've tried calling him several times. Candance's father is thinking about hiring a private investigator to find him."

"Have you tried his school?"

"He took an immediate leave of absence."

As I sipped the lukewarm coffee, I could see the pain in Nicole's face. Her eyes were sad and filled with tears. Not thinking, she wiped tears from her cheeks. Her voice trembled as she expressed her disbelief at the recent events. I got up from my seat and held her tight, trying to control her trembling.

"This is a time in my life when I should be preparing for weddings, not hospitals and funerals," Nicole said.

"Funerals? Come on, baby, Candance will bounce back. From what I know about her she's a fighter."

"I hope you're right."

"You know I am. You've shared so much of your faith with me, Nicole. I think it's time for you to depend on some of that same faith. Remember what you told me, 'Let go, let God.' "

"I know you're right. I've been praying nonstop for days. I just hope God has heard me," she mused out loud.

We finished our coffee and slowly walked toward the elevator when Nicole grabbed my hand and turned to me.

"Raymond," she said in her soft voice. "Do you think Kelvin's bisexual? Was he ever an IV drug user?"

The question hit me like a ton of bricks. I felt my heart race rapidly. My palms were wet with fear. "A drug user?"

"Yes, or maybe he's bisexual or gay. Do you know?" Nicole asked again.

"I can't answer that," I replied.

"Why not? I understand that you two were pretty good friends in college," Nicole said with a question in her voice and face.

I took a deep breath and prayed silently that my legs would support me. "I can't speak for Kelvin, Nicole. I can only speak for myself."

"Speak for yourself. What are you saying, Raymond?"

"I'm gay, Nicole . . . well, I guess you could say I'm bisexual," I stammered.

There was a long pause. Nicole just stared at me in disbelief. Her face became colorless. It looked as though she was drawing on her deepest reserves for strength. When she began to speak again, her voice was clear, her resolve firm.

"You're kidding . . . right?" she asked.

"I'm sorry, Nicole. I know I should have said something earlier."

"Sorry?" Nicole screamed. "Sorry, after you made love to me less than a week ago? Why me, Raymond?"

"Because I love you."

"Love me? How can you love me? You love men . . . isn't that what you're telling me? What did you do, break up with your lover? Is that why Kyle is gone?" Nicole bluntly demanded.

"What does Kyle have to do with this?"

"Well, he's your friend, isn't he?"

"Friend, yes. Lover, no."

"You lied to me, Raymond. I can't forgive that."

"I didn't lie, Nicole. Maybe I just didn't tell the whole truth."

"How could I not know? All the gay people I work with. How could this have happened? How could I fall in love with you? How could I be so stupid?" she screamed as tears started to roll down her face. I reached to wipe away her tears and Nicole put out her hand, stopping my motion.

"Don't, Raymond. Don't touch me," Nicole instructed.

"Nicole, I didn't mean to fall in love with you either. And when I did, I was going to tell you. I do love you."

"But when were you going to tell me? Why not before I gave myself to you?" she screamed at a higher pitch. Her voice was trembling and a horrified stare covered her face. I noticed people around us stopping to glance at the two of us.

"I can change, Nicole. I love you that much."

Anger replaced the horrified look on Nicole's face. Her body wilted like an undernourished flower. "Change? Are you serious?" Her voice dropped lower.

"Yes. Nicole, please give me and our relationship a chance. I love you."

"I don't doubt that you love me, Raymond. Of that I am sure. I mean, I have to believe that you love me. But do you love me enough?" she asked calmly.

"Enough?" The question felt brutal.

"Yes, enough, Raymond."

"I think so."

"Well, right now that's not good enough. I can't base my future on an 'I think so.' "

"Let's not make any rash decisions now. Come home with me and let's talk," I suggested as I walked closer to her.

"Talk. Right now I don't have time to talk," Nicole snapped. "Right now my best friend is down that hallway, fighting for her life. Probably because of loving someone like you," she said as she moved from my reach.

"What are you saying?"

"Raymond, Candance has AIDS."

I stood motionless as Nicole's words confirmed my fears. My body went cold. My eyes darted around the hospital and back to Nicole. I was afraid to see the pain in her face. Her beautiful eyes looked weighted down with sadness. Again they filled with tears. She raised her hand and wiped the tears from her cheeks.

"Are you sure?"

"Yes, the doctors are sure," Nicole said in a quavering voice.

"I'm sorry, Nicole."

"Sorry for what? Sorry for Candance, or for me for falling in love with you?"

Nicole turned and started to run down the long hospital corridor. When I yelled out her name, she seemed to move faster, running away from me. I stood in the same spot for minutes, still as a stone statue, trying to decide if I should give chase or give her some time. My stomach churned with such acute anxiety that I suddenly felt my breakfast coming up. A nurse and an orderly came up and asked if I was all right. The nurse took my hand and led me to a nearby chair and the orderly started to clean up my mess. I sat in a daze and slowly drank a fizzing solution that the nurse had given me. Still in a daze, I walked through the elevator door without even thanking the nurse. Somehow I managed to catch a taxi uptown. I got out on Ninety-fifth, went to my neighborhood liquor store and purchased a liter of one-hundred-proof Stoli. As I walked out of the store, I ignored the Chinese clerk whom I usually conversed with. I stopped at the Love Stores on the corner and purchased a bottle of Sominex. For the first time in my life I wanted to die. I walked quickly up Broadway and to my apartment. Once inside, I quickly broke the seal and drank the vodka straight from the bottle. A few minutes later I poured myself another drink, this time with ice and a small amount of grapefruit juice. I looked out of my window and saw night cover the busy city streets. Just weeks ago I was on top of the world. With a single admission of truth I wanted to find a rock to crawl under. The steady flow of vodka was causing my body to grow numb, but it eased the pain that I was feeling inside. I popped two of the sleeping pills and took another naked drink of the vodka. It had me laughing one minute and crying uncontrollably the next. I had never felt the way I felt now.

About an hour later I was drunk. I heard a knock on my door, and when I opened it, Quinn walked in. I grabbed him and hugged him so hard that my fingers were digging through his shirt. He could tell from my bloodshot eyes that I had been crying. "What's the matter, buddy?"

"I don't know," I mumbled.

"You're drunk, Ray. What happened with Nicole? I've never seen you like this."

"Help me, Quinn," I cried.

"I will," he assured me.

Quinn helped me to the sofa. I saw him walk into my kitchen and heard him rambling around my cabinets. Minutes later he emerged with a piping-hot cup of coffee that he forced me to drink. I was mumbling incoherently, but somehow I managed to tell him what had happened with Nicole and Candance. He told me how sorry he was and then he began to slowly undress me. He then put my arms around his ample shoulders and led me into the bathroom and a steaming shower. I didn't remember much after the shower, but some time later I awoke in my bed with Quinn at my side. Fully clothed. My head was lying against his ribs and his hands were stroking my hair. I could feel his warm fingers glide down my nose to my dry lips.

The numbers on the clock were the only illumination. The darkness was intoxicating, the silence soothing. I could smell the subtle fragrance of Quinn's Perry Ellis cologne.

"How do you feel?" Quinn asked.

"What time is it?" I moaned softly.

"Two-thirty."

"Don't you need to get home?"

"Yeah, I've called. I can stay here if you need me," Quinn answered with sympathetic assurance.

"No, Quinn, I'll be all right. You better get home."

As Quinn rose from the bed and slipped on his shoes, I felt an eerie chill. My bedroom became frighteningly still. It was as though loneliness and despair were settling in for the night. Quinn walked into the bathroom and I heard water running. Moments later he walked into the bedroom and pulled the burgundy bedspread over me. As he prepared to leave, he bent over me, softly kissing my forehead. He slipped a small piece of paper into my hand. "Take care, buddy. Here's my home phone number. Call me if you need me. I love you."

"Me too," I said as tears welled in my eyes.

I watched Quinn closely as he walked slowly out of the bedroom. In the floating darkness his white cotton shirt appeared to be moving alone. When I heard the door close, I wanted to call Quinn back, but deep down I knew only Nicole could ease my pain. I leaped from the bed and went to the kitchen to find my vodka and sleeping pills. They would help me sleep. When I slept, I would no longer feel this powerful pain.

After one stiff drink I was hopelessly depressed again. I crawled from the kitchen into my bathroom and noticed the empty Sominex bottle on the sink. So much for suicide. Disgusted, I stood up and slowly walked to my bedroom.

Before getting into bed, I had a sudden desire to talk with my mother. She picked up the phone after the first ring.

"Mama."

"Raymond. What's the matter, baby?"

"Nothing, Ma."

"Come on now. You were on my mind earlier this evening. I know something is wrong."

I stuttered through the day's events, telling her what had happened with Nicole and about Candance and Kelvin. In the middle of my dialogue, my mother started to pray. She prayed for me, Nicole and Candance. She asked God to watch over all of us in the big unfriendly city we called home. When she finished, my mama with light sobs in her voice said, "No matter who or what you are, Raymond junior, you're my baby and I love you no matter what."

"I know that, Ma . . . but sometimes you need someone besides your ma to love you." Without even saying good night or good-bye to my mama, I hung up the phone and jerked it from the wall.

NINETEEN

Stop the world, I want to get off! The days that ensued became one huge blur. It was as though a dark cloud had descended upon my apartment. I spoke with Nicole, who said she had not decided what to do. Her time and thoughts were with Candance. When I asked how Candance was doing, she replied, "As well as one could be doing in her situation." She also informed me that before we had any discussions about our future, I was to have an AIDS test by her doctor. I told her that I would comply. It wouldn't be the first time I had taken the test. I thought back to the night we made love and how I had gone ahead without a condom because I didn't want to explain why we should use one while we were in the throes of passion. With men, it wasn't a question: you used a condom or you didn't have sex. Quinn and I had had conversations about our sexual past when we decided to proceed with our relationship. I wondered again if most heterosexual women were concerned only with getting pregnant. When I talked with Nicole, I tried to be supportive and not pressure her. I tried to understand the intense pressure she was under. She did tell me that they had found Kelvin back home in Philadelphia and that he was expected in New York any day. I had not been to work in days. I called my secretary and told her I was ill. I didn't answer my phone or my door buzzer. If I could not be with Nicole, then I wanted to be alone. I had never felt the emptiness that I was now feeling. It was a pain that the doctors could not cure. I had never been really physically ill, but I could not imagine a pain greater than the one I was currently experiencing.

Late Thursday evening my buzzer rang constantly. Minutes later there was a knock at my door. When I did not respond, the knocks got louder, as though the person were trying to beat the door down with pure physical strength. About a half hour later the knocking stopped and I got back in bed. I figured it was Quinn. I knew he was concerned, but right now I needed to be alone. After lying in bed for about an hour, I got up to fix another drink. I knew that I was drinking too much, but it helped me sleep or, rather, pass out. My sleep was restless and full of nightmares, but I didn't feel the pain I did when I was awake. While I was in the kitchen, the knocking at my door started again. I stopped my movement so that whoever it was wouldn't hear me. Then I heard one knock, a key turning, and I panicked. I suddenly heard voices when the safety latch prevented entry. I recognized one of the voices immediately. It was my pops.

"Ray!" he called out. "Are you in there?"

"Mr. Tyler . . . this is Mr. Macklin, the building super. Are you all right? If you don't respond, we're going to call the fire department."

I walked slowly from the kitchen to the living room and saw my door half open, with the safety latch holding on for dear life. I walked up and removed it and my pops and Mr. Macklin walked in.

"I'll take it from here," my pops said to the super.

As I stood there wearing only my underwear, my father and I looked at each other in stunned silence. I had not washed my face for days, and my breath must have had a foul odor.

"Pops . . . what are you doing here?" I asked, my body trembling from his unexpected presence.

"Your mother was worried about you. She's been trying to reach you for days," he said.

"I'm okay. I've just run into a few problems."

"You don't look okay. This is a nice apartment. I bet it's more than the mortgage on the house and my office," my pops said while he glanced around my living room.

"Is that why you're here, Pops? To see how I live?" I demanded, raising my voice for the first time at my pops.

"No, son," he stammered, his head down. "I was worried about you too. I know I don't say it . . . but you must know I love you."

A chill surged through my body. Part shock . . . part anger . . .

"You love me, Pops? You don't even know me, Pops. Do you know who or what you're loving, Pops? Do you know me?" I shouted as I beat my chest with a balled fist.

"You're my son and I love you. I may not approve of your life . . . but you're still my son. You're my firstborn."

"Approve . . . approve of who I sleep with, Pops? That's none of your damn business . . . I don't ask you who you sleep with." For a moment we stared at each other and then my father's domineering manner seemed to dissolve. The harsh lines faded from his face, his expression tumbled into despair.

"What did I do wrong, Raymond junior? How could this happen?" my pops pleaded. When I looked at him, I saw something in my pops's face that was unfamiliar. Something I had never seen before, a tenderness, a sorrow. A measured coolness existed in the room.

"Pops, it's nothing you or Mama did. It just happened. Do you think I chose this life, Pops? Do you think I'm this way because you didn't hug me enough or you didn't say you loved me enough? Do you think that you worked too hard and spent too much time away from the house? Do you realize that today is the first time I've ever heard you say you love me?"

I talked in painstaking sentences, trying to lower my voice, to take out the rage.

My pops continued to voice his fears. "Your mother and I have worked all our lives to give you and Kirby the best. We want the best for you. I find myself constantly worried about you now. When you were a child, I never worried about you. I knew that you were my brave little man. I want you to be the man I dreamed you'd grow up to be. I want the best for you, son."

"Maybe this is the best I can expect for myself, Pops," I said in an apologetic tone. "Pops, no matter what you think of me, I'm no sissy. I am the man you raised me to be. My gayness is such a small part of who I've become. Look around you, Pops. I've accomplished a lot in my life. I am making a contribution. I've earned your respect, Pops. Would you be so adamant about coming into my bedroom if I was completely straight?"

"I'm sorry I called you that, son. I don't understand how this happened. Your mom and I are now worried about Kirby. And what about this AIDS shit?"

"Pops, I've been careful. I just wish I could explain it to you, Pops. It's not you. This is the deck that I've been dealt. I'm just gonna have to play the hand I've got. I can't throw away my life because of the cards I hold."

"We can get help, son."

"It's not that simple. Don't you know if there was some cure out there, I would have already tried it. I'm never going to do anything to embarrass you or Mama. More importantly, I'm not going to embarrass myself."

"You never showed any signs of this when you were a little boy. What about all the girls that called you and what about Sela? Was it New York that changed you? Isn't it tough enough being a black man?"

"Pops, it was just something I discovered about myself later in life. Something that brought pleasure to my body. I'm very much a man. I have never had a desire to be anything else. You have succeeded in what you set out to do. I am a proud black man who loves women, but I have loved men too, Pops."

"You didn't let them sc—" My father stopped in mid-sentence and quietly stared at me, his face creased by a question that he was struggling to articulate.

"Screw me, Pops? Is that what you want to know? Would that make me more of a man in your eyes, if I'm the doer?" I felt my rage returning. Why did my father's question cause my anger to return? Should I tell him I didn't let men enter me? Would his knowing this make my sexuality easier to digest?

"I'm sorry, Ray, I have no right."

"You're right, Pops, you don't. It's not a dick-and-ass thing. It's how I feel. I wish you could cut me open and see how I feel. Then I think you'd understand. If you could really see me the way God made me, you'd be surprised how much I'm like you."

"I don't want to lose my son to some disease. I want to be a part of your life like when you were growing up. I want to share your successes and your disappointments."

"A part or all of it, Pops? My gayness isn't something you can touch or see, Pops. Had I not told Mom, you wouldn't be here right now. You can touch me, Pops. This is me . . . it's who I am."

My pops didn't respond. He just turned and walked toward me. When we were eye-to-eye, I saw water in my pops's eyes. I had seen him cry only once, when Pa-Paw died. He took his powerful arms and embraced me as though I were that little boy of so many years before. I went into his arms so easily, as though it were the only place in the world. I felt as though all the anger were being squeezed out of me. I felt tears flow down my dirty face. The tears turned to loud sobs. All of the pain I had felt for years, all the guilt I'd felt about my life came out with those poignant tears. My pops didn't release me until the sobs turned to whimpers. He took his hands and palmed my head. He looked at me and smiled. It was the smile that I saw the first time I called him Pops, the same smile when I scored my first touchdown, the same smile when I finished law school. I imagined it was the same smile he smiled the first time he laid eyes on me. I closed my eyes for a moment and felt a sense of calm come over me. A silence covered the room.

That night my father and I talked and learned more about each other than we had in all the previous years. I shared with him my love for Nicole and how important Quinn had become. He squirmed when I mentioned Quinn, and although his face expressed apprehension, he was tolerant. I think for the first time we understood the pain that my bisexuality had caused both of us. We realized that things and feelings were not going to be changed in one night, but we started to break down the barriers. I tried to put into words why I thought I was bisexual. I thought I had been born bisexual, but that I had managed to suppress it during my adolescent years because of what I had been taught. I shared the theories of some doctors that it was caused during some type of trauma during pregnancy, or that being gay was genetically linked. In either case, I didn't want to blame my parents. When Pops said that all he wanted was for me to be happy, I explained that one day I would be but it would take time. My father encouraged me to be supportive and understanding of Nicole and to give her time. He told me that if she was half the lady I said she was, she would give me a chance to prove my love. When our conversation ventured to law, he congratulated me on my big win and offered me a full partnership with his firm. When I hesitated, he asked me just to think it over. He convinced me to come home for a little time to rest and regroup. On this humid spring evening in New York City, I got my pops back. I was going back South.

Something humorous happened on my father's second day in New York City. I took him to my office for a brief moment and introduced him to my coworkers and senior partners, David and Dan. That evening we went to see *Six Degrees of Separation*, a Broadway show with a shady black gay character. Pops seemed to enjoy it. After the show we went for coffee and then headed to my apartment. When I got home, Quinn was waiting in the lobby. He was concerned about me. At first I was a little bit nervous about the two of them being in the same room, but they really liked each other. The three of us talked about sports, the plight of the black man and living in New York City. Maybe my father had forgotten our conversation the night before. Maybe he didn't put two and two together. Maybe when Quinn showed him pictures of Maya and Baldwin, he assumed he was straight. Maybe he was making an effort to understand. I smiled to myself as the two of them talked like old friends.

I plugged my phone back in, and when it rang, I went to my bedroom, leaving Quinn and my father alone. I answered the phone and it was Kelvin. He said he was doing fine and Candance was *holding her own*. He asked me to meet him at the hospital the next afternoon and to wear a suit. When I asked him what was going on, he simply said he would explain. I didn't question him on his recent whereabouts or his own health. I told him my father was in town and that I had a doctor's appointment, but that I would be there at noon. He thanked me and hung up. When I walked into the living room, Quinn instantly noticed the look on my face. I just said that I had to help out a friend tomorrow. Pops asked if everything was all right and I said, "Yes." He reminded me that he had an early flight, and before I could respond, Quinn offered to take him to the airport. Later in the night, when Quinn had left and Pops was in my bedroom, sleeping, I placed a Stevie Wonder disc in my compact disc player, put on my headphones and sat at my desk to write the most important letter of my life.

My Dearest Nicole,

In a perfect world I would never have to write this letter. In a perfect world there wouldn't be a need for it. In a perfect world this pain . . . absent. In a perfect world we would accept people for who and what they are. No strings, complete honesty, total acceptance, no matter what. In this imperfect world we live in, there is no longer dignity in telling the truth.

This is the hardest letter I have ever written. I know my revelation has caused you great pain. I know you have questions about how and why I'm bisexual. I've spent the last forty-eight hours trying to explain it to my father. I've spent the last eight years trying to understand it myself.

Sorry is such a simple word . . . yet it is the only word that comes to mind in expressing how I feel about what has happened with us. Love is such a simple yet powerful word, yet it's the only word that describes my feelings for you. I love you, Nicole, like I've never loved anyone before. I am sorry that you are hurting. I hurt too. I hurt because I'm hurting you. I hurt because of the pain that my life causes me and others every day. I wish it were different. I feel the pain you're going through because of Candance's illness. I wish I could put into words the pain my bisexuality has caused me. I told you because I wanted our relationship to be unique. Totally honest. There are countless thousands of women out there today in love with bisexual men, without their knowledge. This side of me is such a small part of who I am. Would you please look further into who I am totally? Once I fell in love with you, I decided to share this secret with you. The moment we made love I was convinced that I could be totally happy with you and I thought you with me. The type of love we could spend the rest of our life with. Nicole, you touched things in me that I didn't think existed anymore. I know what it meant for you to give yourself to me. I can't promise you that my desires for men will go away. Chances are they won't . . . but neither will my love for you. If we shared a life together, I would be true to our relationship, no matter what my desires dictated. In a perfect world that would be enough. That love will keep me faithful to you and our future. I know how important your faith is and, therefore, you know how important forgiveness is. I ask you for forgiveness. Not for my sexual orientation but because I didn't tell you up front. Pray for me. Nicole, when you're praying for Candance's recovery, pray for direction. If you do this, I know you will get the correct answer. When that direction comes, be it from above or from your heart, I will live with your decision. When you pray, pray for a perfect world.

Please know that no matter what your decision, I will be forever in your debt for what knowing you and loving you have done for my life. They have allowed me to dream old dreams and they have given me hope for new dreams. They've made me believe in miracles, in one day living in a perfect world. I love you with everything that's me. I'll await your reply.

With all my love,
Raymond

TWENTY

The day Candance and Kelvin married, the June sun climbed to the center of the sky. That next day, when Candance died, the same sky let out a thunderous rainstorm and then a beautiful rainbow appeared. The heavens opened as though they were accepting a new resident.

When I showed up at the hospital on Saturday, I found myself a member of a small wedding party. Candance, a mere shadow of her former self, was dressed in a beautiful white silk nightgown, with Kelvin handsome in a black tux. Nicole, holding a small bouquet of flowers and standing next to Candance, looked gorgeous in a pink silk dress. Candance's parents stood close to each other, looking pleased and pitiful at the same time. A dumpy minister recited the wedding vows and joined Kelvin and Candance in marriage. The next day that same minister would perform last rites. Candance died of an AIDS-related pneumonia less than twenty-four hours after her marriage.

The ceremony in the small, cramped hospital room with motionless drapes was not the way Candance had planned it, but then, she didn't expect to die at twenty-seven years of age. No one cried during the brief ceremony. We were instructed by Candance that only tears of joy were allowed. She was doing what she had always wanted to do, marry the man she loved.

My numb body hid behind a constrained smile as I looked at Candance's frail body, ravaged by this dreadful disease. Instead of offering condolences, I congratulated Candance with a big kiss and gave Kelvin a powerful hug. Nicole was subdued but pleasant. Everyone in the room was functioning as though this happened every day, as though this were the way Candance and Kelvin had planned to get married.

I gave Nicole the letter and asked her to call me in Alabama when she had had a chance to read it and some time to think things over. She smiled and said she would. She then headed back to Candance's room. Halfway down the buzzing corridors she turned and said, "Raymond, how come Candance had to die this way? Why couldn't we tell?"

"I don't know the answer to that, Nicole. The only way you can be certain is to have someone love you enough to tell the truth about who and what they are."

Nicole looked at me and simply shook her head. There would be no funeral services for Candance Daphene Wesley, per her instructions. Her body was cremated shortly after her death. Her parents and Nicole went into seclusion in the Caribbean islands. Kelvin returned to Philadelphia.

As I sat in my apartment all packed and ready to head South, I reminisced over the events of the last six months. I was overcome with a tremendous amount of guilt regarding Candance's death. I was part of a secret society that was endangering black women like

Candance to protect our secret desires. Would this have happened if society had allowed Kelvin and I to live a life free from ridicule? Was it our fault for hiding behind these women to protect our futures and reputations? What responsibility did these women take? Would they have made the same choices in men had they known everything? With the large number of black bisexual men running the streets, how many lives like Candance's would be snuffed out? A lot of these men didn't care to know their HIV status. When men dealt with men, they knew the risk they were taking; most women did not. Though some women were convinced they could spot a gay man, I was not persuaded. Many of us *passed* in and out of their worlds. Asking the questions and hoping for the truth were the only certainty.

A fear loomed over many gay men. The carefree lifestyles they had led in the late seventies and early eighties would lead to demise in the nineties. Not all gay men were promiscuous, but we all were at risk. And this didn't just apply to gay and bisexual men. Until a cure was discovered, everyone was at risk. The only difference was, gay and bisexual men were at least aware of the danger, heterosexual men and women were not. I found a lot of men like myself who tried to conduct their lives like most heterosexual couples—monogamously. When AIDS hit the gay community, many secretly hoped that the epidemic would create more stable gay relationships. It did for some . . . but many found ways around being completely monogamous. Safe sex meant more sex. I thought about Candance and her dying for love. Did she contract AIDS from a healthy-looking Kelvin? Nicole once mentioned that Candance had dated a guy in undergrad from Morris Brown College who died from AIDS years earlier. On the day of the wedding I was there for support, not to question Kelvin on what had happened, not to grill him about his health status. He had asked me to share in an important day in his life. The resentment I felt in the Washington restaurant had disappeared. I remembered looking into Candance's eyes on her wedding day. She really looked happy. Her eyes seemed bigger on her sunken face. She had whispered to me not to give up on Nicole, because she would need me for support. She made me promise to look after her. I bit my lip and held back tears. "I'll do my best, Candance."

I spoke with Kyle. He called while I was waiting on JJ and Quinn, who were taking me to the airport. Kyle felt he was making progress but said it was tough. He said he was really sorry about Candance, Nicole and my problems.

"You're not happy about it?" I asked. "You always said that was I selling out."

"I just want you to be happy, Ray. If Nicole makes you happy, then I say *go for it.*"

He had sublet his apartment to help pay for his treatment and we agreed that he would stay with me once he returned. That way I figured I could keep an eye on him. I told him I didn't know how long I would be in Alabama: "I guess until I get tired." I winced.

I promised to Federal Express him the keys to my apartment and the phone number at my parents' house.

"Make sure that cute Fed Ex man that delivers in your building brings them," Kyle joked.

Right before Quinn came, JJ showed up. I poured her a glass of white wine and talked about how much our lives were changing . . . wondering if things would ever be the same. I noticed that JJ didn't take a single sip of the wine.

"They were some good times," JJ mused.

"Yeah, I guess they were."

When the downstairs buzzer rang, JJ prepared to leave. "I know you and Quinn want to spend some time alone." She smiled.

"I'll see you soon, JJ. You know I'm really happy for you. I've never seen you look happier."

"There is a reason for that," she responded.

"Who, Bernard?"

"Yes, and this," she said as she rubbed her stomach. "I'm three months pregnant, Ray."

"JJ, you're kidding . . . that's wonderful," I said as I hugged her gently.

"I'm very happy about it. I know one day you'll be this happy too. You've just need to decide what you want to do," she said as she walked out my door and Quinn walked in. They exchanged hugs and quick kisses. Quinn looked his usual handsome self in a white warm-up suit. He had a small box in his hand.

"You ready, Mr. Tyler?"

"As ready as I'm going to be," I said as I looked around my apartment, tears forming in my eyes from the morose mood.

"This is for you," Quinn said as he handed me the small, neatly wrapped box. "Open it," he urged.

"What's this?" I asked as I tore open the small aqua-blue box with TIFFANY & CO. embossed across the top. I saw a thin gold chain lying in the bottom of it.

"This way, you'll never forget me. I'll always be close by," Quinn said as he took the small chain and placed it on my wrist above my watch.

"Quinn, this is wonderful. You act like we aren't going to see each other again. I'll be back."

"I don't think so, Raymond. I think deep down you've had enough of New York. Your father told me about his offer. I think you should really consider it," Quinn said sadly.

"I have a job."

"Yeah, but we've talked about that. You have to live in constant fear that one day they may find out and your career would be over.

You and your father have made some great strides and I think you should keep working on your relationship. Besides, he invited me to Alabama anytime I wanted to come." He smiled.

"I don't know. I just have to play it by ear. Quinn, did I thank you?"

"Thank me for what?"

"Saving my life."

"What are you talking about, Raymond?"

"The sleeping pills."

"Oh, they slipped out."

"Yeah, right."

"So, you owe me dinner."

"Bet."

"And a hug."

"No problem," I said. I walked over to Quinn, held him tightly and kissed his forehead before walking out of my apartment.

"You know, even though you won't be close by, I'd like to know I can reach you by phone or air," Quinn said.

"I'm glad you feel that way, Quinn."

"I do, Ray. I really do."

While we drove toward Queens and the airport, I looked over at Manhattan's huge skyline in the distance and then down at my new piece of jewelry. What Quinn said made a lot of sense. But would Birmingham offer me happiness? Would I ever find happiness? Was I leaving it behind in New York City?

TWENTY-ONE

June twentieth, at six o'clock sharp, the doors of the Metropolitan Baptist Church were flung open and there stood Sela. She looked breathtakingly beautiful in a white silk wedding gown and a full shimmering veil that lightly covered her face. The evening sun poured through the stained-glass windows of the packed church as trumpets roared before the wedding march. As Sela walked down the aisle, she appeared to be floating on air. When she walked past the pew in which I was standing, she gave me a thin smile and winked a beautiful eye. A twinge of both sadness and pure happiness came over me. Sadness because I realized I might never have a day like this, happiness because I knew Sela deserved this day. As my eyes began to mist, I suddenly felt my mother's hand grab mine. It was like the first day of kindergarten, my mother's warm hands protecting me.

The large wedding was so different from the one I had been a part of in New York. The air was filled with the smell of flowers and the warm fragrance of the June day. I pondered if this was the type of wedding that Candance had planned. The days after my arrival in Birmingham had been great therapy. My mom and I rekindled our friendship. She babied me as she always did, cooking all my favorites and trying to fatten me up because of all the weight I had lost during my last weeks in New York. We talked about what had happened with Nicole and Pops and what I should do next. She told me how helpless she felt the night I had called drunk with pain. She said, "No mother ever wants to know that her child is hurting from the lack of love."

I had not talked with Nicole since the day Candance died. Quinn had called once, but the conversation was brief. He and his wife and children were thinking about the Alabama Freedom Trail for summer vacation. I thought it would be quite ironic to finally meet his wife at my parents' home. We admitted that the same chemistry that had brought us together would probably keep us apart. Same-gender sex was one thing; that was easy. Same-gender love was something completely different. So powerful, yet so painfully difficult.

My pops had waged a full-scale campaign to convince me to stay at home and join the practice. He was tinkering with the idea of running for the State Senate and conveyed that he couldn't do it without his number one son's help. Kirby was glad to have me home but was immersed in Little League and little girls. He would occasionally drag me through the neighborhood to reintroduce his big brother from New York.

To be honest, I didn't quite know what I was going to do. I was enjoying all the attention from my mama and pops, but I realized that very soon I would have to rejoin the real world. I had taken a month's leave of absence from the firm, and Kyle was due back around the Fourth of July—talk about fireworks in New York City! The last time we had talked, Kyle said he had met a fine black tennis pro, also in rehab. "I still have my *pulling power*," he joked.

The time at home was good and I didn't venture far from there. Several fraternity brothers had called or come by and were convincing me to stay South.

I don't know if I thought being back in Alabama would cure my gayness. The opportunities didn't exist as they did in New York. I still desired Nicole, but I decided that I wasn't going to pressure her. She had a great deal of healing to do.

I received a note from Kelvin thanking me for standing up for him, and saying that he was doing fine. He didn't mention his own health status; maybe Kelvin was positive proof that one could be HIV-positive and lead a normal life.

I guess I was leaning toward staying at home. New York wasn't going anywhere and I still had some healing to do myself. I decided against seeing a therapist, as Pops had suggested. My father didn't know I had once seen a doctor who explained to me that *there was nothing wrong with my sexual desires.* I knew deep down that my desires for men were here to stay. I decided that if I ever met another woman like Nicole, I would be straight-up at the start. No pretenses . . . no deceptions. I realized that this was a stand that I wouldn't get much support for, but it felt right to me and both my parents supported the notion. My mother always told me, "The easiest thing in the world is telling the truth."

I still very much wanted a family and to be happy with one special person. I felt a great deal of responsibility to be a strong role model for my little brother and other young black men. I had to stop beating myself up about my sexual longings. At a time when black men were being maligned, I would concentrate on things that were honorable about me and the qualities that could be an asset to the black community. I felt strongly that I could be of service without people coming into my bedroom. I guess in a lot of ways I was blessed that I could pass in and out of the heterosexual world. Redirecting my thoughts was something I could control. I had made my sexuality the primary focus of my life for too long; from now on, I would allow it to be only a small part of my identity.

Mom and I didn't stay at the lavish wedding reception very long. We both wished Sela and Dewayne the best and took our leave. When Sela and I kissed, she whispered, "I heard you're in love." I smiled. Besides, it was my twenty-ninth birthday, the age at which I had always dreamed everything would come together in my life. I had no idea how difficult a task it would be.

I asked my parents to keep the birthday celebration minimal. Mom cooked a special dinner and there were cake, champagne and gifts. After dinner I stood in the kitchen as my mother put the dishes in the dishwasher. After closing the door on the machine, she sighed, "Finally." She looked at me as we faced each other, separated only by the butcher-block island, and smiled. "What are you thinking about, Ray junior?"

"Ma, what did you think when you found out I might be gay?"

"Think about?" she quizzed.

"Yeah, what did you think? Were you upset, disappointed?"

"Baby, as a mother I prayed that when you were born you'd be healthy and when you grew up you'd be happy. Nothing else matters. Your being gay doesn't make a bit of difference to me and it shouldn't matter to any parent."

"Do you think Pops has really accepted it?"

"The bottom line is, your father loves you. He's just learning what unconditional love is. Lord knows I've spent my marriage trying to teach him."

"Do you think I was born gay, Ma?"

"I don't know, but why does it matter?"

"What would I do without you, Ma?" I asked, and held her tightly in my arms.

"With God's grace, you'll never know," she responded as she rubbed her warm hands up and down my back.

As I left the kitchen and walked down the hallway to retire from an eventful evening, my father pulled me to the side and told me how proud he was to have me as his son. No matter what choices I made about work or my life, he would support me one hundred percent. It was the best birthday present I could ever have received from him. I felt a great peacefulness as we stood huddled in our family room. Just when I was preparing to tell him how much that meant to me, Mama called from the kitchen.

"Raymond junior, telephone!" she yelled.

When I walked back into the kitchen, Mama was holding the phone and smiling.

"Who is it?" I asked. My mama said nothing. She just walked away, smiling to herself.

"Hello."

"Happy Birthday, Raymond." It was Nicole. My stomach started to flutter.

"Nicole, how are you . . . thank you. Where are you?"

"I'm in New York."

"How are you?"

"Better than yesterday, hopefully better tomorrow."

"I'm glad to hear that. This is a wonderful surprise," I said.

"Well, I couldn't forget your birthday. How are you doing?"

"Better. Taking it one day at a time."

"Did you get my letter?" Nicole asked.

"No."

"Well, you will. I just mailed it a couple of days ago and you know the New York City mail."

"I'll look forward to it," I said.

Nicole and I talked for about ten minutes, each of us tentative about what we said and what we asked. She told me that she had gotten the female lead in a Broadway workshop and that she felt pretty good about the show's chances. I wished her luck and we talked about the decisions I had to make. She told me something I already knew: our AIDS tests had come back negative. Her doctor had told her to have another test in six months to be sure. Just when we were preparing to say good-bye, Nicole called my name as she had so many nights before: "Raymond."

"Yes?"

"Well, if the show makes it, you won't forget your promise?"

"My promise?"

"Yes, did you forget? Remember when you said you would never miss my opening night on Broadway."

"Of course I do. Do you still want me there?"

"Yes, I couldn't do it without you."

"Yes you could. But I'm delighted that you won't."

"Raymond, can I ask you one more thing?"

"Please."

"When do you stop wishing for something that may never happen? When do you stop wishing for that perfect world?"

"Never . . . Nicole . . . never," I responded.

With that, Nicole said good night and wished me Happy Birthday once more. A wish that contained the feelings of unspeakable hope, the hope that a new season brings. Tomorrow was the first day of summer.

THE END FOR NOW

Acknowledgments

In addition to the people I thanked in the first edition of *Invisible Life*, I must mention several who made this version possible. First of all, to the thousands who purchased the first edition and requested that bookstores carry the book: thanks for all the letters, I'm still answering them.

A special thanks to Doubleday Super Salesman Chris Grimm for discovering me, and my friend Lillian Yeilding at Oxford Bookstore for her help with securing an agent; three special friends whom I forgot to mention in the first edition, Deborah Chambers, Denise (a.k.a. JJ) Johnson and Joyce Ann Brewer; my beautiful cousin, Jacquelyn Johnson; my sounding board and new friend, Valarie Boyd; my former neighbors, Jessica and Paul; and several new friends who gave me parties and sold books before we even met. Thanks a million, Dyanna Williams, Dee Levi, Carl Cromwell, Ed Robinson, Rodney Lofton, Reggie Van Lee, Mel Smith, Renee Logan, Kym Greene, Tracey Sherrod, KaLavell Grayson, Sadki, Ron Ross, Kathy Hampton and BLSA at Harvard Law School, Mark Johnson, Janis

Murray, Cheryl Jones, Patrick Bell and Jonathan Pollard. Also special mention to my attorney, Linda Chatman, and my photographer, Martin Christopher.

If I have forgotten somebody, please charge it to my head and not my heart. I close by thanking the bookstores and beauty shops that made this book a hit. So here's to: Oxford Bookstore, Shrine of Black Madonna, Folktales, Nia Gallery, Mainstreet, Claris, Lambda Rising, Hue-Man, Giovanni's Room, Insight, First World, Force One, Nelda's, Therapy Salon and Charles, Inc. Thanks also to: ABC, BUILD and IMANI Book Clubs. Blessings to all!

A LETTER
TO MY READERS

Dear Reader:

You've played an important part in making one of my dreams come true, and I want to start by thanking you from the bottom of my heart. Your purchase of this special edition of *Invisible Life* will also assist in helping to realize the dreams of emerging writers through the E. Lynn Harris Charitable Foundation. (I'll tell you more about that later.) Right now, I want to tell you how *Invisible Life* came to be, and what some of the characters might be doing today.

I started writing *Invisible Life* in February of 1991 during a difficult time in my life, both personally and professionally. I was renting a room from a friend in Lithonia, Georgia, and was spending over eight hours a day writing my novel while listening to Barbra Streisand's *Yentl* soundtrack and Aretha Franklin. I had always dreamed of being a writer, ever since I had first learned the power of words at the Little Rock Public Library, where I spent almost every Saturday reading books that transported me to other lands, far from the small clapboard house on East Twenty-first. But as a colored boy growing up in Little Rock, dreams didn't always come true.

The only creative writing I did during my youth were letters to my mother on birthdays and holidays when I couldn't afford gifts. Even today my mama says those letters are among her favorite gifts from me. I never wrote short stories or poems as a child, but I did read almost everything I could get my hands on. One of my favorite books is Maya Angelou's *I Know Why the Caged Bird Sings*. It is important to me for several reasons. First, Ms. Angelou was also from Arkansas, and she was the first real writer I would meet and have the opportunity to talk with. Second, I shared with her my secret desire to be an author, and she encouraged me to write every day even if it was only one word. Great advice that I didn't follow for years.

The idea for *Invisible Life* developed during the AIDS crisis. AIDS was finally hitting home in the African American community. I had lost several friends to the disease and discovered several more were in the final stages. I also found out that African American women were the fastest-growing group of AIDS sufferers, and I started to worry about the women in my life: my close female friends, my sisters, my aunt and mother. I felt helpless and wanted to do something. So I turned to writing letters.

I wrote letters to several of my friends inflicted with the disease. These letters recounted our friendships, the good times and the bad. I didn't want these people I loved so dearly to leave this planet without knowing how I felt. Putting pen to paper seemed like the perfect way to convey my feelings.

A week before he died, my dear friend, Richard, told me how much my letters and friendship meant to him. He told me I had a talent for writing and that I should pursue it. "People have no idea who we are. So you need to tell our story. Let them know we're their brothers, fathers, uncles, cousins, and friends." I promised him I would write, but not for one moment did I truly believe I could keep such a promise. A couple of years after making this promise to Richard, I finally had the courage to at least attempt writing.

Invisible Life was originally called *No Life for Sissies,* and was told from a third-person point of view. The thought of writing such material, using the pronoun I, seriously frightened me. The main character was Courtney Tyler, a young man from New York who's in Arkansas for a family reunion and notices a beautiful young lady who's being crowned Miss Arkansas. Several months later he meets his dream girl, Nicole Springer. On my third day of writing, I made my first major decision and changed Courtney's name to Raymond. The name Raymond narrowly beat Tyrone and Dwight. I wanted a name that sounded proud, powerful, and masculine.

After writing a couple of chapters I mustered up enough courage to show them to a friend whose judgment I trusted. She thought I was definitely onto something, and gave me some valuable advice. She said, "You have to become Raymond to tell his story." So despite my fear, I tore up the three chapters and started over. This time I told the story from a first-person point of view, as if I, E. Lynn Harris were Raymond Winston Tyler, Jr.

I can't tell you the fear I felt the first time someone asked me if I was Raymond. Of course I answered "no." But then I started receiving letters from young men and women telling me how much this novel had helped them and I realized how important it was that I be forthcoming about the similarities between Raymond and myself. Every time I answered this question I became stronger and my courage grew.

I decided to rewrite the novel with a different premise. What would happen if two men, close friends from college who had shared an intimate sexual past, bump into each other by chance on the eve of one of the men's marriage? This revised first chapter became Chapter Three in the final book, the chapter where Raymond bumps into Kelvin and his bride-to-be Candance in a New York department store.

Another friend loved this chapter but wanted to know how Raymond and Kelvin met. I quickly learned that as a novelist, I needed to be able to answer any question the reader might ask. So I drew from my own experience; something I learned was not uncommon for first-time novelists.

Several years earlier, I had a dream about a man I'd seen at a fraternity party. I did not know his name, or if he was a student at the university. A week later, I literally bumped into this handsome stranger. Our meeting led to my first serious relationship with a man. I was a senior in college.

Even though I respected my friend Dellanor's advice about the importance of "becoming Raymond" I wanted Raymond to be the man I sometimes wanted to be. I wanted him to be attractive and athletic; the kind of man both men and women would be strongly attracted to. I wanted Raymond to come from a strong two-parent household. I did not. I wanted him to be middle class. I'm not from a middle-class background and at the time I was writing I was on the last of my unemployment checks. I thought Raymond should be a lawyer. I was briefly interested in a career as a lawyer, not because I had a burning desire to practice law, but because I thought it was a respected career and I would make a lot of money. It would also give me an entrée into the middle class. And since I knew the novel would be controversial, I wanted to separate myself from Raymond as much as possible. If people rejected the novel, they would be rejecting Raymond, not me. Once I knew who Raymond was, I started writing again, this time without fear.

When it came to creating my heroine, I didn't look any further than one of my best friends, Lencola Sullivan, a beautiful former Miss Arkansas and Miss America runner-up. Lencola and I were never involved with each other but we still share a wonderful friendship that I treasure more and more each day. Nicole can't hold a candle to Lencola, although Lencola loves the fact that I used some of her wonderful innocent and caring qualities to create the shell of one of my most lovable creations.

Kyle, the character readers seem to love the most, is a composite of five people I had the honor of being friends with while I lived in New York in the 1980s. I actually met a couple of them in the Nickel Bar during our regular Friday evening get-togethers. In the eighties, New York was filled with festive bars and engaging characters who could dance, drink and spout witty one-liners all at the same time. These people became my mentors and tour guides and helped me navigate my way through a world that was as foreign as Spain to me, a man from Little Rock, Arkansas. But there was one major difference between my new friends and that character that would become Kyle: none of them were ever addicted to drugs or worked as call boys. They were all college-educated and held professional positions. I just wanted to add a little spice to the novel.

John Basil Henderson, my most asked-about character, is the man people love to hate. Although I'm convinced more people feel sorry for him than actually hate him. I based his character on a man I met while I was living in Chicago. This man moved through my life like a speeding bullet, remaining like Basil a total mystery. Since the success of my novels, I have met several Basil clones.

I finished the first draft of *Invisible Life* a little after the Fourth of July 1991. I was both excited and nervous. Although my family and friends were supportive, very few knew what the novel was about. At that point, I had never had a conversation with my mother about my sexuality. But a reaction from one of the most important people in my life led me to believe that I had something powerful and healing with *Invisible Life*.

My Aunt Gee, my mother's sister, was the only person in my family with whom I discussed my personal life. I often shared the joy and pain of being gay. I called Aunt Gee when I was dumped by my first love. And she was the first person in my family to receive a copy of my manuscript. Why did I choose my aunt, rather than a supportive sibling or cousin? I valued Aunt Gee's opinion and I knew I would need her to prepare my mom for what to expect when I came back to Arkansas for my first book signing.

A few days after I gave my aunt the novel, she surprised me by calling around midnight. This was strange because Aunt Gee is usually in bed by nine. She said, "Oh, baby, I'm so sorry. I didn't know what you have gone through. This book is wonderful! It's going to help a lot of people understand."

Through my tears of absolute joy I thanked my aunt, a strong Christian lady, who had always supported me, but also held out hope that prayer would change my orientation. Her feelings, I think, are similar to what a lot of mothers and fathers feel about their gay sons and daughters. They worry much more about how the world will treat their children than they do about a family's possible feelings of shame.

After a couple more drafts, I eagerly sent out my manuscript (with wonderful cover letters) to publishers and agents via Federal Express. Weeks later my novel would be returned, the pages so in place I knew it had not been read. Lying neatly on top would be a nice "thanks, but no thanks" rejection letter. At the same time friends were reading the novel and enjoying it, but I wasn't sure if I could really trust their opinions. I got helpful editing suggestions from close female friends, Tracey Huntley and Janis Lunon, even though I had yet to discuss my sexuality with them. Not only did they help make the novel stronger, they gave me clues about who the readers of my book would be.

I started to seek out what I called *blind* readers, people who didn't know me, or what the book was about. While the rejection letters continued to depress me, the response from my blind readers (mostly African American women) encouraged me tremendously.

These everyday readers gave me the courage to self-publish the novel, when it looked like the commercial publishing world wasn't ready for my story. I was warned that self-publishing a novel would be a turnoff to major publishers, and if I wanted a long-term writing career I should wait until the right editor discovered my novel. But I couldn't wait. I had discovered my calling; my mission for living.

I have often said writing saved my life. In many ways it did. Self-publishing a novel is one of the most difficult experiences in the world, but to me it was also a great joy. During the first month of the publication of *Invisible Life* it was not uncommon for me to deliver a novel right to the front doorsteps of a reader who had heard about the novel from someone else. A young man, K'Lavell Grayson, started telling his clients about a book that they *had* to read but couldn't purchase in a bookstore. Before I knew it, K'Lavell was selling more than twenty copies of *Invisible Life* a week. And the rest, as they say, is history. Well, not really. I spent the next two years peddling my book everywhere I went, hitting every African American beauty shop I could find. I did the Black Expo circuit and found out that people weren't always so certain they wanted to read a novel like *Invisible Life*. I even went to house parties from Atlanta to Philadelphia! When I traveled to cities outside of Atlanta, I had only one goal in mind—to sell enough books to get home! Sometimes I did and other times I would simply seek out the nearest beauty salon and sell the balance of my books to complete my mission. For the first time in my life I was starting to believe that with hard work, friends, family, and an abiding faith in prayer anything was possible.

Now, some five years later, I can honestly say I have the best job in the world. In what other profession do you get to meet people from all different backgrounds, white, black, Asian, Hispanic, male and female, gay and straight, who feel they know you from reading your work? How many jobs allow you to change the way people feel about themselves and other people? Looking back on my youth in Little Rock, I realize I had no idea of the healing power of words. But as an adult I've discovered writing is the one medium that's so personal, so one on one, that it's impossible not to understand the power of words. All the reader has to do is open his or her heart and mind. I have often said it is not my intention to change the world with my writing, but I would be lying if I said it isn't my hope to change people's hearts and the way we feel about each other.

Enough of my New Age thinking. What about the characters in *Invisible Life* who didn't find their way into my second novel, *Just*

As I Am or my new novel, *Abide with Me?* Kelvin, Raymond's first love, is now married and living and teaching in Minnesota. He's having a difficult time since he just revealed to his wife of five years that he's HIV-positive. With the new drugs currently available, Kelvin remains in good health, and his wife, Mandy, has decided to stick with him. Quinn, Raymond's married lover, is still married and still keeping his wife in the dark. Quinn knows a couple of men who are married as well, and sometimes they take long weekend *fishing* trips.

JJ, or Janelle, is still married to Bernard and has two children, a little boy and girl. She recently got her master's degree from the University of North Carolina and has just opened up a day-care center in Charlotte. Bernard has recently started college and has dreams of becoming an accountant.

So there you have it. I'd like to end this letter by once again thanking you for all your wonderful support. Keep those cards and letters coming, and I will keep writing novels you'll enjoy reading.

E. Lynn Harris

For information regarding the E. Lynn Harris Better Days Foundation, forward your request to:

P.O. Box 78832
Atlanta, Georgia 30309